SLASH AND BURN

SLASH AND BURN

COLIN COTTERILL

Published in 2011 by
Soho Press, Inc.
853 Broadway
New York, NY 10003

Library of Congress Cataloging-in-Publication Data

Cotterill, Colin.
Slash and burn / Colin Cotterill.
p. cm.
ISBN 978-1-61695-116-0
eISBN 978-1-61695-117-7
1. Paiboun, Siri, Doctor (Fictitious character)—Fiction.
2. Coroners—Fiction. 3. Older people—Fiction. 4. Laos—Fiction.
I. Title.
PR6053.O778S57 2011
823'.914—dc23
2011030330

Printed in the United States of America

10 9 8 7 6 5 4 3 2 1

ACKNOWLEDGMENTS

With very special thanks to Charles Davis who taught me more about helicopters than I'll ever need to know, and to his marvelous journal of those Air America days: *Across the Mekhong*. Kudos and thanks too to other veterans of an era in Southeast Asia that some would like to forget, but many are proud to recall. For their help on this book I thank: Edmund McWilliams, MacAlan Thompson, Wallace Brown, Denny Lane and Dr. Amos Townsend.

Special thanks to You Jia Zhu and her brother Jin Zhu, Polly Griffith, and Steven Schipani.

Ongoing thanks to my usual suspects: Dad, Tony, Lizzie, Valérie, Kye, Kay, Martina, Robert, Bambina, Leila, David, and Jess.

CONTENTS

SLASH AND BURN

You know? Being shut up in a cage with a live bear was a piece of cake compared to being drunk and high in charge of half-a-million dollars' worth of flying metal. The full moon beckoned, hanging there like an ivory wok in a vast steel-gray sky. It spread the landscape with an eerie monochrome like daytime to a dog. Medium-gray jungle against dark-gray mountains. Patches of charcoal and slivers of silver off the rivers. Boyd could make out every leaf, every rock, as clear as creation day. He was a god. Oh, yeah. A deity on a mission. The almighty protagonist in the movies they made before they could afford colour: starring Boyd Bowry in his never-ending quest for . . . cheese.

"Cheese, little buddy," he'd told Marcos. "I'll bring you back a hunk of moon cheese. They let you scoop it right out. You want fries or something with it?"

"Man, you shouldn't leave me here with that," was all Marcos could come back with. Boyd remembered being at the door of the cage then. He'd stopped, looked back at the bear: drunk, snoring, farting, head in her feed trough.

"She'll be cool, man. Fix her a cup of coffee in the morning. Tell her it was great. Leave your phone number."

Marcos had done one of those non-military salutes. That's why that finger's so long, you know? Gets all the exercise. That was . . . what? An hour ago? Half an hour? Time lost all its credibility at ten thousand feet with no colour in the world. Someone oughta write a PhD about that. The relationship between . . . between hue and chronology. The colour of minutes. He'd heard Marcos yelling some Filipino double Dutch at him as he walked away. The little guy was mad. Smiled a lot, but. . . .

No, wait. Marcos? That's not right. Marcos is the goddamned president. The guy's about to be eaten by a bear. The least I can do is remember his name. I've known him for. . . .

OK, don't be distracted now.

Focus.

Cheese.

Ignition and all that instrumental hoo-ha had been instinctive and that was just as well 'cause he couldn't recall doing any of it. He'd cranked her up, left the ground, and here he was heading off to the heavenly moon deli service. A Sikorsky was a hell of a lot safer than a Chevy in so many respects. Never drove a Sikorsky into a fire hydrant, for one. And if you did, the cops would never catch up with you, for two. And, what else? A Chevy never surfed moon rays like a Sikorsky H34.

Oh, no.

Oh, yeah.

What a trip. What a goddamned trip. Just hanging in the gray, looking at the moon. It was cosmic. What happened to nights like this? What happened to love and harmony, man? No peace and quiet for those monkeys down there in the trees. For those big lizards on the rocks. "Sorry guys." At least he didn't have to listen to his own engine growl. He had his headphones connected direct to the cassette player. The Who: Brits, but complex, man. Percussion like the punch of anti-aircraft flak.

And even though the music went straight into his brain and dead-ended there, he got it into his head that the words were being broadcast all over Nam to the east and Thailand in the west and some karmic interpretation service was sending the message to farmers in their bamboo beds. He shouted over the music, "You were deceived, brothers, but you can see what we've done, right? You've got the magic eyes? You know we'll get ours in some other life. You've got that damned right. What do we know?"

And that was when it happened; the actual date and time when the sky fell on Chicken Little. There was a thump first, then an odd lack of vibration. One second the scenery was holding him up, the next a trapdoor opened in the universe and he fell through it. Gravity. What a concept! The fuel light was flashing like Christmas. There were "procedures." He could probably send out a mayday. That was on the list. But who in their right mind would be up at 2:00 A.M. waiting for some dopehead on a magical mystery tour to call in? And timing, man. He was in fourteen thousand pounds of metal heading down to earth with twenty canisters of volatile substance on board. Some rescue that would be. He disengaged the rotors, waited for stability, unclamped his belt and rose from his seat. He smiled at the briefcase sitting in the copilot's seat but he didn't have time to take it with him. He had barely thirty seconds of the rest of his life to look forward to. To sort it all out.

"Use your time wisely, man."

Who should he think of? Who to pledge his love to? Who to hate? No, that last one was easy. That son-of-a-bitch was one day away from getting his. And now, look at this. Goddamn it. A one-way express ticket to some big old Boyd barbecue. All in the timing. He worked his way down the crawl space to the cabin and staggered around in there. He'd seen men die in all kinds of ways. He knew what St. Peter's first question would be.

"How did you go down, son? Were you calm about it? We don't want no screaming girl scouts up here, boy."

So Boyd opted for cool. When you're cool, death doesn't seem that final.

There was a village and all were asleep save two. They saw the chopper come down, not like a rock, not plumb straight, more the way a slab of slate might slice through water. They both saw the wheel hit the tree tops then a spark and the big bird exploded—spewed out a whole galaxy. One of the insomniacs smiled and clapped his hands but he could never tell anyone what he'd seen. The other was so shocked she fell out of a tree, hit her head on the way down and knocked herself blind. But the last image that projected itself in her mind was as certain as the earth. She'd seen it. A dragon had collided with the moon. It had burst into a million shards and the pieces cascaded across the jungle and there would never be lightness again at night.

1

ANOTHER FINE MESS

Dr. Siri and Madame Daeng sat on the edge of the smelly bed and looked at the body hanging from the door handle opposite. They were a couple not renowned for silence but this one lent itself most splendidly to speechlessness. They took in the too-red lipstick and the too-tight underwear. They breathed the whiskey fumes and the scent of vomit diluted with disinfectant. They'd both seen their share of death, perhaps more than a fair share. But neither had experienced anything like this.

"Well," said Daeng at last, uncomfortable in the early morning quiet. The foggy mist rolled in through the window and rasped the inside of her throat.

"Well, indeed," agreed her husband.

"This is another fine mess you've gotten us into, Dr. Siri."

"Me? I didn't do it."

"No. Not *it* exactly. *It* you didn't do, I grant you. But the consequences that led to *it*. They've got your fingerprints all over them."

"Madam, judging from the evidence in front of us, I'd say this would have occurred whether we were here or not. And it didn't even have to have happened here. This was a tragedy begging to be let out of the bag."

"Again, you're right. But if you hadn't volunteered yourself, volunteered us all, we'd be at home now beside the Mekhong eating noodles in relative peace. We wouldn't be in this room with this particular body, about to be embroiled in an international scandal. This would be someone else's problem. Someone in good health capable of handling it. But oh no. One last adventure before I retire, you say. What can go wrong? you say. Everything's perfectly safe, you say. And look at us now. Five weeks ago we were perfectly content and now we're up to our necks in dung."

"Come on, Daeng. Be fair. What could I have done to avoid it?"

"What could you have done?"

"Yes."

'Torn up the note."

Five Weeks Earlier

It was true, just five weeks before, things had been normal. Well, normal for Vientiane. But first there was the haunting, then the note, then the Americans. And somewhere between the three life had become complicated again. That was Laos in the late seventies though, wasn't it? What can you say? The place had always been mysterious, always been a victim of its politics and its confused beliefs and its weather. While the north experienced a premature dry season, the southern provinces were being flooded by Typhoon Joe. Worst hit was Champasak, the show province where almost half the country's farming cooperatives had been established. All of them had been rained into submission and, once again, the locals were convinced that Lady Kosob, the goddess of the rice harvests, was displeased with government policy. The collectives program was doomed. This came as a blow to the ministry of agriculture who'd nationalized all the old royalist estates in preparation for this great socialist plan.

If the weather wasn't bad enough, the country's close proximity to Kampuchea, once a cultural and commercial partnership, had become a liability. Refugees fleeing the Khmer Rouge were flooding into Thailand and southern Laos. The Lao government had issued twenty official statements denying KR claims that they were allowing Vietnamese troops to cross Lao territory. They absolutely weren't amassing at the border in preparation for an invasion, which, of course, they were. But as there were still no actual laws, the Politburo could logically argue that they weren't breaking any. The forty-six-member Supreme Council had been working on a national constitution for eight years and had barely made it beyond the design of the front cover. This general disorder, plus the fact that money was harder to come by than a cold beer, resulted in an estimated 150 citizens crossing the river to Thailand every day—120 successfully. An editorial in *Pasason Lao* newssheet informed the 40 per cent of the country who could read and the 2 per cent of those who could be bothered, that the People's Democratic Republic of Laos had never had it so good.

During the month of July in 1978, people did the morgue at Mahosot Hospital a great favor by not dying mysteriously. They merely passed away as people do and no questions were asked. No motives sought. It was almost as if they sensed that Dr. Siri Paiboun, the country's only coroner, was reaching the end of his unasked-for tenure and they didn't care to trouble him. The good doctor had been putting in his notice every month since the Party first manhandled him into the job three years earlier. His boss, Judge Haeng, little in so many ways, had ignored the requests. "A good communist," the man had said, "does not let go of the plough halfway across the paddy and leave the buffalo to find its own direction. He eats with her, tends to her injuries, and sleeps with her until the job is done." Siri had resisted the temptation to spread the word that the Party was advocating bestiality. He'd known his time would come. But when it did, he'd been only a heartbeat away from occupying his own slab. He'd met the departing spirits eyeball to eyeball, and they were waiting for him. After the horrific events of May that year, he was still deaf in one ear and could barely feel his right hand. His few hours of sleep were plagued with nightmares. Everyone agreed that after his run-in with the Khmer Rouge, Dr. Siri had earned his retirement.

If he could stay out of trouble, Siri had under two months left on the job. Then, the leisurely life he'd dreamed of through decade after decade in the jungles of Vietnam and northern Laos would be his; coffee mornings overlooking the Mekhong, leisurely noodle lunches at his wife Daeng's shop, long evenings of talking rice whiskey nonsense with ex-Politburo man Civilai, and nights stretched out against a triangular pillow in his illicit backroom library reading French literature and philosophy. Dallying through to the early morning with comrades Sartre and Hugo and Voltaire. Really. All he had to do was stay out of trouble. For anyone else this might not have been much to ask. But this was no simple man. This was Dr. Siri Paiboun: seventy-four years of age, forty-eight years an unconvincing member of the Communist Party, host to a thousand-year-old Hmong shaman spirit, culturally tainted beyond redemption by ten years in Paris. Emotionally numbed to the horrors of injury and death by years of battlefront surgery, Dr. Siri felt he had earned himself the right to be an ornery old geezer. And, no. Staying out of trouble for two months was no easy task for such a complicated man.

He'd had just the one case since his retirement notice was accepted. Compared to some of his adventures, it was barely worth mentioning as a case at all. The children at Thong Pong middle school had become unhinged. A number of them had started to vibrate uncontrollably and speak in languages none of them knew. The local medical intern had seen nothing like it and requested assistance from the Ministry of Health. Stories in Vientiane spread like atomic bomb fallout and word very quickly found its way to the morgue where Dr. Siri and his staff had been sitting lifeless for several weeks. Almost immediately, Siri had set off to visit the school on his Triumph motorcycle with his faithful nurse Dtui and lab assistant Geung squashed together behind him. As religion and superstition had no place in the new regime, nobody voiced what everyone suspected: that the school was haunted. Both doctor and nurse feigned indifference when they arrived, even though both were keen to discover a supernatural source for the peculiar epidemic. Dtui was one of only a half-dozen people who knew of Siri's dalliance with the beyond and she had no doubt in her mind that there was a malevolent ghost at play in the school.

According to the head teacher, every day after morning assembly, up to forty children would become zombie-like, ranting and drooling and shaking without control. At first she'd considered that this was merely a student prank to get out of studying Marxist-Leninist theory during the first period. A number of other ruses had been uncovered by the embedded political spies from the youth league. But this was too elaborate. Some of the children had even begun to utter obscenities in voices that, without question, did not belong to twelve- and thirteen-year-old children. To Siri it sounded very much like some mass shamanic hysteria. For some reason, the pliable minds of the children were being hijacked

by wayward spirits. But there had to be some unseen interme-
diary to channel the demons.

"Tell me," he said to the head teacher. "What normally happens
during your morning assembly?"

"The usual ceremony, Doctor," she replied. "The children line
up in their grades, I make announcements, the flag is raised and
the school band plays the new national anthem."

The new socialist national anthem, coincidentally, had the same
tune as the old royalist national anthem. Only the words were
different. Although badly metered and slightly misleading, as far
as Siri could ascertain there was nothing inherently evil hidden
in the new lyrics. So he asked to look at the musical instruments.
The head teacher unlocked the music department footlocker and
it was there that Siri found the culprit. He pulled out the exor-
cism tambourine with its tassels and bottle cap rattles and smiled
at Nurse Dtui.

"Do you know what this is?" he asked the principal.

"A tambourine?" she guessed.

"A shamanic tambourine, Comrade, used in séances," he said.
"And fully loaded, I'd say. Any idea how it fell into your possession?"

"Someone from the regional education office brought it," she
recalled. "Said it had been confiscated from some royalist. Why?"

"I'd wager this is what's been causing the hysteria," he told her.

"But . . . but it's just a musical instrument," she protested.

Siri smiled at the Mao-shirted woman. She was a cadre from
the northeast with a black and white upbringing and no toler-
ance for dimensions beyond the usual three. And so it was that
in both Siri's report and that of the head teacher, the problem
had been attributed to tainted sweets sold by a rogue vendor
outside the school gates. Yet, once the tambourine had been
removed there was no repeat of the insanity.

The instrument now sat on Siri's desk at the morgue and he flicked the little bells from time to time just for the hell of it. Nurse Dtui and Mr. Geung would look up from their unimportant tasks and sigh. Siri would apologize then ring it again. His only other annoying habit had been pulled out from under him. Dtui had removed the clock from over their office door because the doctor had begun to count down the minutes to his retirement in reverse order.

"Only seventy thousand five hundred and forty-five minutes to go," he'd sing. Dtui knew that the effects of this after a day or two would have driven them all into the same moronic stupor as the pupils at Thong Hong. So she'd come in early one day and had the hospital handyman take down the clock. She'd told Siri it was off being serviced. As she never lied, he didn't question her.

At her desk, Nurse Dtui had her Thai fanzine open in front of her. To anyone walking unexpectedly into the office it would appear she was merely fantasizing her size fourteen frame into a size seven swimsuit as worn by the Bangkok television starlets on photo shoots. But hidden between the pages of her magazine were her Med. 1 Gynaecology notes in Russian. Despite a sudden unexpected pregnancy and the arrival of Malee, now five months old, Dtui had yet to give up her hopes of studying in the Soviet bloc. Unsolicited initiative was considered by the hospital administration to be a suspicious characteristic, a sign that you were not satisfied with your role in the new republic. So she studied surreptitiously. Even though she had no intention of abandoning her baby or her husband and running off to Moscow, she continued to prepare herself for that far-off day when she might take over the morgue. When times were hard, it always helped to have a dream. And times in Vientiane were certainly hard.

But not for some, it seemed. In the corner of the office, behind a desk and a chair he rarely used, Mr. Geung stood rocking gently back and forth in a blissful Down's syndrome trance. His condition had one of two effects on onlookers. Some were appalled that a moron should be allowed to work at a hospital. Others, like his many fans around Mahosot, were envious of the apparent lack of complication in his life. Devoted to his work. Loyal to a fault. Friendly and honest. Mr. Geung seemed perfectly happy with a no-frills, budget lifestyle. But they all wondered what was going on in his head. How could a middle-aged man with such a terrible affliction seem so at peace? And recently his serenity had risen to a cloud way beyond that elusive number nine. Only Siri and Dtui knew the reason for the elevation. Although Mr. Geung himself was not letting on, his morgue mates could tell. It was romance. Birds did it. Bees did it. And, clearly, Mr. Geung did it too.

Others might have interpreted the marks on their friend's neck as an allergic reaction to the washing powder in his shirt collar. But Siri and Dtui worked in the morgue. They knew teeth marks when they saw them. They didn't exactly condone the practice. "One step away from vampirism," Siri had called it. But neither begrudged Mr. Geung his first taste of romance, albeit in bitten form. Tukda's arrival at the staff canteen had at first enraged Geung.

"She's Down . . . Down's syndrome," he'd said, with the same condescending tone he'd heard all his life. "Sh . . . she shouldn't be working here."

But there was no mistaking the fact that Comrade Tukda was a pretty young lady and sweet natured. None of Mr. Geung's protestations persuaded his coworkers that he didn't find her attractive. And Geung and Tukda, through those mysterious corridors and hidden passageways of the syndrome, found each other.

What they did and where and how and if, nobody knew. Only the washing powder allergy on Geung's neck, and the sappy grins when they mentioned her name, gave anything away. He answered no questions on the subject. Denied all accusations. It was his . . . their secret. But there was no doubting the fact that Mr. Geung was a very happy man.

And this was how the members of the morgue team filled their days. Siri counting minutes. Dtui conjugating. Geung rocking. Then, all of a sudden, on one hot July morning, a note arrived. That such a flimsy slip of paper could have the effect it did would have been hard to imagine.

The morning crowd was silently engaged in the serious act of consuming Madame Daeng's noodles. It was like watching a herd of buffalo—albeit seated—working their way through a garden of lush grass. Extra stools had been imported, dotted willy-nilly around the tables but still there wasn't enough seating. Daeng and Siri encouraged diners to leave as soon as possible so others might enjoy their breakfasts, but Madame Daeng's noodles were not to be rushed. They were the *cordon bleu* of soup noodles. If Michelin had been allowed into the country they would have been hard pressed to find enough stars with which to decorate her nameless noodle establishment. Yet, in spite of her popularity, Daeng never once considered raising her prices or reducing the size of the servings. She was a pro.

Siri stood beside her, gazing proudly at the lake of hunched shoulders and bobbing heads.

"Looks like I won't have to worry about us starving to death when I retire," he said.

Daeng looked up from the boiler, gently tossed a wire basket of pasta, then lowered it back into the bubbling water. She was a fine-looking woman with a mop of gray hair that always made her seem as if she'd been racing a fast-moving motorcycle, which often she had.

"And there I was wondering how we'd ever make do without your thirty-thousand *kip* a month contribution," she smiled. "What is that on the international exchange market these days? One dollar fifty?"

"Two eighty. But let's not forget all the other perks."

"A dozen mosquito coils. Four kilos of weevil-infested rice. The occasional gardening implement. Socks. Six rolls of self-dissolving toilet paper. I don't know how we'll survive."

"And the petrol allowance."

"Two litres a month. You'll have to start riding my bicycle."

"I'll have nowhere to go. I'll just be hanging around under your feet like this—day in day out. You always said you wished we could spend more time together."

"I don't think I meant all of it. Couple of hours in the evening would be nice."

"I shall be yours twenty-four hours a day to do with as you wish. Your love slave around the clock."

Daeng laughed and scooped noodles into a bowl of broth. As there were no more stools, the customer collected the dish and sat with it on the bottom step of the staircase.

"Siri, you could no more stay put for twenty-four hours than I could. You'll be poking your nose in here, gallivanting there. And to tell you the truth, if I wanted a love slave I'd find myself a much much younger man. A body builder. I get plenty of offers, you know."

"Ha! He'd have to go through me first to get to you. You hear that, you lot?" he shouted. "Anyone here tempted to run off with my wife will have to fight me first."

"No problem," said Pop, a wizened old bean stick whose weight more than doubled after one of Daeng's spicy number 2s. He was probably the only customer in the shop older than Siri and he looked it. "Look at the state of you," he said to Siri. "Barely a fortnight out of your sick bed, broken hand, scars and bruises all over. Huh. I reckon I could take you with one hand, especially if Daeng was the prize. One blow with this teaspoon and you'd be on your back."

"Is that right, Comrade?" Siri replied. "Then let's see about that."

He grabbed a chopstick from the jar with his functioning hand and went at Pop with a fencing parry. Pop got to his feet and held out his teaspoon. A utensil duel ensued, egged on by the clatter of chopsticks against tin water mugs from all around them.

A teenager in a white shirt stepped in off the dusty sidewalk and sidled nervously across to the noodle seller, bemused by the mêlée.

"Comrade," he said, "I have an urgent note for Dr. Siri Paiboun. They said I'd find him here."

"That's him," she said. "Over there. The little boy with the white hair and messy eyebrows brandishing a chopstick. They're fighting over me, you know?"

The boy wasn't together at all.

"Go ahead. Give it to him," she told him. He reluctantly walked up behind Siri and tapped him on the shoulder. Siri turned and Pop, not one to miss an opportunity, whacked Siri on his lobe-less left ear with his spoon. Siri cried in mock pain and sank to his knees. The percussion of sticks on mugs heralded Pop their champion. In the throes of an ignominious teaspoon death, Siri seized the note from the lad's outstretched hand and died on the noodle shop floor. It was just another day at Daeng's noodle shop.

2

MEANWHILE, IN METRO MANILA

Nino Sebastian had done very nicely for himself out of his stint with Air America. He'd lived frugally, made a little extra here and there by selling things that weren't exactly his to sell, and unlike the Romeos at the Udon base, he didn't pump his salary into the bars and massage parlours. When it was all over he'd come back to Manila, built a house and a service station, and married a girl who'd never have looked at him twice without the forty thousand dollars in his pocket. His mother and father pumped gas, his sister looked after the canteen, and he and his brother Oscar ran the garage. It was all sweet. Life. Love. Grease. There wasn't the excitement but that wasn't a bad thing. Excitement just meant there was a chance you'd get your testicles blown off. He could do without that kind of excitement. Here he had boxing and *jai alai* to get his pulse racing.

There was a match tonight. Jets vs. Redemption. He had money on the reds. He'd take the truck over there. Pick up his cousin Poco on the way. It was a sticky night. He'd already taken a shower and put on his lucky turquoise shirt but he was sweating so bad he was thinking of taking another. He looked out the kitchen window and was pissed off to see the light on in the garage. Oscar was away in Samal so he guessed some customer had come in hoping for a rush job, had the nerve to turn on the light. Some people had more balls than manners. But no matter how much the guy offered, he wasn't going to get service on *pelota* night.

When Nino walked in the back door of the service area, a dark-skinned man was standing looking under the hood at the 1961 Cadillac engine Nino and Oscar had been sweating over for a month.

"Sorry, guy," Nino said. "Nobody working tonight."

"That's OK," said the man. "I was just passing through, wondering if you might have a job opening."

Nino looked the stranger up and down. He wasn't dressed like the type of man who enjoyed getting grime under his fingernails. He was too . . . finicky looking. He had a comb stuck in his hair at the back like he'd been grooming that morning and forgotten it was there. Some of the kids today thought that was a statement. Nino thought it was stupid. And, of all things, in spite of the heat, the guy was wearing a jacket and showed no sign of sweating.

"We do all our own repairs here, pal. Me and my brother. We only take on work the two of us can handle. Sorry."

The stranger shrugged.

"No problem. Thought I'd ask anyway." He took one more look at the engine. "Excuse me saying so, but you do realize you've screwed up the carburetor assembly?"

"What are you talking about?" Nino had never screwed up anything to do with an engine.

"Here," said the guy. "You've put the throttle lever in upside down."

Nino hurried over to the car and looked under the hood.

"Are you crazy?" he said. "That is a perf—"

He barely felt the pin prick of the needle in his neck and, in a breath, it was all over for Nino Sebastian.

3

PEACH

The rainy season, which usually fell between April and August in the north of Laos, had begun in March this year and run out of juice by June. Although the Mekhong was still bloated with flood-waters from China, and storms were lashing the south, rain hadn't hit Vientiane for a month. Lao meteorologists, recently trained in East Germany, were saying that industrialization in the West—but most likely in North America—was altering the environment. They were calling for a symposium of Communist states to discuss the role of capitalism on climate change. There was very little the Americans couldn't be blamed for in the People's Democratic Republic of Laos and, to be fair, most of the accusations were warranted.

Vientiane was a city of red-dirt side streets and paved main roads laid by the same Americans who were now screwing up the weather. The continuous early rains of 1978 had flushed the dirt out of the lanes and onto the main roads. Gardens and rice paddies and empty dirt plots had spread to all points of the compass. The entire city had been reclaimed by dirt. The gutters were clogged.

The potholes were concealed. The footpaths, where they existed, were no higher than the roadways. This massive mud pie was baked beneath a scorching July sun and inevitably the dust arrived. A cat passing in front of your house could kick up more dust than a herd of wildebeests galloping across the Kalahari. There was too much to sweep away. Hot though it was, people shuttered their windows and closed their doors. Those with hoses and who were connected to the main supply were out front every sunrise washing down the street. But by midday the red mist was back. The official dust season was several months away so there was a real threat that Vientiane might just vanish completely; unrecognizable as a city in satellite images.

Siri had his spare sarong wrapped round his face to keep the dust out of his mouth. He wore his old dark-lens goggles and a Castro hat and looked like a very suspicious character when he pulled up in front of the Ministry of Justice. He'd had a choice, of course. The note from his nemesis, Judge Haeng, had simply told him to be at the judicial office by one. He could have torn it up. He was retiring. What could they do to him? But Siri had a mischievous streak and he enjoyed nothing more than rubbing his boss the wrong way. He wouldn't have many more opportunities. The guard at the gate saluted. The boy had no weapon and his uniform was three non-matching shades of green. Siri, still disguised as a terrorist, climbed from his bike and walked up to the booth.

"Do you know who I am?" he asked the boy.

"No, Comrade," came the reply accompanied by another salute.

"So, for all you know I could be here to assassinate the judge and the minister. I might have dynamite strapped inside my jacket."

The boy looked doubtful.

"It . . . it's possible, I suppose."

"And I still get a salute?"

"It's what they told me to do, uncle."

"Just that?"

"Yes."

"Heaven help us," Siri grumbled, walking away from the guard and up to the steps of the ministry. "What a system," he said aloud to nobody. "All cock-a-doodle and no do. The place is falling down around us and all we get are salutes."

He kicked the dust from his sandals at the top of the steps and walked through to the reception area. The place was deserted. There were eight typewriters without typists and one large administrator's desk without Manivon, the ministry secretary. Siri was certain that if an enterprising burglar were to have stumbled into the ministry that day, he could elicit the aid of the guard out front to carry the machines to a waiting *samlor* bicycle taxi. The place was going to the dogs. He'd be well off away from it.

His mood no better, he strutted along the open air corridor and pushed open the door to Judge Haeng's office without knocking. The door slammed into something large and soft, then gave way. Siri stepped inside the small room which was lit only by one window with a bank of cracked louvres. Amongst his illicit books, Siri had a thick pictorial travelogue of the world's wonders and he noticed how the sunlight squeezing through that little window cast Stonehenge-like shadows in a room filled to bursting with enormous Westerners. Some were seated, some standing, some wore uniforms, others merely sweated in clothes inappropriate for a July room with one ceiling fan. There were men, all oily white, and two women. One of the latter reminded Siri of a bewigged Sumo wrestler in a sundress.

This thought notwithstanding, he didn't want to forget his manners. He walked from person to person shaking hands and saying, *sabai dee*—good health. All returned his handshake—not a dry palm in the house. Some repeated the greeting. Others made remarks in what he recognized as English, which was one of the many languages he didn't speak. As he circled the room he felt like a tourist amongst the giants of Easter Island. At the far side of the room he encountered Judge Haeng sitting at his desk holding on to a tired smile. His greasy hair hung over one puffy, acned cheek. This was a condition Siri knew to be exacerbated by heat and stress. He guessed the little judge was feeling both.

"Siri? Is that you?" he asked.

At first it seemed like a bizarre question, as if the man had become sightless overnight. But then Siri remembered he was still disguised. The room became a little lighter when he removed his tinted goggles, and cooler when he took off his hat and scarf. The guests in the room also seemed somewhat more at ease with him unwrapped.

"What's all this then?" Siri asked the judge.

"Americans."

"They're back? Did they forget something?"

"It's a delegation, Siri."

"What do they want?"

"I . . . I'm not . . . I. . . ."

"You don't know."

"Of course I do. I'm just. . . ."

"You don't speak English, do you?"

"I know a good number of phrases. I'm just a little rusty, that's all. What about you?"

"Can't speak a damned word of any importance."

"I thought you were in western Europe?"

"France. Different language entirely. The only English I know I picked up from sailors in dockside bars." He said loudly, "Rule

Britannia," and held up a thumb. All he received were stares of incomprehension. "See? No use at all. None of them speaks Lao?"

"No."

"What type of delegation travels without an interpreter?"

"There seems to have been a bit of a hold up. The minister ushered them all in here and told me to entertain them till the interpreters arrive."

"Have you shown them your impersonation of Richard Nixon yet?"

It was a line wasted on a man bereft of a sense of humor.

"I don't do—"

"So, how have you been entertaining them, Judge?"

"We didn't have any fizzy drinks. I sent Manivon off to get some. I wasn't expecting them, you see? The rest of the staff are preparing lunch. These have been here for fifteen minutes, just standing around."

Siri laughed again.

"But you, Siri," Haeng changed his tone, "you're late. I told you to be here at one. It's now one-fifteen."

"They took my clock away. I had to estimate the time by the position of the sun and it was too dusty to see it. Judge, you do realize it honks in here with all this meat stewing? Any chance of turning on the old A/C?"

"It's been out of order since last Wednesday."

"Can't we put them outside under a tree?"

"They aren't sheep, Siri."

Siri smiled at the wilting guests.

"I bet they'd be grateful for some air."

"The minister said—"

And at that moment the office door was thrust into the backside of the same man accosted at Siri's arrival. He hadn't changed his position so it appeared he enjoyed being hit with doors. A blonde girl burst into the room all laughs and fluster. The space was suddenly filled with her language; brief introductions, shared comments, and an overall atmosphere of relief offering hope that the delegation might be allowed out. After one cursory circuit of the room she turned at last to Siri and Haeng and performed a most splendid *nop*, palms together at the chin, her nose just a fraction above her fingernails, upper torso angled toward them.

"Respected gentlemen," she said in beautiful Lao. "Good health. I'm extremely sorry for my tardiness."

Siri and Haeng, in spite of their ages and status, found themselves returning the *nop*. Siri did so with a smile. Haeng blushed with embarrassment. The Politburo had condemned the gesture as a bourgeois throwback to the days of royalist-instigated servitude. But here was a white imperialist using his language and gestures in *his* country so this intrusion had really left him no choice but to retaliate. His unease was compounded by the fact that she was uncomfortably attractive.

"I have a class at the *lycée*," she continued with a smile. "It should have only taken me ten minutes to get over here but my bicycle had a flat tire which I had to repair, hence the dust on my skirt and the sweat smudges on my face. I'm usually a lot neater. Really."

If Siri had shut his eyes he might have been listening to the musical lilt of a young lass from the north of Luang Prabang. It was by far his favorite accent. Even the largest women in Luang Prabang with the hairiest toes could turn a man's heart with such an accent.

"Where did you learn Lao?" he asked her, fascinated.

"My parents were missionaries in Ban Le on the Luang Prabang border. I was born there," she said.

"You're a Lao," he laughed, without a hint of condescension.

"My heart is, yes," she said. "But my passport has an eagle on the cover and I have to live in this big awkward *farang* body. Officially I'm one of them."

She looked around at the damp delegation. They spoke. She replied. There was suddenly an impressive display of fine dentistry. She'd obviously said something to please them. She was as inspiring politically as she was physically. There really was nothing awkward about her body. She was long-boned like a young race-horse, and fresh-faced. She would undoubtedly break many men's hearts if she hadn't done so already. Although it was hard to tell the age of Westerners, Siri put her down as no more than sixteen or seventeen. She told them her name was Peach, which only served to make her appear even more delicious.

Judge Haeng, whose penchant for young women was legendary in the few surviving nightclubs of Vientiane, seemed to have arrived at the same conclusion. He'd renovated his flagging smile and was sitting with his chin leaning on his palm like some vain author's publicity photograph.

"You're very beautiful," he said. An old lecher's remark.

"Thank you," she said. "But it's merely a temporary bonus of youth. I'll probably find myself eating and drinking too much and turning into a Chinese doughnut before I reach thirty."

She smiled and the room became brighter. Siri was fascinated. A mythical creature from whatever the Americans called their version of the Ramayana had landed in his midst and could speak his language. And it was true, despite her fluency in Lao she was alien. Perhaps it could be attributed to her youth but she had none of the modest charm of his countrywomen. She didn't defer to the male of the species. She was rough-hearted like a soldier and Siri suspected she'd happily bite off the head of a mate when she was done with him. Judge Haeng would be sorely out of his depth if he thought he could use his standard courting rituals on such a creature.

4

SUMO IN A SUNDRESS

The Lao Justice Minister's office had an adjoining suite with a conference table made of teak. It was so large and heavy they'd had to cut it in slices in order to get it up to the third floor. Its reassembly hadn't been terribly successful and there were two incongruous lines of Happy New Year adhesive tape stretching across the table top to disguise the joins. At this table sat the American delegation to one side, and the Lao to the other. There were two perfectly good table ends but it appeared nobody was allowed to sit there. Instead, they faced off like American football teams. There were seven Americans, not including the interpreter, and eight Lao.

Siri wasn't terribly surprised to learn that the Lao simultaneous interpreter, Judge Haeng's cousin Vinai, was in bed with laryngitis. To the vice-minister's displeasure, the meeting was conducted through the competent but unverifiable translation of Peach, the missionary's daughter. But so confident was she in her interpretation that both sides soon settled into a seamless row of pleasantries and introductions. Like all very good translators she quickly became invisible; invisible that is to all except for Judge Haeng who ogled and grinned at her from across the table.

Like all the leaders, Minister of Justice Bounchu was a military man. For some, the transition from camouflage to charcoal gray had been an uneasy one. He'd been fighting for most of his life and living in the caves of Sam Neua throughout the revolution. It was obvious he'd be more comfortable with mortar fire exploding around him than he was in diplomatic circles. Despite his bulk and his ferocious countenance, there was something timid about him, like a polar bear shaved and put in an ill-fitting suit. This ministry was his sweet fish reward at the end of a heroic life, more a position than a role. He smiled and nodded and left all the details to his minions. He sat opposite the Sumo-in-sundress head of the American delegation, Representative Elizabeth Scribner, Democrat, Rhode Island. Selected for this mission presumably because of her bulk, Mrs. Scribner was not a smiling, all-friendly politician. In fact, one would have to assume she was elected to congress as a result of intimidation.

Siri, still with no idea why he'd been called for, listened to the minister's address with its pompous language, then to the reading of the early communications between the Chief of Mission of the United States consulate in Vientiane and the Ministry of Foreign Affairs of the Pathet Lao Government. Saigon had fallen to the Vietminh in April of 1975, and the Pathet Lao claimed the prize of Vientiane eight months later during a well-orchestrated handover. Being good sports, they invited the US consulate to remain in operation, insisting only on the removal of CIA personnel. That left a grand total of six, all confined to Vientiane with the odd trip across the Mekong for shopping in Nong Kai or other pleasures in Bangkok. The US State Department had attempted to sneak in one or two spooks as cleaning staff or book-keepers but the PL had a comprehensive list of the names and backgrounds of CIA operatives provided by the very resourceful Soviets. Apart from a little housekeeping, the remaining consulate staff were an ornamental lot. They had nothing much else to do but send memos to the PL. No consulate personnel had been allowed to travel around Laos. The US aid agency—USAID—compound had been closed and its employees hustled onto flights out of the country. So only a few dozen US citizens officially remained. Some were teaching, or married to Lao citizens, or working for the Quakers or Mennonites.

According to the communications, it appeared that a year earlier the consulate had made a request that they be allowed to investigate claims of US citizens held in captivity in Lao prisoner-of-war camps. The Lao had pointed out that following a unilateral program referred to as Homecoming, all known military and political prisoners in Laos and Vietnam had been handed back to their delegations. They added that the war was over and there was absolutely no point in hanging on to them anyway. But the Missing In Action—MIA—lobby in the US was strong and evidence was constantly materializing to indicate that there were indeed American ex-servicemen on Lao soil. In a number of memos, the PL had reminded the consulate that, according to US policy following the Treaty of Geneva in 1962, there were no American military on Lao soil to begin with. As there were officially no ground troops or US air force personnel active in Laos, with tongues in cheeks the PL had asked how these MIAs had been clumsy enough to find their ways into prisoner-of-war camps in the middle of a neutral country. The notes back and forth appeared to have reached a stalemate.

As they were unable to travel and had no permission to

investigate MIA claims, the US embassy in Bangkok invited Lao citizens to bring evidence of downed aircraft and/or remains of airmen to their Vientiane consulate where officials would check their veracity. There were rumors, none confirmed, that they were offering cash rewards for genuine finds. They could never have envisaged what a stampede this would produce. The queues extended around the block. Citizens had gone to great lengths to secure laissez-passers to travel to the capital to present their souvenirs. Others sent packages through the unreliable post with details of where to forward the checks. One clerk from the Central Identification Laboratory in Bangkok was responsible for sifting through a mountain of bones—most of them from pigs—and teeth: some from elderly relatives who hadn't quite finished with them. There were dog tags fashioned out of beer bottle tops and photographs of Uncle Dtoom who was albino but from the right angle looked just like an American airman. One hopeful claimant sent the front fender of an old Ford which he swore had fallen from the sky whilst he was working in his paddy.

Despite their obvious inauthenticity, all of the claims had to be labeled and documented. The site of a supposed discovery was marked on a map and after six months there were more crosses on that map than were military personnel active in the US armed forces. It was as if every village in Laos had its own downed airman. Yet, in all that time, not one positive identification was made and the program was abandoned. The Washington lobby was not amused so the US embassy in Bangkok moved on to its Plan B, to arrange for joint US/Lao teams to go off into the countryside to investigate claims in a professional manner.

All these recommendations were read out in painful detail during that long morning in Minister Bounchu's meeting room. Each guest had his or her own bottle of syrupy green Fanta for refreshment, and bottomless cups of lukewarm tea were available. The Americans, unaccustomed as they were to Lao all-day meetings, drank thirstily. The Lao barely touched their drinks. After an hour and a half it became apparent why. There was a good deal of seat-shifting and leg-crossing from the American contingent and it was obvious that they were in need of a toilet break. Yet the seriousness of the day's affairs called for strict adherence to protocol. Nobody wanted a gaffe of etiquette to stymie the talks. Being the first to go to the toilet could be seen as a sign of weakness. So they held it in. The cadre reading the reports had not yet reached March 1978. There were still four months of communications to go and faint smiles on the faces of the Lao delegation.

But after another half an hour Congresswoman Scribner had apparently reached her limit. She cleared her throat, nodded politely, and sighed before beginning a serious conversation with the interpreter, Peach. The Lao, unused to interruptions during official gatherings, looked at her in astonishment. Peach, well aware of the infringement, apologized several times before passing on the Congresswoman's message.

"Congresswoman Scribner would like to point out that both sets of delegates already have copies of the various communications between the two sides," she said, nervously. "She humbly suggests that, without further ado, we get to the point at hand. The Americans wish to know whether the recommendation has been accepted. She. . . ."

At this point, Peach blushed and everyone on the Lao side could tell they were due for another hiccup of protocol.

"Go on. Say it," Siri urged her. "It can't get any worse."

All heads turned to Siri who smiled and shrugged. Peach continued.

"The congresswoman would like to remind the minister that the US consulate currently has a request for aid in the form of cash for the procurement of rice to stave off the effects of last year's harvest failure. It was signed by both the prime minister and the president. The congresswoman would . . . would not like to think that such an important decision might be stalled by the lack of agreement over a small MIA request."

The Lao present broke into a flurry of smiles but only Siri's was genuine. Apart from reading his address, the minister had found little to do at this meeting but his moment had come.

"Little sister," he said to Peach in a low, husky voice, "please tell the fat woman that she isn't in Washington now. This is Laos. We'll do things the way we do things. If she doesn't like it, she can go home."

And with that he gestured for the clerk to read on. The congresswoman came to the boil like a pressure cooker and continued to bubble throughout the remainder of the morning. It was almost lunchtime before the government's response was read. The US delegates were bloated as dumplings, their leader visibly stewed. It was the vice-minister of defence who finally read the cabinet's decision.

"The Central Committee and the Politburo of the People's Democratic Republic of Laos have considered the request of the United States of America to conduct one single mission in the north of the country to search for a supposed downed airman. The Lao Subcommittee for Post Conflict Affairs is pleased to announce that your request has been accepted. A joint Lao/American task force will be dispatched to Xiang Khouang province in the northeast of Laos where an investigation will be conducted into the disappearance of civilian helicopter pilot Boyd H. Bowry. As per your description, Comrade Bowry apparently went missing in August 1968, whilst on a"—he cleared his throat as if the cough were written in the script—"'humanitarian aid mission' in the area around Long Cheng. After careful scrutiny, the subcommittee has approved eight of the fifteen names provided by your consulate, thus:

"Major Harold G. Potter—US Military, retired—as team leader;

"Dr. Donald Yamaguchi—forensic pathologist attached to the University of Hawaii;

"Sgt. John Johnson—United States Marine Corps attached to the United States consulate in Vientiane;

"Mr. Mack Gordon—second secretary of the United States Embassy in Bangkok;

"Mr. Randal Rhyme—journalist with *Time* magazine;

"Miss Peach Short—interpreter.

"These six may later be joined by Senator Ulysses Vogal the Third—United States Senator, Republican, South Carolina, and Miss Ethel Chin, secretary to the senator.

"The People's Democratic Republic of Laos will be sending the following ten officials to work on an equal, counterpart basis with the United States team. Its members are. . . ."

Siri listened to the reading of the list with little surprise. It was the type of cronyism he'd come to expect from his government. He recognized most of the names and their familial and professional connections to people in high places. The majority were incompetent or, at best, redundant. The only name that jumped out at him as being a marvelous choice, a true professional medical man with a stunning record, was his own tucked down there at the bottom. So, that was why they'd dragged him along. They didn't even have the good manners to consult with him beforehand. Well, he thought, I'll be taking a dip in the Mekhong with rocks tied to my old fellow before they get me on a joint task force to Xiang Khouang. Dream on, Politburo. Unless. . . .

To the great, almost visible relief of the delegates, the vice-minister announced they'd be breaking for lunch and would talk about details and dates early in the afternoon. A room never cleared so fast. In seconds, only Siri and Minister Bounchu remained. They'd been through countless campaigns together. Siri knew the general to be a sincere but simple man. He knew the soldier saw Siri's educational background as a barrier between them, as did many of the jungle elite. Siri's lack of respect for the Party line didn't help to bring the two old men together. They admired each other for their respective skills; Bounchu's expertise at inflicting damage on men, Siri's at repairing them. But they had never been, and could never be, friends.

"You're going to make this difficult for me, aren't you, Siri?" Bounchu said, leaning back on his creaking chair. He avoided looking into Siri's emerald green eyes. Eyes that intimidated so many.

"Not at all," Siri replied. "I'm going to make it dead simple."

"You can't not go, you know?"

"Oh, I can."

"You'd embarrass the Party, Siri. Not for the first time, I know. The Americans are aware we have just the one coroner. They specifically mentioned your name."

"They're looking for bones, Comrade. I don't know a humerus from a whale's appendage."

"Listen. If you didn't go, they'd be the experts."

"They *are* the experts. I'm a converted bush surgeon. They have a decorated forensic pathologist on their team. A real one."

"Well, for some reason, they hold you in esteem, Siri. They know about the cases you've worked on. It's what they believe you are that counts, not what you consider yourself to be. We need someone there who can keep a professional eye on them. Like it or not, you're the only one we've got."

"Don't you read the *Pasason Lao*, Comrade Bounchu? I've just come back from a very traumatic holiday in Cambodia." He ran a finger across the tick-shaped scar on his forehead. "I'm not fit for service. I'd never pass the medical."

"Yes, I've heard all about it. It was unfortunate, I give you that."

"Unfortunate? You're right. Torture and starvation and near death could get a little troublesome. By rights I shouldn't be here today. And it's for that very reason that I don't have to take any more damned fool orders from you lot. You can't do any worse to me than the Khmer Rouge did. What were you thinking, Bounchu? That you'd drag me into this meeting stone cold, show me no respect, and expect me to be so fired up with national pride after a morning with the enemy that I'd gladly traipse up north on a bone hunt? It might work with your young brainwashed cadres but I'm over the hill and happily rolling down the far side. I'm a renegade. Out of control. So you either shoot me for disobedience or put up with me telling you where you can stick your task force."

Siri drank his green Fanta as a sort of visual exclamation mark. It was warm and syrupy and he wished he hadn't but it was a fittingly dramatic touch. Bounchu wasn't the type to fly into a rage. One of his qualities as a leader was his poker face. You could never tell whether he was about to shake your hand or shoot you. It wasn't until he smiled that Siri knew the minister wouldn't be reaching for his Kalashnikov.

"Siri, old friend," he said. "We've been through a lot together."

A drastic change of tactic, Siri noted. He recognized the sudden lowering of the red flag and the hoisting of a white one in its place. Now they were old friends?

"I'm really in a tough situation here," Bounchu said softly. "The prime minister really wants this mission to go well and he insisted I do everything humanly possible to convince you. I don't want to put any pressure on you, comrade. I know what you've been through. But, surely for old time's sake you could help me out just this once. Five days in the north? Is that too much to ask?"

Siri shook his head slowly.

"I don't know," he said.

"I'd consider it a personal favor."

"There might be a way."

"Name it."

"So, tell me again," said Madame Daeng.

"No matter how many times I tell it, the story won't change," Siri assured her. "Unless of course you ask me again in three weeks by which time I will have forgotten the original story and be forced to come up with something far more entertaining to tell you."

Siri was attempting to understand American culture by reading Henry James's *The American*, translated into French. But either the translator lacked the ability to extract the precious ore from the dense seams in James's prose, or James learned his craft writing radio scripts for Thai soap operas. Either way, Siri's confidence was beginning to ebb. He doubted the book would help him understand Americans in the three weeks he had left to familiarize himself. He was thinking of switching to Melville. He had other translated works in his secret library: Harper Lee, even Scott Fitzgerald. He firmly believed that you could learn most about a people by reading the works their academics convinced them were worthy of the title "classical."

"Then let me just see if I've got the facts right," Daeng continued. She was standing in the doorway of the Paiboun memorial library—their back bedroom—with her arms folded. "Call me cynical if you like. . . ."

"I would never dare."

"But, for some reason, none of this seems to ring true."

"Then I must be lying. I'm hurt."

"Siri, I would never accuse you of lying even if I know for a fact that you were. It's not what a good wife does. But you do have the ability to leave out strategic parts of stories and what remains, although not exactly a lie, plays a substantially different tune to the truth."

"So sing me what you have."

"Minister Bounchu calls you into his office and asks you to lead a team—"

"Technically, General Suvan's the team leader."

"Right. But he drools a lot and forgets where he is. He's obviously only on the team as a charitable political appointee. His name was next in line for a junket."

"A fair appraisal."

"And, with no pressure whatsoever from you, no coercion or bribery, the minister accepts the list of names you put together for a task force to head off into the jungle with the Americans. And your list just happens to include your wife, your nurse and her husband, your morgue assistant and your best friend."

"And Commander Lit from Vieng Xai."

"Who you befriended on a case."

"He's a good man."

"And Minister Bounchu said, "Good one, Siri. Nice choices.""

"Something not unlike that, yes."

"Siri?"

"Yes?"

"Did you blackmail the Minister of Justice?"

"How could you even suggest such a thing?"

"Threaten to expose something from his past? Things only a doctor would know?"

"I told you about that?"

"Siri?"

"Absolutely not."

"You know I'll find out eventually."

"Yes, but I enjoy your interrogation methods. Come on, Daeng. We'll have a grand old time."

"Which brings me to the purpose of this mission; what you've been calling our group vacation to the northeast. We are to team up with a bunch of American professionals and head off into the jungle to look for the remains of a downed aircraft."

"And its pilot."

"And you believe this trip won't be stressful? You do remember you're convalescing?"

"A stroll in the cool forests. A little scoop here and there with a trowel. Lunch and a little rice whiskey with friendly local hill tribesmen. What better than a week in the cool fresh mountain air of Xiang Khouang? In Europe they pay huge sums of money for alpine spa retreats and here we are getting paid to attend one. Explain to me how that could be a bad thing, Madame Daeng. Nothing to worry about at all."

"I'd like to believe so. Because it might have escaped your memory but not two months ago you were knocking on death's door . . . from the inside. And trouble finds you, Siri Paiboun."

"Trust me. Nothing can go wrong this time."

5

CUEBALL DAVE

Cueball Dave still insisted on the ponytail. He got comments about it all the time. They called him pathetic. Guys over fifty don't put their hair in a ponytail, they said. It's an act of desperation, they said, especially when the top of your head's as white and shiny as a cue ball, hence the nickname. But Cueball Dave didn't care what they thought. He didn't want to look like all those other old fogies. It gave him a style. Told them all he wasn't a bank manager. Told them he had a wild background. And the girls in Pattaya loved tugging on that little tail of his.

He had a comfortable life. He'd lived in Thailand for ten years and couldn't speak a word of Thai. Waste of time. Stupid tones he couldn't get his tongue round, and besides, all the night people spoke some kind of English. He had a condominium room he'd bought and paid for, had shares in a restaurant he ate at, a regular bar he drank at, and a dozen or so regular serious night-time relationships. He had a wife and kids somewhere back in Boston, and a pilot's licence, canceled, in some bureaucrat's drawer in DC. Life had become very simple for Cueball Dave. There were those who could only dream of such a life. But Dave was always looking for more. Always had his eye open for something better. And then, in a moment of brilliance, he made it happen. Things were about to change.

He was out on the town celebrating his good fortune. He was in a Johnny Walker atmosphere vacuum where everything outside the bubble wasn't really happening. He might not have been in that bar at all. In front of his nose were the ankles and too-large stiletto heels of a girl in a bikini, dancing—kind of. Some sixties rock was bellowing out of the speakers and there was a sweaty stale strawberry-tinted smell in the air. A dozen cheap air-fresheners hung behind the bar like decorations. A well-groomed homo was making eyes at him from across the stage. There was a gibbon on a chain begging drinks. Someone had rung the free-shots-for-everyone bell by accident earlier and the bar stewards had beaten him up when he refused to pay. Dave was on his third beer mat. The first two were his fretwork initials now. The drunk he'd been talking to had vanished. He wondered how long he'd been alone. He held on to his glass as if he might tip backwards off the stool should he let go of it. Then someone stepped inside his vacuum.

"Excuse me."

Cueball Dave swiveled his neck around slowly as if it was starting to rust and saw the homo standing there. He was dressed as a man but any Asian in a place like this was after something.

"Look, son. I don't—" he started.

"I'm sorry to trouble you, but aren't you David Leon?"

"I might be."

"You don't remember me? I was one of your flight mechanics at Udon. Manuel Castillo. Manny. From the Philippines?"

"Well, yeah. Sure," said Dave. He had no idea who this boy was but he didn't want to make himself sound like he thought all Asians looked the same. Young for a field mechanic though. Perhaps he'd met him. Too much of a coincidence for it to be a pickup line.

"I'm so happy. I knew it was you," said the young man.

Manuel Castillo, or whatever his name was, threw his arms around the ex-pilot before the old boy could get out of his way. His cufflink caught on Cueball Dave's neck. Then the lights went out.

The Baby Booby Agogo didn't exactly close. It wound down and then wound back up again depending on how many customers were there and how much money they were spending. Cueball Dave wasn't spending any money and he was taking up valuable space. He'd been unconscious on the countertop for an hour and he made the place look low class. The *mamasan*, a sprightly old lady whose makeup appeared lime green under the mood lights, decided that, regular customer or not, Dave had overstayed his welcome. She shook him roughly but he didn't react. After her second attempt to rouse him, she felt for his pulse. She was a woman of vast experience so her next reaction was to take out his wallet, remove all but twenty *baht*, replace the wallet and shout for the bar manager. Another customer had chosen the Baby Booby as his final resting place.

6

THE EAST WING

The Friendship Hotel in Phonsavan, designed like a hunting lodge, so they say, had originally been called the Snow Leopard Inn. It was very close to the old airfield and a short walk from one of the many jar clusters on the Plain of Jars. The hotel was built and occupied for many years by Corsican drug dealers in the heyday of the plain's notorious opium trade. The building served as a warehouse for pressed opium and the mafia pilots made daily stops at the heroin processing plants before delivering their wicked wares to the poor saps fighting in Vietnam. When local politics and war forced the Europeans out of business, the building was renovated and rooms were added. There was nothing remarkable about the Friendship Hotel other than the miracle of its continued presence. It stood amid a landscape of craters in the most bombed area of the war. It somehow avoided the total decimation of every recognizable structure from hospitals to pig pens and nobody could explain why it was still standing, not even allowing for the well-documented lack of expertise of the Royal Lao bomber pilots. There was overwhelming evidence of near misses. The surrounding countryside was littered with unexploded ordnance and large signs at the hotel perimeter warned guests not to venture beyond the fence. The signs were written in Lao and Russian.

Whether the USMIA task-force members were aware they'd be sleeping in the one-time hub of the Indochinese drug trade was hard to say. But they'd certainly been briefed on the dangers of taking leisurely strolls through the countryside. The hotel manager, a small bubbly Hmong by the name of Toua, had assured the government that the grounds had been cleared of explosives before the extra bungalows were erected behind the main building. Even so, as they hurriedly assembled the bamboo chalets for the MIA teams, a worker had run his hoe into a cluster bomb and lost a foot. He'd become a member of a sizeable club. Few of the residents of Phonsavan could claim a complete set of limbs or appendages. Between 1964 and 1973 there were some 500,000 bombing missions in Laos. Two-point-three million tons of ordnance were rained upon the land. Almost half of this was in the form of cluster bombs; "bombies" as they were affectionately known. And a third of those hadn't gone off. Not yet. Since the ceasefire, the sly little devils had claimed another twenty-thousand victims. Operation Rain Dance had begun to pepper the Plain of Jars with bombs in 1969 and no clearance operation could ever rid the region of the danger. To everyone's relief, nothing untoward had happened since the arrival of the Lao and American delegations at the Friendship Hotel. But manager Toua was keeping his three remaining fingers crossed.

The key personnel of the two delegations were billeted in opposite wings of the lodge in rather basic but clean rooms. Those considered to be of a lower status were put up in the bungalows at the rear. These decisions had been taken by Judge Haeng, who, despite his socialist background, was ever conscious of class and status. The security detail comprised two elderly gentlemen with antique muskets who appeared to be on twenty-four-hour shifts as they were ever-present. Even with the noisy generator rattling and clunking at full throttle, electricity was only available from 6:00 until 9:00 P.M. Thence, the guests were left to their own devices. Flashlight beams sabred through the curtains of the American west wing and loud but incomprehensible voices were carried away on cool breezes into the tar-black night.

In the east wing, General Suvan, the Lao team leader, had retired early. The old soldier spent a good deal of his time either napping or being completely asleep. Even when he was awake he had that saggy facial skin that made him look as if his features were permanently drowsy. Judge Haeng and his cousin Vinai, the Lao interpreter, were sharing a double. Mumbled secrets could be heard through the stucco walls of their darkened room. These three had been the only "non-negotiable" members of the Lao delegation. Minister Bounchu had to maintain some face, after all.

At the furthest extremity of the east wing, a circle of lit candles inside a circle of people illuminated a dozen bottles of rice whisky. The bottles had handwritten labels and cardboard stoppers wrapped in plastic so their pedigree was in no doubt. The taste, however, was exemplary. The mixer of choice was locally produced papaya juice and the finger food was corned beef from cans and graham crackers, both pilfered from the huge stock of supplies brought in by the Americans.

"Exactly how long are they planning to stay up here?" asked Civilai. The ex-Politburo pain-in-the-backside had beaten his best friend Siri into retirement by twelve months. He'd spent most of that time eating. For many years no more than a stick figure with a balding globe at its apex, Civilai's parts were slowly starting to swell, led most triumphantly by his stomach. Not fat by any stretch of the imagination but the old gentleman carried his paunch around proudly like a monk with a new silver alms bowl.

"Theirs is an eating culture," Siri explained to him. "Like the Thais. Whereas we're more of a drinking culture. Good luck!"

He raised his glass and all those seated around on the grass floor matting mirrored the gesture and echoed "Good luck" in hushed but enthusiastic tones. They swigged their fruity nightcaps.

"And here's to Malee," Siri continued. "Beautiful daughter of Nurse Dtui here and her handsome beau, Inspector Phosy." Again the group raised their glasses and swigged. "Malee is experiencing her first week away from her parents. Let's hope she doesn't get into any bad habits at the state crèche."

"Here here," said Dtui.

"And," Siri said, "as the scene at Wattay airport was characteristically chaotic and I didn't get a chance to introduce him properly, allow me to welcome our old friend, Commander Lit from the security division. The Minister insisted we have someone from security on the team and I could think of nobody better."

The applause was deliberately muffled as nobody wanted to alert Judge Haeng to their soiree. Lit was a tall, gangly bespectacled man, stiff as a teak plank. His smile was easy and his eyes keen.

"Lit has recently been promoted and transferred to the third garrison in Vientiane, " Siri added. "I had the pleasure of working with him in Vieng Xai and I know he'll be a most splendid member of our team."

Siri could have added more. He could have mentioned, for example, that the young officer had been so taken with his Nurse Dtui during that trip that he had asked her to marry him. As Dtui had turned him down and as her current husband was now sitting beside her, Siri decided nothing would be gained from that announcement apart from a little sport with Inspector Phosy. But that could wait. "Lit," he said, "there are some people here you don't know. This gentleman to my left is our morgue expert and the most hard-working person in Vientiane: Mr. Geung Watajak. Geung, you really don't have to stand u—oh, very well."

Even though he was drinking nothing but papaya juice, Geung made standing up look difficult. The flickering of the candles seemed to disorient him. His balance secured, he held up his glass and said, "I . . . I . . . am very proud."

With that he knocked back his juice like a Glaswegian downing a dram of Scotch and they never did learn what he was proud of. Given Geung's "situation," Siri had expected him to take time over agreeing to accompany them north, or even to refuse to come. But Geung's loyalty to the Mahosot morgue, a commitment which had on one occasion almost killed him, was unshakeable. He'd never been invited on a field trip before. He was always the man left behind to sweep away the cockroaches and welcome new guests into the freezer. So when they announced he'd be coming along, his face had lit up like the floodlights at the That Luang Festival. Romance was obviously a minor league activity for Mr. Geung. He'd been able to talk of nothing but the trip for two weeks and had taken that long to pack. It was astounding how a man with no possessions could fill a large suitcase as he did. The morgue seemed a lot emptier once he'd loaded up his bag. They all toasted him, upended their glasses and leaned into the circle of light for refills. Geung lowered himself back onto the mat and Siri continued the introductions.

"Beside Nurse Dtui, who you know," he said with a wink, "is Vientiane's one and only competent police officer, Inspector Phosy." Phosy always looked a lot smaller than he was when compared to his large rosy wife. But he was all muscle and brawn. He received his applause with a deep, overly respectful *nop*.

"Next," said Siri, "a legend in the underground resistance forces against the French, a spy of many faces, never discovered by the enemy, a woman with an intellect so high that she married me"—riding the groans—"and the maker of the best noodles on this and probably every other planet, I present you, Madame Daeng."

After accepting her applause, Daeng reminded Siri that the candles had grown a lot shorter since he started speaking.

"Right," he agreed. "Which fittingly brings us to the last of our team, a young lady who—"

"What do you mean, the last?" said Civilai most indignantly. "What about me?"

"What about you?"

"Don't I deserve an introduction?"

"You always told me you're a man who doesn't need one, old brother."

"That only applies to people who've heard of me."

"I thought everyone had heard of you. Good and bad."

"I've been out of circulation. Even the memory of the brightest star fades in the night."

"Very well," said Siri. "This old gentleman, this fading starlet, used to be Comrade Civilai of the Politburo. He was once fully twinkling—a somebody. He is now commander-in-chief of the larder. A politico of pies and pastries. A diplomat of the dining room table. A—"

"They get it," said Civilai, helping himself to another corned-beef canapé.

"And now to our guest," said Siri. "We welcome to this informal first night meeting, Miss Peach Short. Yes, undoubtedly a spy from the far west wing, but as Judge Haeng has already discovered, a spy easy on the eye."

After very polite thanks at being invited to join the Lao team, Peach looked seriously around the table.

"You do realize I'm underage for all this drinking, don't you?" she giggled.

"Ha!" said Civilai. "Age is far too abstract a concept to be "under." This is Laos. We mature much faster over here. Nurse Dtui's daughter has already won the crèche cocktail mixing competition two months running. And this is an initiation. This is where we find out just how Lao you are. You can obviously talk the talk, but can you drink the drink?"

"He's right," said Daeng. "Unless you've made a complete fool of yourself in public at least once, you can't really be called one of us."

"At least once," Civilai added.

Peach took a deep breath, threw back her drink in one gulp, and reached for the bottle. The cheer was a little over the top. With luck, the sound of the Americans yelling at each other might have drowned it out.

"Exactly how old are you?" Dtui asked.

"Seventeen and eleven months."

"You see?" said Civilai. "If she was from the tribes she'd have four children by now. But how did the daughter of a missionary learn to drink, little daughter?"

"Mom and Dad did the remote village thing," she told him. "They schooled my brothers and sister and me at home and let us run wild with the local kids. When we grew up they trusted us to have the common sense to know what was right. But by then our right was more the village's right than theirs. We did stuff we still haven't gotten around to telling the folks about. Best they don't know, I say. I guess it's what you deserve for naming all your kids after fruit."

"Boys too?" Civilai asked.

"Melon and Mango."

"Poor lads."

"And where's your family now?" Daeng asked.

"They were asked politely by the local cadre if they wouldn't mind leaving the country. Most of the independent missionaries were thrown out when the PL took over. They were too poor, I guess. Your authorities only turned a blind eye to the religious groups with enough money to invest in development projects."

Siri smiled. She was fearless. If ever Haeng stopped drooling for five minutes to listen to what she was saying, he'd hate her.

"Why didn't you go with them?" Phosy asked.

"Where to? Indiana? No way. I wouldn't know what to do there. I don't know those people. This is my home. I applied for a teaching job on local rates and got it. Not enough to live on but these little junkets sustain me when they come along. Mom and Dad are pissed at the communists. They're fund-raising right now to support the insurgency. How Christian is that?"

"I don't think you should be telling us," said Dtui.

"What can I say? You can't choose your father."

"A father's goodness is as big as a mountain," said Daeng, who had a Lao saying for most occasions.

"I had my own ears and eyes, auntie," Peach replied. "First you hear it, so you must see it. Once you've seen it, so you must make a judgement with your heart. This is my judgement. I'm staying here."

A counter Lao saying.

"Very well," Siri said. "As Madame Daeng quite rightly points out, candles are not forever. So, before we are forced into our bunks, probably to be blown to kingdom come if any of us walks in our sleep, I've asked Peach to tell us what she's learned from the American contingent about the mission we're here for."

"At last," said Comrade Lit.

"I'm glad somebody knows," said Civilai.

"All right," said Peach. "Your Judge Haeng was supposed to pass all this on but he's not in the mood, for some reason. He asked me if I'd do it. This is what I've learned. Or, at least, what they told me at the briefing. We are here to find one Captain Boyd Bowry or his remains. When he disappeared in 1968 he was twenty-four years of age, which would make him thirty-four if he's still alive. He was a helicopter pilot attached to the Air America program out of Udon Thani in Thailand. I assume you all know about Air America?"

"Perhaps you could give us a quick overview so we know how the Americans see it," Siri suggested.

"OK," Peach went on, "I hope I can remember it all. Briefly, Air America was—still is, for all I know—an airline funded and operated by the CIA. They flew what they called "aid" missions inside Laos after the Geneva accord banned foreign military personnel. Of course the CIA continued to recruit military people, mostly marine pilots like Bowry. They took them out of uniform and maintained that they were civilian pilots working for a private company. They carried a lot more than rice, mind you. Captain Bowry was flying helicopter missions in and out of Laos for two years. As I'm sure you know, not a hundred kilometers from here were two CIA bases. One was at Sam Thong where there was a refugee camp for displaced hill tribe families. The other was at Long Cheng, the home of the CIA's secret army. It's where General Vang Pao and his Hmong troops were based. It's where the CIA trained them up to fight you guys. At one stage, Long Cheng, with all its troops and US advisors and pilots, was the second most populated city in the country after Vientiane. There were so many spies there it collected the name Spook Heaven or Spook City.

But that's the big picture. We're all here for the little picture. Captain Bowry."

"Why him?" Phosy asked. "I mean, of all the airmen they claim are missing, why is this man at the top of Washington's list?"

"Good question." Peach nodded. "And as far as I can see, it pretty much comes down to influence and pressure."

"And money," said Civilai. "It always comes down to money."

"You might be right, sir," Peach agreed. "Captain Bowry is or was the son of Senator Walter Bowry from South Carolina. It appears he's had people searching for his son for ten years. He sits on a couple of important committees and has a lot of clout in foreign policy. It's probably due to his cronies there that money was freed up from the aid budget to offer funding to Laos. There was a lot of opposition to it. "Why should we be feeding the enemy?" That kind of thing. It really flew in the face of anti-communist feeling. So you can be sure he had some kind of pull."

"Why this burst of excitement after ten years?" Daeng asked.

"On June tenth, someone sent the congressman photos purportedly taken inside Laos," Peach told her. "They showed a Caucasian peering out of a bamboo cell. In one of the pictures he seems to have a briefcase or something with him which might be relevant. He could have been in his thirties. He was bearded, suntanned and a lot thinner than the father remembered, but he believed it was his son. The picture quality wasn't that clear and other relatives weren't so certain but the congressman was positive."

"But he wasn't standing beside a road sign," Civilai said. "Wasn't holding a copy of the national newspaper?"

Peach shook her head.

"Just him in a hut, as far as I know," she said.

"Then there's absolutely no way to tell where or when the photos were taken," Civilai went on. "A hut is a hut is a hut. Could be at a theme park in Hong Kong for all they know. Am I right?"

"You're always right," said Siri. "But the important thing is that the photographs caused a reaction—money was made available and through just a little diplomatic extortion, this mission was instigated. And here we are, an ace team selected on merit on the basis of all the solid investigative work we've done in the past. The Party couldn't have chosen a finer band of professionals to find young Boyd and bring a little peace of mind to his family."

They toasted to this testimonial.

"What do we know as fact?" Lit asked.

"About the disappearance?" said Peach, flipping open her notepad. She paused to take a long sip of her drink then ran her finger down the page.

"It was the night of August eighth, 1968. Bowry and his Filipino flight mechanic, Nino Sebastian, had been drinking excessively at the forward air controller canteen at the Long Cheng base. They were with a pilot called Mike Wolff. He was with the FAC, the forward air control, also known as Ravens. It appears that they got hold of some LSD from somewhere and went out of their minds. At one stage, Bowry and Sebastian climbed into a cage with the mascot, a black bear, who was fortunately already sleeping off the effects of a heavy night of beer. Then, about two or three in the morning, Bowry announced he was going for a joyride in his chopper. Sebastian tried to talk him out of it but was too wasted to go after him. That wasn't the way it was written up in the official Air America report, by the way. Officially there was engine trouble and the helicopter went down in the mountains. Our version is from interviews with eyewitnesses; the FAC pilot he'd been drinking with in the canteen and the mechanic. That was the way they recalled it. Boyd Bowry headed off into the night sky and half an hour later they heard an explosion. They sent out search and rescue teams at first light but as they had no idea what direction he'd gone in, and there'd been no mayday signal, and there was no sign of wreckage, they abandoned the search after five days."

"If they heard the explosion he couldn't have gone very far," said Lit.

"And nothing else until the photos turned up?" asked Dtui. "No sightings? Reports?"

"Not a thing."

"Any ideas who sent the photos?" Phosy asked.

"They arrived at the US embassy in Bangkok in a sealed manila envelope care of the military attaché. No stamp. No frank mark. It was just there in the box along with the regular mail. The words "Laos, 78" were written on the back of the photos."

"In English characters?" Commander Lit asked.

"Yes. No identification of the sender."

"So, it wasn't from a bounty hunter hoping to get a reward," Civilai remarked casually. "It's usually about the money, you know."

"So you've said," Siri smiled. "How did the embassy identify the airman?"

"From one of the pictures," Peach told him. "It showed the tail section broken off the helicopter. It had the registration number H32. That was Bowry's."

"Does the American delegation have the photos with them?" asked Madame Daeng.

"I could ask."

"It might help to identify the area," Phosy put in. "Vegetation."

"Different plants growing at different elevations," added Commander Lit.

"If there are any locals in the pictures we might be able to identify their clothing," said Daeng. "At least we'd know what ethnic group we're looking for."

"Even the pilot himself," Siri added. "After all these years he'd be wearing the clothes they provided. That could give us a clue."

"The weave of a sarong," said Daeng.

"Just the style of putting together the bamboo hut," Phosy suggested. "Unique to different regions."

"Really," Commander Lit agreed, "there's a lot to be picked up from photographs if you know what you're looking for."

The group was suddenly aware of their American guest staring wide-eyed at the interaction and smiling warmly.

"Have you had a thought?" Siri asked.

"No."

"Then. . . . ?"

"You guys. You're. . . ."

"What?"

"Capable."

"Be careful now," laughed Civilai. "Such lavish praise might go to our heads."

"No, I'm serious. There I was thinking Dr. Siri put this guest list together so his friends and family could have an all-expenses-paid trip to the mountains. Nepotism, you know? That wouldn't have surprised me at all. But, you guys. . . ."

"Yes?"

"You're the real thing. You actually know what you're doing.'

'Too kind," said Daeng. "This calls for another round."

"I'm serious," said Peach.

"As am I," said Daeng. "And it wouldn't surprise me if you saw one or two other flashes of brilliance from us before the week's out. Hold on to your hat."

Siri smiled at this interaction, impressed at how Peach slotted so naturally into a Lao setting. She seemed mature and wise beyond her years.

Corned beef and crackers turned out to be a very appropriate complement to Xiang Khouang rice whiskey, especially with a good dollop of mustard. They refilled and re-drank and the conversation meandered around a myriad of subjects and drunkenness arrived with the night mist. Before they staggered off on their separate ways, they vowed not to rest until they found their young airman. Siri reminded them to use the signposted latrines rather than hopping over the back fence. Prostheses, said Civilai, after several stabs at the word, had come a long way since the peg but were still very poor substitutes for actual legs. The only people not to head off in search of their rooms that night were Siri and Daeng. Siri had tried to leave but Daeng reminded him that they had hosted the meeting in their own room. To be honest, she only remembered that at the last moment when she saw her corduroy working trousers hanging from the curtain rod. As the guests had taken one candle each to see their ways home, only two stunted candles remained on the grass mat. The room was a salon of slow dancing shadows.

"It's cold up here," said Daeng.

"We should huddle together for warmth," Siri suggested.

Siri's attempts at blowing out the candle flames left him coughing and wheezing.

"That's not a very promising sign for huddling," said Daeng.

"I'll be fine. It only happens when I exhale violently. I'm rather good at inhaling."

He licked his fingers, pinched, and the last flame died. The room could have been draped in black velvet, so rich was the darkness.

They skirted the island of bottles and glasses and made their way to the bed. As was his habit, Siri took the window side. The bed was covered with a quilt so thick that he almost needed a tire lever to lift it and insert himself underneath. He reached for his wife.

"My goodness, you aren't cold at all," he said.

"Patience. I'll be with you in a few seconds," she replied.

To his surprise, her voice had come not from the bed but from several meters away.

"Oh dear."

Siri extricated himself from the quilt as quickly as he was able.

"What's wrong?" Daeng asked.

"Do we have a flashlight in the bags?"

"Of course."

"Then we should turn it on. I think I may have just been unfaithful to you."

After a good deal of searching Daeng unearthed the lamp and shone the beam on a lump in the bed covers.

"Who on earth. . . ?" asked Daeng.

"Well, I tell you it certainly isn't one of the men."

He heaved off the quilt and there, sleeping like the dead, was Peach Short.

"Siri?"

"I didn't know. Honestly."

"Couples have been divorced over less."

"I thought she was you."

"When exactly did you realize she wasn't . . . no, perhaps you shouldn't answer that. We should take her to her room. She has a big day tomorrow."

"She looks so peaceful. Perhaps we should let her. . . ."

"Siri!"

"That was a joke, my dearest."

Despite all the lugging and manhandling and door opening and laying out, Peach didn't awaken from her drunken slumber when they sent her home. But by the time they got back to their room, Siri and Daeng were completely tuckered out. The only sound as they held hands under the covers was of their chests rising and falling. A new adventure was about to begin. The only thing certain about tomorrow was that their young American interpreter was going to have a very serious hangover.

7

THE ICE-BREAKER COMETH

The knock on the door might as well have been directly on the inside of Siri's head. Somebody was in his skull with a wrecking ball trying to get out. The groan from Daeng's side of the bed told him that she wasn't faring any better. If it was morning, the day was doing its damnedest not to show it. An early mist had oozed in through the open window and was swirling around the bed like dry ice. In the distance could be heard the thump of artillery fire as the joint Vietnamese/Lao forces began their daylight offensive against the last stubborn pocket of Hmong resistance at the Phu Bia mountain. While the Americans slept soundly in their beds, their discarded allies fought for their lives. The sound was the only sign that dawn had officially cracked. The knocking continued.

"Go away," said Siri, both to the hangover and the unwanted visitor.

"That rice whiskey. . . ?" said Daeng with a voice like a shovel through pebbles.

"I forgot to mention the day after," Siri confessed.

"I feel like. . . ."

"Me too."

"Was that a knock at the door or my eyelids banging together?"

Siri shuddered as he left the warmth of the quilt and quick-stepped across the cold floor to the door. Peach stood in the doorway with a massive smile on her face.

"Morning, Doctor," she said brightly and slid past Siri into the room. "I was gonna bring you doughnuts and coffee but the nearest deli's nine hundred kilometers away."

Daeng peered over the quilt.

"How on earth can you be this jolly?" she asked. "You were paralytic last night."

"I have a missionary's constitution. We get back on our feet really fast."

"Do you . . . er, remember anything about last night?" Siri asked.

"Absolutely," she smiled.

"Oh, really?"

"Yes. I remember taking a quick nap on your bed then waking up in my own. I guess showing off with fuel-injected rice whiskey isn't such a smart idea. Who. . . ?"

"Me and the doctor," said Daeng, unburdening herself of the bedcover.

"Well, I appreciate it."

"All part of the service. To what do we owe this wake-up call?"

"Orientation. Remember?" I told you I'd warn you what to expect at the start of each day? She opened her notebook. "OK, today will begin with the 'Getting to know you' breakfast at seven thirty. Once we all know each other we fly off to Long Cheng."

"Because?" Daeng asked.

"I guess because that was the last place anyone saw Boyd Bowry alive."

"And they think they might have misplaced him in a cupboard somewhere?"

"I doubt there are any cupboards left," Siri said. "I get the impression there isn't much remaining of the original outpost. Lost to mother nature and pillaging once the place was overrun, so they tell me."

"Maybe so," said Peach, "but, for whatever reason, that's where the surrounding villagers have been told to assemble with their war booty. You've heard the heavy artillery? It means we have to take a very circuitous route to avoid the hostilities. It should take over an hour to get to good old Spook City. The task force sets up a base camp there and we go through the stories and evidence until we get a plausible lead. Then we head off to investigate."

"I assume we'll have a packed lunch?" asked Daeng, massaging her temples with her thumbs.

"I don't think we'll need to worry about food on this entire trip, Madame Daeng," Peach laughed. "The chopper that brought us here could barely lift off from the weight of the provisions. They had the team all squashed up at the front. 'Leave not one can of spam behind' was the call."

"And everyone on the list turned up?" Siri asked.

"Pretty much. Senator Vogal and his secretary Miss Chin are on standby."

"What does that mean?"

"Well, it means he may not come. But they still needed to get official permission for the both of them, just in case."

"In case of what?"

"Success. If we rescue the pilot or we find his remains, he'll show his face up here. Right now he's slumming it at the Oriental in Bangkok for the five days of the mission. If he gets news of a breakthrough, they'll fly him in. He'll pose for pictures, shake a lot of hands, give quotes to the press. There'll be maximum exposure back home. Headlines. I doubt he'll stay here overnight. They'll fly him back to civilization the same day and he can go home. Job done."

"And why should he be involved at all?" Daeng asked.

"Well, he's big on the MIA lobby, for one. If they find a live one there's a lot of bucks to be had to keep looking. It's a sensitive issue in Washington. Big political strides to be made by supporting the vets, and, in turn, the military. And, two, he's Senator Bowry's best pal. Their kids played together. He knew Boyd. The family want him over here keeping tabs on the investigation."

"But he doesn't want to roll up his sleeves and help us dig," Siri remarked.

"It doesn't matter," said Peach. "He's in Bangkok. If you're on your recliner TV chair in the States that's every bit as good as being in the Lao jungle. "Senator Ulysses Vogal the third is in Southeast Asia supervising an MIA joint force mission." Good line. Nobody questions whether he's in the sweaty forests of northern Laos or doing cocktails in the lounge. Just the word "Asia" is scary enough over there. He'll be a hero. If we find Boyd it'll be his photo on the front page of the *Post* with his arm around the young man, sweat stains around his armpits. You and your team won't so much as crack a mention. "Local diggers" they'll call you."

"What if the boy's dead?" Daeng asked.

"Same difference. 'After a prolonged search, Senator Vogal sadly carries the remains of his best friend's war hero son across the bitumen to board the TWA flight home.' Votes a-plenty there from the female electorate. He'll do great in farming communities."

"You're impressively cynical for such a young thing," Daeng smiled.

"Madame Daeng, you try growing up white in Southeast Asia during an American war. The lines between them and us and right and wrong get real fuzzy. It was people like Vogal who decided there should be intervention over here to stop the communist takeover of the world. It was a policy experiment to prop up the fading popularity of the president. Another snow job to con the gullible general voters of North America."

There was a long silence in the misty room.

"Very well," said Siri. "As we haven't even begun to look for the pilot, we're still quite a way from finding him. It's possible we won't have to disturb the senator from his cocktails. Let's take it from the introduction breakfast and see how we progress from there. Little Peach, do you foresee any disasters over our communal rice porridge?"

"Do you really want to know?" she asked.

"Major Harold Potter would like to welcome all the Lao delegates and says that he greatly respects the People's Democratic Republic of Laos for everything the socialist administration has achieved in the past three years."

Judge Haeng's cousin Vinai, the director of the Office of Interpretation Services, was standing at the end of the dining room at a beautifully carved but wonky dais. The audience sat at two long parallel tables. The Friendship Hotel restaurant had once been the entire building. It was constructed of sturdy hand-sawn lumber and its pillars were sunk deep. But the tin roof had been replaced with concrete tiling and, apart from the doors and window frames, very little wood had been used to complete the new lodge. Perhaps this was why only the dining room felt comfortable. It was as if the laid-back ghosts of the Corsicans watched over their inn from the solid rafters. Even the inevitable breakfast speeches seemed mellow.

Siri turned to Daeng.

"The major said all that in four words?"

"You'd have to assume English is a lot more succinct than Lao," Daeng decided.

Siri had studied French at a Lao *lycée* then become fluent during his years in Paris, but he'd had no cause to dally with the English language. Cousin Vinai's English rendition of the American major's comment had sounded authentic but he had no idea how accurate a translation it was. It was the conflicting word count and the bewildered faces of Peach and Nurse Dtui that alerted him to the possibility that something might be amiss. Cousin Vinai had been allotted the role of senior interpreter for the mission, yet since their arrival in Phonsavan he'd avoided all contact with the aliens. The judge suggested this was because of Vinai's laryngitis and that he wanted to preserve his voice for the first day of activities. That day had arrived and he had supposedly translated General Suvan's opening address word for word from his own script.

To Vinai's left at the VIP table, which was resplendent with plastic hibiscus, sat General Suvan in full dress uniform. In fact, Lao full dress uniform was not as impressive as it sounded. He might have been mistaken for a postman in any other country. Although the same age as Siri, the balding old man made the doctor look like a teenager. His movements were languid and his reactions showed a lack of reflex. In front of him on the table was the three-page speech he'd just delivered. It was dog-eared and crumpled so he'd either slept on it or it was a well-used address. Vinai had his own copy. During the speech, the fried eggs and crispy bacon and steaming pots of instant coffee arrived and, as there was still a pervading atmosphere of nervous cultural tension between the two groups, nobody tucked in. So the guests watched their food slowly cool in front of them. Another half an hour would render the meal inedible which probably explained the brevity of the American major's own greeting. But, to their horror, Judge Haeng seated to the general's left reached into his own brief-case and pulled out a wad of paper twice as thick as that of the general. Cousin Vinai produced a translation of equal thickness. The judge slid back his chair but Siri got to his feet before him.

"With respect, Judge," he said, wondering whether that counted as an oxymoron. If looks could kill, Judge Haeng was standing over Siri's body with bloody fingers.

"As this is a special occasion," Siri went on, "I suggest that it would be a courtesy to our American guests if we followed their culture and ate while we listened to your probably insightful and humorous early morning discourse."

He still had little idea about American culture or whether they ate during speeches in the United States—Henry James certainly didn't—but he was hungry. Judging from the ensuing round of applause once the translation had reached the visitors' table, they were hungry too. And so, Judge Haeng's speech and its purport-edly English translation were all but drowned out by the clattering of American knives and forks and the hum of conversation. Nobody failed to notice the fact that Haeng glared at Siri the entire time. Siri seemed not to care. He was taking the opportunity to study the colorful assembly of Americans opposite.

The retired major, Potter, wore a large flowery Hawaiian shirt, green shorts with an impressive collection of pockets, huge boots, and a Dodgers baseball cap. Siri could think of no better word to describe his complexion than "ripe." He was flushed and bloated like a man dropped into boiling water and left there to simmer, the result of blood vessels expanding. His nose was a crimson golf ball. He was, Siri decided, a man lost to alcoholism. This vora-cious appetite extended to food. Peach, seated beside him, looked on in amazement as he forked a mountain of potatoes into himself.

"Honey," he said.

Peach looked around for the bar girl he might have been soliciting. She saw nobody.

"Are you talking to me, Major?"

"You're the interpreter, right?"

"I am."

"Then shouldn't you be telling us what these two guys are saying?"

"Well"—she looked over her shoulder—"one of these guys is Judge Haeng and he's giving a long talk about the tolerant nature of the Pathet Lao to former imperialist oppressors. And the other guy is translating it into English."

"What?" The major put down his fork for the first time and cocked an ear in the direction of cousin Vinai. "That's English?"

"Apparently."

"I can't understand a goddamned word. Can't they get the interpreter to do it?"

"Comrade Vinai is the head interpreter, Major."

"What about the big woman?"

"What big woman would that be, sir?"

"The one they put on our chopper yesterday. She spoke pretty good."

"On our helicopter?"

"Yeah, you didn't see her? She was the only Laotian on board."

"I was stuck at the back behind a wall of cans, but, no, can't say I noticed her."

"Well, she was damned good."

Once the Judge Haeng/Cousin Vinai double act was over and the plates emptied, everyone sat with their coffee waiting for the main event. Peach tapped the major's arm.

"You're up, Major," she said.

Potter wiped his mouth with a paper napkin and inflated to a standing position. He said something loud and full of expression and then paused. There was an embarrassing silence. All eyes were on Cousin Vinai who was burrowing down into a bowl of rice soup. He waved his spoon at Peach.

"You take it, little sister," he said. "This is the first chance I've had to eat."

So, once again, Peach assumed the mantle of interpreter. She explained that Major Potter had planned a small activity as an icebreaker for the two sides to get to know each other. It was an adaptation of the game charades, of which none of the Lao apart from Siri and Civilai had heard. Siri gritted his teeth. For charades to be fun—if it ever truly was—you had to be three sheets to the wind, not hungover and stone-cold sober at breakfast. But there was no fighting it. Sergeant Johnson, perhaps the blackest live man Siri had seen in Laos, handed out cards apologetically. He was a marine based at the US Consulate in Vientiane. He had a booming sugary voice. He leaned into his walk like a meatless Nebraska Man in a hurry to catch up with evolution. But his gait put his smile out in front of him and it was a marvelous smile. It fitted on that handsome face with its gleaming eyes that took in everything around them.

The names of all those in attendance had been written in both Lao and English and the cards had strings attached so they could be hung around the neck.

"Oh, heaven help us," said Civilai. "Didn't the Chinese do something like this during the cultural revolution? What humiliation."

"Get into the spirit, brother," Siri said.

"If only I could."

But to make matters worse, the Americans all stood and pushed their tables and chairs back to the wall. The Lao assumed they were supposed to do the same so the moment arrived when both teams were standing facing each other with no barriers between them. The symbolism was poignant. Whether this was his idea or a directive from Washington nobody would know, but Major Potter stepped forward and said, "*Kwoi soo* Harold."

The Lao looked on in amazement. Had the major actually announced in Thai that he had a fighting penis? It was a bold statement if true. But they racked their brains for another possible meaning. It was Dtui who found it.

"Ah, *koi seu* Harold," she said. "My name is Harold."

The Lao echoed the utterance in relief and the ice began to break quite accidentally and all by itself. You couldn't go downhill from there. The point of the game was to give your name in English and Lao and then mime what you did for a living for the other team to guess. The major launched into a gala performance of marching and shooting and saluting and the Lao kept silent. Everyone knew he was a retired major but they wanted to draw out the embarrassment. Oddly, the more he mimed the happier he appeared to be and the more the US contingent laughed. They were an amusing bunch with apparently no shame at all. It was Judge Haeng who finally called out enthusiastically, "He's a soldier."

This was translated and the Americans and Mr. Geung applauded and whooped.

"He's a soldier," laughed Mr. Geung.

This delighted the Lao who were now officially into the spirit of the moment. Even General Suvan came to for the event. His mime of a soldier was remarkably similar to that of the major, albeit slower, but he was delighted when somebody guessed correctly and he slumped back into a chair from the exertion. The game continued and was a success at many levels. Civilai had several lewd suggestions, none of them translated by Peach. All on the American side knew that Daeng was having a joke with them when she mimed that she was just a noodle seller and Mr. Geung could not resist adding sound effects as he sawed through the rib cage of an imaginary corpse. Peach was the last to go. Her hand gestures of two people talking led to Mr. Geung's guess that she was a duck farmer and that heralded the biggest laugh of the morning.

By the time they were due to file out of the dining room, despite the odds and the temperature, there was no ice left to break. The two groups merged and mingled and attempted their few words of the others' language. They shook hands and smiled and laughed at nothing in particular. If only the war had been conducted under similar rules.

Only one man, it seemed, was not humming the melody of peace and love. To date, Judge Haeng had not engaged Siri in conversation. In fact they hadn't spoken since before the doctor made changes to the team list. But here, with everyone in a milling mood, he made a beeline to the old coroner and grasped his left hand like a claw crane engaging a sack of rice. He smiled, but not for Siri's benefit.

"I haven't had a chance to thank you for adulterating the personnel list that I'd spent a month finalizing," he snarled behind his teeth. "I don't know how you did it, Siri, how you forced the minister's hand on this, but I promise you I will not forget it. Never. I'm the wrong man to get on the wrong side of and you are firmly on that side, Siri Paiboun. You have tossed able men and women from this work detail, respectable cadres with status and influence and you have replaced them with morons and housewives and senile sociopaths." (Siri took the latter to mean Civilai rather than himself.) "And you embarrass me further by including my name in your circus ring. It's all too too bad. A good communist does not shake his comrade by the hand and stab him in the back at the same time."

Siri matched the man's smile.

"I imagine I'd need a very long knife with a curve on it to achieve such a feat," Siri said. "Or perhaps a scythe. Yes, that might work. Otherwise I'd have to let go of the hand then run round the back. But, by then you'd know what my intention was, wouldn't you."

"What are you. . . ?

"Dear Judge Haeng, I don't need to do anything behind your back. If you ever threaten me again with your menacing hand-shake, or insult my friends and family, you'll have me to deal with face to face. What you've experienced of me so far is nothing compared to what you'll get if you don't back off. You aren't my boss any more. You're just another annoying civil servant."

He removed his hand from its clammy nest, and left a fuming judge smiling at himself.

Before heading off to the helicopters, Major Potter singled out Cousin Vinai from the herd and put his arm around the inter-preter's shoulder as if they'd been friends for years. The major yelled to get everyone's attention, pointed at Vinai and said a few words. There was something in Vinai's eyes that Siri recalled witnessing in the expression of a deer they'd cornered in a dead-end gorge during the fighting. It was that "on a spit by supper time" look. He gazed around desperately for Peach but she was nowhere to be seen. He was on his own.

"The . . . er, major would like to say how impressed he is with the record of the Pathet Lao over the first three years of their administration," said Vinai.

Judge Haeng and General Suvan clapped but a worm of suspi-cion had already crawled through the minds of the other onlookers.

Siri looked at Dtui who shook her head. Major Potter spoke again. Vinai, still scanning the room for Peach, said, 'The major is saddened when . . . he sees so much destruction in this area . . . caused by the bombing."

Haeng and Suvan clapped again. Siri sighed.

"Vinai, please tell the major we're interested to know whether he's been to Laos before," Civilai shouted.

"No, this is his first trip," said Vinai, without translating.

"Ask him," said Civilai.

"I. . . ?"

"Ask him."

Vinai turned to the major, looked up into his puffy face and spoke very quietly. Potter listened attentively then seemed to ask for clarification. Vinai spoke again. The major removed his arm from Vinai's shoulder and looked around, presumably for Peach. The American spoke once more, slower, enunciating every word with such precision that Mr. Geung could have understood it. Vinai, aware now that his grasp on credibility was slipping, said, "The major was here . . . on holiday."

Like the US cavalry, Peach arrived at that moment and fell into a discussion with Potter. It appeared the major wanted to wish everyone good luck on the day's mission, lay down a few simple ground rules and inform the teams of the subgroups they'd be working in. Nothing at all about holidays. At some time during this housekeeping talk, Cousin Vinai slunk away.

When the others were loading the choppers, Siri, Commander Lit, Phosy and Civilai found him hiding in his room and surrounded him. Phosy had been designated the roles of good, bad and only cop while the others looked menacing.

"Comrade Vinai," said Phosy.

"Yes?" said Vinai.

"The English language."

"What about it?"

"Do you speak it?"

"I am the head of the foreign languages department affiliated to the Ministry of Justice."

"Congratulations. But the question was, do you speak English?"

"I've translated entire documents into Lao."

"From English?"

"Some."

"And so you speak it?"

There followed a long pause during which Vinai appeared to be searching the ceiling for an answer.

"Not exactly," he said.

The Lao felt obliged to inform the Americans of this turn of events. In fact, they had no choice. The loss of an interpreter was crucial to their work. They found Peach and took her to the major's room where the team leader was sitting on the edge of his mattress going over a map of the region. The corner of a crate of whiskey peeked from beneath the bed between his feet. He crossed his legs to hide it. They tried to be as diplomatic and humble as possible, explaining that although Vinai was a leading authority on English language text, he had little opportunity to listen to the spoken form and he found the American accent to be almost incomprehensible. The major seemed unfazed by this news.

"Major Potter says it's no big deal," Peach translated. "We should just use the big woman."

Siri assumed the major was referring to Dtui. Yes, she was . . . not fat exactly but casually ovoid. Definitely not big by American standards. And she most certainly had a vast repertoire of vocabulary that would be ideal when dealing with the forensic surgeon. But he didn't understand how the major would know such a thing. He stared at Phosy whose buckled eyebrows seemed to mirror his own confusion.

"How does the major know about Nurse Dtui's English skills?" Siri asked Peach.

"He's not talking about Dtui," she said after a short interlude.

"Then. . . ?"

"He means the large gruff Lao woman who traveled on our helicopter yesterday. I didn't notice her myself. The major says her English is fluent."

"There weren't any Lao scheduled to travel on your flight apart from the pilots," Commander Lit said. "I checked the security arrangements."

"This one turned up late. Your chopper had taken off and she hitched a ride with us."

"But our team was complete, too," Phosy said, shaking his head. "That's why we took off. Nobody was missing."

"And where is she now?" asked Civilai. "I didn't notice any strange Lao in the breakfast room."

Peach asked the major who laughed and got clumsily to his feet, nonchalantly back-heeling the crate under the bed as he did so. He put his arm around Civilai and led him to the window. He'd obviously missed the cultural sensitivity day at orientation. He pulled the flimsy curtain aside and pointed to a spot way beyond the back fence almost twenty meters into the no-go area. There on a deckchair in a one-piece orange bathing suit was a rotund woman in dark glasses and a sunhat. All this, irrespective of the fact that the morning sun had barely made a crack in the early mist.

"What on earth. . . ?" said Commander Lit. "None of that land out there has been cleared of unexploded ordnance. Didn't she see the signs? What's she playing at? Is she mad? Who is she?"

But the other Lao in the group knew only too well who had followed them to Xiang Khouang, and it wasn't a *she*.

Auntie Bpoo was as common a figure around the downtown area of Vientiane as Eros was to London and Jesus to Rio. A man, most certainly; deep voiced and pot-bellied and solid as a wad of sticky rice, but a slave to cross-dressing. He read palms and predicted the future on street corners and fooled nobody with his zebra-striped tank tops and lime green hotpants. But put him in a silk suit, plaster him in make-up and stick a permed wig on his head and he might just fool a helicopter full of Americans. Because that's what had happened.

Far from being angry, Siri was impressed that the fortune-teller had been able to pull it off. The doctor hadn't an inkling that Auntie Bpoo spoke English, but that didn't surprise him either. He, she—and she preferred to be called "she"—was a remarkable . . . woman. Although she pretended that her soothsaying was a scam, that she just wanted an excuse to sit and talk to people, to make friends and be accepted in Lao society, Siri knew for a fact that she had an uncanny gift. Tangled deep in her quirkiness and her unfathomable poems and her mood and gender swings, was a person who actually could see the future. Siri needed someone like her to help explain his own untrained connection to the spirit world. Yet so far she'd played dumb. He wondered whether, here in the wilds of Phonsavan with no escape, he just might be able to get some sense out of her. All that could come later. For now they had to convince her to put on something respectable and take a ride with them to Spook City.

8

SPOOK CITY

The two choppers were nearing Long Cheng. They'd just flown over Sam Thong, ten minutes to the north. It was deserted now but in the early seventies it had housed 150,000 refugees. The US would fly journalists there to view the USAID humanitarian program. They wanted the world to see what a solid job they were doing to help the masses of poor people displaced by the fighting—fleeing the Pathet Lao, they called it. What the administrators didn't mention was that the refugees were actually fleeing US bombing. Entire areas were evacuated so the CIA's Hmong fighters had an empty playing field for combat. Chased from their homes, all these displaced people had become dependent on US airdrops. Another thing the journalists didn't know was that a few kilometers over the ridge was the real war effort, the launch pad for the forward air arm leading up to a thousand sorties a day—Long Cheng.

The choppers crossed over a saddleback mountain and were careering down into the Long Cheng valley. The highlight of the macadam airfield was a drastic limestone karst at the end of the runway. Fliers called it the vertical airbrake because if you over-shot, it was a most effective method of slowing down, albeit terminal. Many of the surrounding huts had been stripped of their tin roofs, and bamboo shacks, victims of neglect, extended far up into the surrounding hills. But there were signs of domestication here and there, suggesting that life might return to the place one day. The heli-copters landed beside the old runway. A few dozen ponies were tethered to pipes and shrubs. Already, several hundred people were milling around the ruins of Spook City. They'd probably heard the erroneous rumors about the Americans paying a thousand dollars for old bones and wreckage. Some had traveled for days to this isolated outpost. The theory had been that only the really serious claimants would go to that much trouble. If they'd set up their camp in a town on a main road the searchers would have been inundated. And, as Commander Lit had rightly said, if the explosion of Bowry's helicopter had been heard from Long Cheng, he really couldn't have gone that far. The villagers approached the two helicopters and stood with their eyes closed as the rotors kicked up dust. The teams carried their equipment down a shallow dip and along a narrow path. For convenience, they would be working out of General Vang Pao's old residence. It was a concrete, two-story outer-suburb motel of a place, as incongruous as the shirt-and-tie spooks who'd built it. Although the furniture had been removed, it wasn't that much less comfortable than the Friendship Hotel. And, as most of the bombing in the region had originated from here, it was quite possible to stroll around without the fear of being blown up.

Siri remained at Auntie Bpoo's heels on the walk across the compound, looking for an opportunity to get her alone. When they passed the shell of a concrete hut, he grabbed her arm and dragged her through the open doorway.

"I could scream, you know," she told him.

She made a move for the doorway but Siri blocked her path.

"They're used to screams up here," he said. "Nobody would notice."

"Well, what if I smacked you one across the chops?"

"Smacked me? Really, Bpoo. There are times when you aren't feminine at all."

"Whatever makes you think I'd want to be feminine?"

"You're wearing a sarong and a brassiere."

"You forced me to dress in a hurry. I had a frock laid out for today."

"And that isn't feminine?"

"They're merely garments. Outer coverings. Clothes do not a gender make. If you wore a saddle, would you be a donkey?"

"If I had a wardrobe full of the things, I'd expect to be called an ass, yes."

"Honestly, Dr. Siri. Ancient as you are, you still care what other people think of you. You're so vain."

"Why are you here?"

"You threw me into a helicopter."

"I mean Xiang Khouang. What possessed you to stow away?"

"I'm very fond of Americans."

Siri turned and headed out through the doorway. The word *bpoo* in Lao meant crab and anyone knew there was no blood to be had from a crab. Experience had taught him that you couldn't get information from Bpoo if she wasn't in the mood to share it. He'd just stepped into the sunlight when he heard, "You're going to die, Siri."

He turned back and smiled.

"Madame Daeng and I have already picked out the coffin. It has a battery controlled fan inside in case it gets stuffy. That's an extra expense, of course, but I think I'm worth it."

"I mean in the next five days."

"And you've come to watch?"

"I've come to stop it."

"Where were you all the other times I died?"

"This isn't an "almost died." This is the real thing; dodo, door-nail, dinosaur . . . that kind of dead."

"Real? But I thought you were a charlatan. You told me you make it all up."

"I am. I do."

"So?"

Auntie Bpoo sighed, hitched up her sarong and sat untidily on a pile of breeze blocks.

"Siri, you are so annoying. You and all those heebie-jeebie spirit characters you drag around with you. They know you're too dense to talk to them but they're stuck with you. How do you think they feel when their portal to the living is boarded over with a very thick plank and padlocked?"

"How do you know about them?"

"I get the odd message."

"Then teach me. I'm willing. I want to communicate with them. I want to know what they're trying to tell me. I'm tired of their cryptic clues. I want to sit down over a cup of instant ether and learn from them."

"Honey, you've either got it or you haven't. I've got it with bells on. They show me things I'd really rather not see. You? You haven't got it at all. Your spirit shaman fellow really blew it when he set up shop in you. You're a dead end for the spirit world."

Siri came over and sat cross-legged on the dirt floor in front of Bpoo.

"Who are they? Who have you seen?"

"A whole lot of them."

"For example."

"Oh, dull, dull. All right. Your mother, your ex-dog, a dozen or so confused spirits you've picked up along the way. And there's some really old character who stinks of history."

"Yeh Ming. My shaman spirit. Do they talk to you?"

"Every now and then. I mean the ones that used to be people. The dog just snarls and drools a lot. I have no idea what he wants."

"Can you tell me what they say?"

"No."

"Why not?"

"Because I don't want to be your telephonist. "Oohoo, Dr. Siri, there's another call from your mother. Will you accept the charges?" Come on. I have a life."

"Not much of one."

"Bastard!"

She stood and stormed to the door.

"I'm sorry," he called after her. "Really I am. I didn't mean it. I'm sure your life's grand."

"It is."

She stopped in the doorway but didn't look back.

"I knew it. So . . . when am I going to die?"

She was silent.

"Bpoo?"

"Soon, I imagine. Day or two."

"Any idea how you're supposed to prevent it?"

"None whatsoever."

"Well, good luck anyway. I'm supporting you a hundred per cent on this one."

Bpoo turned around and leaned against the door jamb.

"I . . . er. . . ."

"What is it?"

"I think it might have something to do with sticking a finger in your ear."

"The death or the antidote?"

"I'm not sure. Does it mean anything to you?"

"It doesn't sound like a pleasant way to die."

"You're right. Look, I might have got that part wrong. I'll keep my ears cocked in my bad dreams until I get something more specific."

"Thank you."

"You're welcome. Would you like a poem now?"

"It's the very least I can do."

There really was no avoiding Bpoo's traditional yet meaningless poems. Luckily they only ever ran to one stanza. Some might have analyzed them to see what hidden meaning they contained, but it was invariably better to nod, say "Interesting," and walk on.

She began:

Tomorrow sees,
> *Unease blow from the middle east*
>> *The Arab beast*
> *Takes lives   the holy gash*
> *Exploding aunts*
>> *Lance of fire*
>>> *Our daughters, ash*
> *The guiltless ones*
>> *Sons dashed in God's name.*

"Finished?" Siri asked.

"Yes."

"Interesting."

* * *

It was Nurse Dtui who first commented on the makeup of the crowd gathered for the day's show-and-tell. They were either women, children or men over sixty. The war had wiped out an entire generation of able-bodied young men. And for what? She admired the resilience of the types who'd journeyed up through the hills with hope of a modest reward. She wanted to pay them all but she had little more than they did. Probably all of them would be returning to their villages empty handed. She doubted any would bother to take their offerings home with them. Some had brought half shell casings full of parts on the back of goat carts. Others had spread tarpaulins on the ground and laid out their non-matching bones in the shape of complete skeletons in various cartoon poses. Others had brought souvenirs. One wore a helmet lining that sat on his head like a lampshade. Another was in combat boots five sizes too big for him. An old couple had brought their blond-haired, dark-skinned grandson to claim child support. The atmosphere was that of a large MIA boot fair more impressive than anyone on the Lao team had imagined. There were a lot of desperate people in the northeast.

The teams set up three separate reception areas and taught the locals the fine art of queuing. A number of claimants thought this meant they had three chances. Rejected at one table they'd make their way to join the queue at another. Communication was also a problem. Many of the villagers came from different ethnic groups and few spoke fluent central Lao. Inspector Phosy was competent in three northern languages, Judge Haeng in two. Dtui spoke Khmu well enough and Cousin Vinai—thankfully not completely useless—spoke four different Tai dialects passably well. Lit and Siri (when the spirits were in harmony) also spoke Hmong. Information was passed through these convoluted channels down to the American team who had Dtui, Peach and Auntie Bpoo translating for them.

By noon on day one it was quite obvious that merely sifting out the scam artists and career bounty hunters would take far longer than the five days allotted to them. They needed some way to eliminate the frauds. As often happened at such moments, Dr. Siri had an idea. He vanished into the hills at lunchtime with a can of corned beef and a rope. When he returned half an hour later, that rope had a dog attached to it. It was a large, feral, dirt-gray animal. After seven or so years of being ignored it seemed bemused by all the sudden attention. It was half-starved and quite clearly the corned beef had elevated Siri to sainthood in his mind.

"Siri, that is one very ugly dog," Daeng laughed.

"You're right," Siri agreed. "He needs a bath."

"A bath will just make him clean and ugly."

"Then clean and Ugly he shall be."

Siri threw Ugly into one of the cement sections that doubled as a water trough and scrubbed him down with a straw broom. He emerged still dirt-gray and no less ugly but his head was held high and he smelled better. Siri walked him once around Long Cheng at the end of the rope allowing him to sniff wherever he wished. The doctor then arranged for the rumor to spread: Ugly was a US military bone dog. He could sniff out animal and Lao remains like a hog to truffles. All those who had brought bones to be assessed would be asked to line up for Ugly to get a good sniff. Anyone found to be deliberately fobbing them off with bear tibias or dead auntie's scapula would be imprisoned and probably end up in front of a firing squad.

It was merely gossip but the reappearance of the enemy on Long Cheng soil gave credence to such a rumor, and before Ugly's second lap of the compound, some two-thirds of the villagers had disappeared, leaving their parts behind. The task at hand now seemed far more achievable. When Peach passed this news on to Major Potter, he came in search of Siri with his arms outstretched. Only Ugly's attempt to bite off the major's right hand prevented Siri becoming another hug victim. But Potter and all on the American team gave him a peculiar collection of *nops* in thanks for making their work easier. Still, they worked through till five thirty, interviewing claimants, inspecting the souvenirs they'd brought along, attempting to pinpoint locations on a map. Yet, by the time they clambered back into the helicopters, there was a prevailing feeling that the day had produced nothing of any value. Four days to go.

It wasn't until they were in the helicopters that Judge Haeng recognized Auntie Bpoo. He was beyond shock. She was another thorn in his hoof.

"What in Lenin's name are you doing here, man?" he asked, shouting above the whirr of the rotor.

"I'm very well thank you, Judge, and you?"

"I asked you a question."

"So you did, and very rudely too. Let's start again with manners, shall we?"

"Show me some respect. You know who I am and what I am capable of. In fact, I'm going to have you arrested. Put in prison."

"On what charge, my little magistrate?"

"Trespass. Illegal encroachment on a government project."

"Ah, but I have a booking."

"A what?"

"A reservation, at the Friendship Hotel. I always sojourn in the north. I was enjoying my holiday when the nice red major invited me to join him up here. How could I refuse?"

"I do not believe this is a coincidence. How did you get here?"

"On the bus."

"Show me your laissez-passer."

"It's in my room. But of course you knew that, you cunning devil. Any excuse to get into a girl's bedroom."

"How dare you? Listen, you are a freak. There's no place for your type in the new republic."

"Oh, I see. So there is a place for Vannasack Symeaungxay, Thidavanh Bounxouay, and Doungleudy Phoudindong but not for Auntie Bpoo?"

Haeng leaned backwards and the colour fell from his face.

"How. . . ?" he began.

"I know that those are the names of the young ladies you have established in rooms around Vientiane. In December there'll be another, Latsamy Thongoulay, but you haven't met her yet. Even so, I believe the ministry would be interested to hear all about them."

Haeng lowered his voice.

"This . . . this is blackmail."

"Not yet. I haven't quite decided what I want from you. When I do, *then* it'll be blackmail."

They were leaning close to be heard in the noisy helicopter. Before Haeng could react, Bpoo kissed him on the cheek. He fell away from her and moved to another place wiping the lipstick from his face and cursing. One disastrous trip, two hoof thorns. No respect. People had no respect. But he had his plan. Before the mission was over they'd envy him, admire him for what he was about to do. Yes, respect. From each and every one of them.

Back in Phonsavan, most of the Lao bathed from scoop jars in the communal bathrooms. The Americans opted to wait until the generator was switched on at sundown when the pumps would deliver water to the ensuite bathrooms. Only Judge Haeng in the Lao wing shared their patience. Dinner that evening was at seven;

a fusion of Lao and Western cuisine as interpreted by Hmong kitchen staff working for a Hmong manager and his wife.

The Hmong was a divided people. Those who had lost the toss and sided with the Americans were now fleeing through refugee camps or making a last futile stand in the mountains. Those who had supported the communists lived a life not terribly different to how it had always been. Many were dragged down from their mountain homes to till fields and work in towns. Some succumbed to diseases they'd not known at higher elevations. Others, like Mr. Toua the Friendship manager, put their knowledge and industrious nature to more commercial ventures. He believed this joint US/Lao mission was just the start of a tourist influx that would turn Phonsavan into the Luang Prabang of the northeast. So all this effort would be worth it.

There were no longer two islands of tables in the dining room. They were now dotted around the room like in a regular restaurant. And, after a day in the field together, an American journalist might find himself sitting with a Lao soldier, a Lao policeman and his wife with a black sergeant, a Japanese-American forensic pathologist with a transvestite of unknown origin, a Lao general and an American major with a young interpreter.

"Tell him I was in Nam, honey," said Potter. He'd somehow managed to get himself a happy whiskey glow even before supper and Peach leaned back to avoid his breath. She passed on the news to General Suvan.

"Six years, six goddamn years I was there," he continued. "You tell him."

She told him. There were no thoughts or reactions coming in the other direction. It was all Potter.

"They were all—and excuse my bluntness—chinks and dinks and zips and gooks to us."

"I might have trouble transl—"

"Just do your best, honey. I know you're trying. But the point is this. We only knew 'em by pejorative terms 'cause that's what the Pentagon told us they were; ruthless, uneducated nameless heathens. That's how they ran their wars. There wasn't a Ngoo Yen or a Fat Dook, not a husband or a father or an ex-schoolteacher. Just a bunch of gooks. That's why we underestimated them. How can you fight people you don't understand? How can you kill people you don't love? That was my point. There has to be a passionate reason to kill a man. You know what I mean? None of us had that passion. Hey, honey. I'm way ahead of you here. You wanna catch the general up on some of this?"

Peach wasn't sure how to go about translating Potter's point, nor was she certain the general was listening. There was beer on the table and he'd guzzled his first glass with more gusto than she'd noticed from him all trip. The Americans had brought in a dozen crates of Bud on their chopper. It was chilled, having spent the day in the cool water trough out back. With beer being so hard to come by, it was a treat, a honeymoon to consummate this morning's first date. The Americans had the art of seduction down to a fine point.

"This is what we should have been doing all along," Potter said, spearing a frankfurter. "Engaging. You're all nice guys deep down, and you know what I like? You don't gloat. We gloat. You don't gloat. You know what the Vietcong did after they kicked our ass out? They sent a bill for damages of fifty billion bucks. They wrote it on a restaurant invoice sheet and addressed it to Kissinger. You gotta admire that. Ha! A goddamn bill. I bet the general's got a heap of questions he's been dying to ask an American soldier. Am I right?"

Peach asked. The general smiled, spoke briefly and took another slurp of beer.

"The general can't think of anything just now," she told him.

"I bet he can't. I bet he can't. These are emotional times. I relate to that. It took me some while to come to grips with my emotions too. To find and exorcize my demons. All that unnecessary slaughter. The destruction. I said to myself one day, "Hey, these are people we're strafing here. There's gotta be a better way." And this is it, honey. This is that way. Beers across the table. Loving thine enemy. I'm so proud to be here. Cheers." He lifted his glass and the general tapped it with his own. "Yes, sir. You got it. You certain he doesn't have any questions?"

Peach didn't bother to ask nor did she comment. She knew that Potter wasn't exorcizing his demons. He was drowning them one by one. And now they were holding onto his ankles and dragging him down with them. She couldn't let this go on. He was unsuitable for his role. People like Potter had to be removed. She could make sure of that.

Siri, Daeng and Civilai didn't have an American. They felt a bit left out. At the next table were two of them huddled together. The second secretary from the Bangkok embassy, Mack Gordon was late thirties and overweight with an outdoor look like a hairy dog on the back of a pickup truck licking at the wind. His smile spread from ear to ear and his tongue seemed too big for his mouth. Talking to him was Randal Rhyme from *Time* magazine. Siri and Civilai knew Woody Allen from his films, of course, and were certain Rhyme was his brother; Woody being the taller, tougher-looking older brother with more hair.

"It's racism," said Civilai. He attempted to crush one of the cans but the Budweiser corporation obviously reinforced them before sending them off to remote areas. He was able to dimple it quite fearsomely, however.

"They've probably heard about you two," Daeng said. "Who's going to volunteer to come to this table to be victimized?"

"We'd be very pleasant, wouldn't we, Siri?" Civilai protested. "Why does everyone else get one and not us? They've obviously had orders to mingle, to make us all feel like family. It's all been orchestrated to lull us into a mood of love and peace. I wouldn't be surprised if they've put something in the beer."

"Hmm. This is a Civilai conspiracy theory I haven't had the pleasure of hearing before," Daeng laughed. "While the Russians and Chinese and Vietnamese are attempting to conquer us with money and consumer goods, the Americans sneak in under the radar and win us over with love and tourism."

"They've tried everything else," Civilai reminded her.

"So, if that's true, why aren't they here wooing us?" Daeng asked.

"Exactly. They're damned clever. They know that I know their plot so they're holding back. It's a double . . . something or other. I've a good mind to go over there and crash their meeting and show them some assault hospitality of my own."

Siri laughed. "If I didn't know you better . . . and I obviously don't, I'd say you were just miffed 'cause we haven't got an American to play with. You're jealous."

"And I bet you half a dozen cans of free beer that you don't dare go over there," Daeng added.

"You won't find the word 'dareless' in the Civilai dictionary, madam."

He rose majestically, grabbed three unopened cans of beer from the metal tray table beside him and marched to the neighboring table. Without missing a beat, Secretary Gordon pulled out a chair for their invader and they all shook hands.

"He seems to have done it," said Siri.

"And they've apparently found a common language somewhere between them," Daeng noticed. "They're laughing."

"Well, you wouldn't catch me selling out to the other side," said Siri.

"Me neither."

"There isn't enough water in the Mekhong that would make me talk to one of them."

"I'd sooner run head first into a bramble bush."

"I'd pull you out."

"Thank you." She looked around as she sipped her beer. "Tell me, the *farang* with the shiny head and glasses, he's a journalist, isn't he?"

"Yes. Why?"

"Well, don't look over your shoulder now but he's coming this way."

"Fight him off, Daeng."

"It's too late."

Rhyme from *Time* stood over them—only a little over them—and produced an irresistible smile. His blue eyes were magnified to double their size by his thick lenses.

"Wow!" he said, and then, in fluent French, "Madame Daeng and Dr. Siri Paiboun in the flesh. This is very exciting for me. A great honor I can't tell you how much I've looked forward to meeting you two."

Siri leaned across and pulled out a chair.

9

THE DRAGON'S TAIL

Day two of the mission began very much as had day one. The choppers landed at the site, the teams carried their equipment to Vang Pao's house and set up the folding tables. Upon the arrival of Saint Siri, Ugly wagged his stub of a tail so frantically he threw himself sideways. Siri had saved him some breakfast so the relationship was cemented. The food, the newspaper it was wrapped in and a few mouthfuls of dirt were gone in ten seconds.

Whether the queues had remained in place overnight was hard to say but there appeared to be no changes in the lineup on the second day. The teams split into their groups and began to investigate the claims. An impressive array of objects was collected: tin ration trays, bootlaces, a complete arsenal of Zippo lighters, and, remarkably, a Charley Weaver mechanical bar tender without batteries. Where it actually came from nobody knew, although its owners claimed a pilot had given it to them as he was escaping a burning helicopter. You had to admire them for trying.

An hour had passed and still nobody had found a verifiable link to Captain Bowry. That was until the arrival of a group of old men and young boys dressed in black with spare sarongs worn as turbans. They had fashioned some sort of litter out of bamboo. On it, tied down with rope, was the tailplane of a helicopter with its directional rotors still attached. They carried it solemnly, like pallbearers, lowered it respectfully onto the ground in front of Vang Pao's house, and stood back.

"My word," said Siri. He left his table, abandoning a group of Hmong women who were trying to sell him a gold tooth. He stood beside the litter and was soon joined by all the other team members. Someone let out a low whistle. The tailplane had apparently been torn from the helicopter by an explosion. The metal at its base was jagged and black. The rest was dark green and had no military insignias but the figures H32 in white were clearly visible.

"That's it," said Dtui. "That's the one in the photographs. H32."

Major Potter had shown them the embassy pictures on the first day and now he was holding up the tailplane photo to compare with this new arrival. His excitement confirmed it was a match. He didn't know who to hug first. He barked something to Peach who, in turn, asked the pallbearers in Lao where they'd found this wreckage. They smiled and nodded, but nobody answered. They attempted the same question in Hmong, Kang and Lu before Phosy finally hit the jackpot with his Phuan. The Phuan had once had their own kingdom in the region. But as hostility and violence weren't their strong points they were eventually decimated by the warlords around them, finally to be forced into slavery by the Siamese. According to the ethnicity poll of 1977, there were barely ten thousand left in Laos. But this had to be a very isolated group if they had no other major languages between them. Phosy led the group to a chicken's earrings tree, arranged for water, and as they drank they recalled their two-week journey with the dragon's tail. The inspector showed them a map and although the group had no concept of how a vast wilderness could be shrunk and flattened onto a square of paper, they were able to guide Phosy's finger via the setting and rising suns and the mountains and valleys and rivers, to their home.

After twenty minutes, Phosy joined the others. All interest had turned to the new arrivals. Phosy showed them a spot on the map, Ban Hoong to the east, where the group had apparently begun their journey. It was a mere forty-minute helicopter trip from where they now stood.

"They're closer to Phonsavan than to here," Dtui remarked.

"Their sorceress told them to come," Phosy translated. "Said she'd seen a sign in a dream."

"I take it there isn't the slightest possibility she caught the government announcement on the radio?" Civilai asked.

"I doubt it," said Phosy. "She's been dead for seven years. It was her final request that they deliver the dragon's tail to the wealthy overlords at Spook City."

Peach was translating for the Americans.

"I guess that would be us," said the major. "Did they tell you anything about how the dragon's tail came into their possession?"

Phosy continued the story.

"There was an explosion one night and they woke up the next day to find this thing had fallen through the roof of their meeting hut. The sorceress told them that she'd been sitting in a tree—I get the feeling she wasn't really in control of her senses—and she saw a dragon collide with the moon. The moon broke into a million pieces. They couldn't convince her otherwise because she'd gone blind that night. Given the evidence, the head man in the group's more inclined to believe it was a helicopter."

"Was this the only part of the chopper they found?" Lit asked.

"Apparently."

"How come only their sorceress saw the explosion?"

"There was always a lot of air activity in the region: bombings, anti-aircraft fire, crashes, the dumping of undelivered ordnance. They'd been visited and threatened by both sides during the war. All their young men had been forcibly recruited to fight. They were afraid. They weren't about to go rushing out in the middle of the night to investigate an explosion. Just pulled the blanket up and hoped it would all go away."

When word of this made it around the Americans, Sergeant John Johnson stepped forward.

"Did anybody hear anything before the explosion?" he asked.

"One woman seemed quite animated about the topic. She was awake that night," Phosy said. "She was afraid of the helicopters and this one had circled overhead a number of times. She was sure he was looking for their village. Then, she says, the aircraft just went quiet, as if it was hiding in the silence of the sky. Then there was the bang."

Johnson asked how long the gap was between the engine cutting out and the explosion.

"She says about ten breaths," Phosy told him. "Does that mean something?"

"It could do."

"Did the villagers find a body?" Siri asked.

"No," Phosy told him. "But the vegetation around there is pretty dense."

"Has the tail been in their village all this time?" Major Potter asked.

"Pride of place in the meeting hall where it landed, apparently," said Phosy.

"Then do they recall anyone coming into their village and taking a photograph?"

Phosy asked the group and showed them the photographs from the embassy. They confirmed that it was taken in their meeting hall but didn't recall anyone with a camera. None of the villagers had one, they said. Neither did they recognize the huts nor the American.

"Then I see just the one option," said Potter. "We head off to their village and set up shop there, that's if General Suvan and Judge Haeng agree, of course."

Haeng told the interpreter that he was just about to suggest the same thing. The general nodded and asked about lunch. That just about summed the pair up. And so, with tens of disappointed but ultimately dishonest people sent packing from Long Cheng, the two Russian Mi8 helicopters with their young Lao pilots headed east in an arc to avoid the no-fly zone. Aboard were twenty mystified Phuan villagers scared out of their wits their first time in the sky. Four of them had started to be violently sick in the plastic bags provided even before they took off. The rest joined them in midair. The second chopper carried the tail section of a Sikorsky H34 suspended from a hammock.

As the old men and boys of Ban Hoong had never seen their village from the air, and the pilots had barely five hundred hours of flying time between them, it was left to Sergeant Johnson to guide them there from the maps and from landmarks on the ground. He leaned out of the open hatchway like a stuntman and signaled to Peach who was connected by headphones to the pilots. To everyone on board the carpet of green seen through the smudge of cloud and mist seemed featureless, but the sergeant had a knack and led them directly into the bosom of Ban Hoong. The village was so ramshackle, the kick of the rotors almost leveled it. They touched down in a clearing between the huts. As they climbed down from the choppers, Siri wondered whether the place was

deserted. Nobody was about. The villagers in the helicopters realized where they were and gratefully leapt from the craft even before
the rotors had slowed. One by one, women and children emerged
from the stilt huts like field mice after a monsoon. Despite the fact
that their elders and children had been away for two weeks, the
homecoming was subdued.

Siri had seen many such villages in his days in the jungle. It
was a collection of single-room grass-mat structures on stilts,
each with a bamboo ladder. In the gap beneath the huts were
humble family looms and well-used farming equipment and varied
livestock. The site was a dip into the distant past. Only the corrugated iron roofs stopped this being a two-hundred-year-old
community tableau. But the setting was idyllic. It wasn't yet 10:00
A.M. and not all the mist had burned away from the surrounding
mountains. The sun was still a fuzzy egg yolk behind a lace curtain.
The air was fresh and tingled the back of Siri's throat. The sound
of running stream water provided the soundtrack. The second
hands on the watches on the wrists of the Americans began to
crawl more slowly around the faces. Time had altered.

It was too much for some. The US embassy personnel, Rhyme
from *Time*, Judge Haeng and Cousin Vinai took one of the choppers to Phonsavan where they would queue at the post office to
make their long-distance phone calls to Vientiane. It was time to
pass on news of the amazing development of the day. Meanwhile,
the others set up their folding tables under the still-damaged grass
roof of the meeting hall. Siri, who liked to understand his environment, strolled around the village with Ugly at his heels. The doctor
smiled at people he couldn't talk to and inspected the sad garden
fences and unloved plants that marked the boundaries of each family
property. He looked hopefully for something to admire but was left
with a feeling that this village had died along with its sons.

Perhaps the only anomaly in an otherwise normal village was the boy who dominated the tiny village square. He was fifteen or sixteen and he sat cross-legged on the dirt. Two or three bugs buzzed around his head. In front of him were a dozen bottles of various origins: Coke, soda, a petroleum jelly jar, all glass. And in each bottle there was an insect, different species, varying sizes from a beetle to a horsefly. And if a visitor looked carefully, he'd see a fine thread feeding down through the bottle's stopper and tied around the abdomen of each creature. The result was that when released from their prison they could fly only to the end of the thread. And if a visitor was to take the time to notice, he'd see that the bugs buzzing orbits around the boy's head were attached by thread to his base-ball cap. The lassoing of the insects would have taken a great deal of patience. The doctor tried to speak to him but the boy laughed deep in his belly and ignored the old man. Ugly was fascinated by the display. It wasn't long before other members of the team had gathered around the insect cowboy. Two of the Americans took pictures. Everyone agreed it was extremely cruel, but terribly cool. Ar, the head of the village, stepped up to claim the boy. Both father and son had cheekbones you could stack plates on.

"My youngest son, Bok," he told Phosy. "Never been right in the head. Can't talk."

"Is this all he does?" Phosy asked.

"He thinks if he can get enough of 'em he'll be able to fly," said Ar. "But of course they all die the same day. So he spends all his time hunting for new ones. I tell him he'd need a thousand of them to lift him off the ground but he never gives up. If only we could find something with a longer life span. . . ."

Ar had obviously given the proposal a good deal of thought. It was as if somewhere at the back of his mind he believed that if the insects lifted his son the boy might become normal.

But you can only stand and watch beetles on leashes for so long. Both teams gathered in the meeting room to discuss the next plan. Ar pointed in the direction in which their sorceress had seen the dragon crash into the moon. After lunch they would take a hike across that ridge to the crash site.

"You do realize," said Civilai, looking off into the distance, "that if the explosion actually took place over there and the tailplane found its way here, the odds of finding even a little piece of this pilot are less than finding a gram of common sense in the Politburo."

"Not necessarily," said Lit. "He was in a confined space surrounded by metal. Even if there was a fire there could be some remains inside the cockpit."

"I don't know," Dtui said. "All this expense and bother for one man. It seems unfair to me. These hills are littered with the dead relatives of families who can't ever hope to reclaim their bodies."

"Oh, Dtui," said Civilai, about to launch into one of his famous, "You don't think. . . ." tirades. "You surely don't think this is a mission to find a body? This is much more than that. This is the empty coffers of Vientiane cooperating with the bankers of Wall Street."

"Good, Civilai," said Daeng. "We're doing this for the money."

"Common sense, young Madame Daeng. Because we ride fearlessly on the back of the Vietnamese tiger we have to join them in their condemnation of China. Last month our prime minister stood up in parliament and said that China was a bunch of international reactionaries. As a result we are going to lose one of our most generous benefactors."

"I thought you hated the Chinese more than anyone," Siri laughed.

"Not true. I hate all evil-minded usurpers in equal measure.

But any fool, even you, Siri, could not fail to notice that with Peking on its way out our beloved leaders have begun making overtures to enemies past. The Thais, a nation of corrupt capitalist pornographers, have suddenly become our useful allies. Cracks have appeared in our resolve and televisions and motorcycles are leaking through them. Cultural exchanges are being arranged. A famous short-skirted pop singer has been invited to sing at our next That Luang festival."

"Nan . . . nan . . . Nanthida, I like her," said Mr. Geung.

"You be careful, Geung," said Dtui. "We don't want anyone getting jealous, do we now?"

Geung blushed the colour of a week-old chili.

"See?" said Civilai. "Corrupted already. And now we're encouraging a CIA comeback. Next thing you know they'll bring their Beatles over here to subvert our youth."

"I think you'll find the Beatles are English," Dtui told him.

"All much the same. Cultural terrorism."

"I hope you had a chance to say all this to the embassy fellow last night," said Siri.

"Obviously he did," said Peach. She'd snuck up on them from the American team. "Major Potter was asking whether you might join him at his table for dinner this evening, Uncle Civilai. He's very interested to hear your theories."

"Just me and him?" Civilai asked.

"Well, unless you pick up English in the next six hours, or him, Lao, I guess I'm going to have to be there too. Sorry. But I'll try to be as gecko-on-the-wall as I can. What do you say?"

"Your dream has come true," Daeng laughed. "One on one with an imperialist tyrant."

"Tell the major the match is on," said Civilai.

"That's good," said Peach. "In fact, if the guys from the embassy get through to Bangkok you might even have a state senator to play with too. He'll stay in Vientiane tonight then fly up here tomorrow. I'm sorry we can't get you the president."

"Wow, a real senator," said Dtui in her best American accent.

"Why's everything suddenly moving so fast?" Daeng asked.

"The discovery of the tailplane, I guess," said Peach. "The scent of a photo opportunity? The helicopter wreck and a whole bunch of ethnic people gathered around. In a day or two he might even have a skull to put on his lap. All powerful stuff."

"Wall Street," Civilai mumbled.

Just a little beyond the village, Auntie Bpoo had laid out her grass mat, changed into her bathing suit, and was attempting to catch some rays. The villagers came to look at her. Some of them believed their sorceress was right. The sky had opened and all the misfit angels had fallen down upon them. But they had nobody to blame but themselves. They should have buried the dragon's tail while they had a chance.

10

le plain des alambics

The best part about being the only living burglar in Vientiane was the fact that the population had become so certain they'd never be robbed that they'd stopped locking their doors. Admittedly, very few had anything worth risking your neck for. These were frugal times and valuables had long since been exchanged for foodstuffs. Eg missed those nights when he'd have to pick a tricky lock or climb into a precariously situated window. He was built for burglary, was Eg. Forty-something with a face so bland nobody could ever identify him. Not even people who'd known him most of his life. He was slim and knotty with muscles, quick and light on his plimsolled feet. His eyes became used to the dark rapidly so he didn't use a torch, the downfall of many a burglar. Testament to his skill was the fact he'd never been caught. Whereas all the villains with records languished in the prison islands on the Nam Ngum reservoir, Eg had been left to ply his trade in peace. He had to be careful, of course. The PL patrolled with guns and shot at anyone out after curfew.

Some householders made life so easy for him he wanted to chuckle. Take this morning, for example. A padlock on the shop's metal grille a four-year-old could open and an advertisement, "Madame Daeng will be away until August 31st. Apologies to our regular customers." Shops on both sides closed. Nothing but the bloated Mekhong opposite. It was 2:40 A.M. and the street patrols, if they could be bothered, were on the hour. A piece of cake. Eg walked to the side street, hopped over a low wall and crossed the yard abutting that of Madame Daeng. He peeked over the wall. There were a dozen chickens and some big peculiar-looking bird that he imagined would look good on a spit. Obviously somebody came in during the day to feed them all. No dog. No alarm. No problems. And, would you credit it? Leaning against the back wall was a ladder. They wanted him to rob them. It was a community service he'd be providing.

The birds barely squawked when he dropped silently into the yard and edged the ladder across to a window. In seconds he was up and sliding a chisel between the wood and the frame and the window popped open like an old clam. Seconds more and he was inside. There was a musty, schoolroom smell to the place. He closed his eyes tight, counted to five, then opened them. And there they were, all around him—books. More books than they had in the national library. And not just books these, but foreign books with raised lettering he couldn't read. He sat cross-legged in the middle of the room and grinned. It was his lucky night. Sometimes good fortune just dropped into your lap. Madame Daeng, the spirits bless her, had a whole room full of illegal books. Five to ten years for possession. He knew the Ministry of Culture would be very interested to learn about this. Oh, yes. Eg the burglar was about to embark along a brand new career path.

Cross-cultural integration had become an art form by dinner time at the Friendship Hotel. Almost everybody had a new buddy. Even

couples had split up in the cause of socialization. Each table had
its own 750 mls of Johnny Walker Red and a battalion of soda
bottles. As the Friendship had only three hours of electricity there
was no ice but after the third glass it was of no importance. The mood
needed elevating. The teams had reached the end of the second day
but had come up with not a single molar. Not a rotor or a seat
spring. There was one empty table. The men who had traveled to
Phonsavan to report the day's finding were presumably still stuck
in the queue at the post office. They'd been there for six hours so
their patience would have been wearing a little thin by the time
they returned. A smiling Johnny Red awaited them.

Auntie Bpoo had brought a lit candle to the dining room. She
had sought out Dr. Yamaguchi and attempted to use her physical
presence to hustle him away from the others to a table in the
corner—just the two of them. From her wardrobe she had selected
a splendid crimson silk gown with noodle-thin shoulder straps.
She was a good five centimeters taller than the pathologist, thanks
to a pair of matte-black stiletto heels. Phosy had witnessed this
attempted kidnapping and, feeling sorry for the old man, he and
Geung went to sit with them. Bpoo was clearly not amused. It took
a while to get her to agree to translate. But once she did, Phosy
enjoyed his evening with the American. In a still photograph, even
though he wore no glasses and his hair was ungreased, Yamaguchi
would have looked as Japanese as Emperor Hirohito. He had that
same strained expression that comes from carrying the weight of
a three-thousand-year-old dynasty. But Yamaguchi was as American
as bubblegum. It was evident from the very first moment he swag-
gered into a room. His posture was good from years of being the
nail that wouldn't be hammered down. But the feature that made
him stand out was volume. It was Civilai's theory that the Americans,
like the Chinese, placed their elementary school teachers too far

from the students' desks. As a result they were trained to shout at one another from an early age. Most Lao schools had no furniture so the pupils could sit around the teacher and communicate at a civilized volume. Yamaguchi's meal banter had a decibel level above that of a foghorn.

At five minutes to nine, the wheezy generator rattled and clunked its intention to retire so Siri, Ugly and Civilai took half a bottle of Johnny to the hotel veranda. The post office gang and their helicopter had still not returned. Siri, locked in an excruciatingly dull evening with General Suvan and his confused reminiscences, had noticed two odd things. One was the distinctive smell of smoke. It had been present earlier but he'd merely assumed it was the cook burning the evening meal. By eight it had become so pervasive that he'd excused himself to walk around the hotel to make sure the place wasn't on fire. Toua the manager assured him it was probably just villagers nearby burning off the top growth to prepare the fields for planting. Siri was well acquainted with slash and burn agriculture. For centuries, nomadic tribes had burned off stretches of thick undergrowth and allowed the ash to fertilize the soil. The earth would offer up good harvests for three or four seasons until the soil was degraded, then the tribes would move on. In ten years the land would have replenished itself and be ready for the next migrating farmers. The three main crops for the surrounding Hmong were rice, maize and opium, and each required this shifting cultivation. But the manager's answer didn't sit right on Siri's mind.

Then there was the air activity. Shortly after eight the flights had begun, fifteen or so, all told. Siri was certain he recognized a number of different craft. They were all heading west. It was remarkable, given the inexperience of its pilots, that the air force would choose to fly at night. The manager hadn't been able to give an explanation for that particular mystery.

Siri and Civilai sat on two creaking rattan lounge chairs by the hotel entrance staring out over the Plain of Jars. Except there was nothing to see. To either side of them were the room-bound flashes of lamps and the shadows of candles, but directly ahead was nothing. It was the blackest black they could remember. Civilai commented that it was like staring out at the edge of time. He was remarkably poetic on Scotch whisky. The low clouds had obliterated the moon and stars and, as people retired for the night, one by one the rooms vanished. Soon, there was a perfect quantum state where Siri and Civilai and Ugly were just a part of the universe, blended together in one big black porridge of nature and meta-nature. It was a moving moment spoiled only by one of the ever-attentive maids who brought them a candle in a glass globe. She placed it on the table between them and fumbled her way back inside. The light barely reached the fence posts with their swirling mist founda-tions. But the two old boys could see each other quite well. It was cold and they wore jackets, but their feet were bare. They watched their toes wiggle, listened to the coughs and yawns of people priming themselves for sleep, and to the slobbering sounds of Ugly cleaning his equipment. They sniffed in the smoky night air and the nectar of the neat whisky.

"Daeng not joining us?" Civilai asked at last.

"Today was a bit much for her arthritis," Siri told him. "She thought we'd be sitting behind a table taking notes all day so she didn't wear her boots. Ugly's standing in for her."

"How are *you* holding up?"

"A bit tired but I'll survive."

They enjoyed the quiet some more.

"They're out there, you know," Siri said.

"Who's that?"

"The jars."

"Right. If we had tourism I'd put fluorescent lamps on each one so you could sit here and look at them; those lights that change colours, you know? Pinks and lime greens. Perhaps fireworks; those little sparkly ones."

"Tasteful."

"And none of that nonsense about burial urns. Guaranteed to kill off tourism at the first mention."

"You don't believe they are?"

"Siri, who in their right mind would allow their dead relatives to be folded up and squashed into a jar?"

"Some of those jars are two meters across."

"Even so. Complete waste of labor when you have a wake to attend."

"So, what's the Civilai theory?"

"Well, it seems obvious. This region was famous for its dog racing. Traders came from all around to watch the heats. Gamble their life savings away on the nose of a mongrel."

Ugly looked up, probably coincidentally.

"So, seeing all this potential from the new tourist trade," Civilai continued, "the locals set up stalls. They made themselves jars, the bigger the better, and brewed rice whiskey."

"So they're stills?"

"Absolutely."

"*Le plain des alambics.* The plain of stills. Hmm, I like it."

"Except rice whiskey ferments naturally so it doesn't need heat. Once you've built your jar everything takes care of itself."

"You have heard of the famous French lady archaeologist who made an extensive study and concluded they could only be burial urns?"

"Of course she did. She was a well-known prohibitionist. She wasn't going to go home and tell everyone how she'd discovered an ancient civilization of debauchers and fornicators, was she? She had to make something up."

"Good point. Except she found human remains in the jars."

"Siri, those jars are enormous. The strongest whiskey is always at the bottom. The vendor just keeps topping it up with water. So your serious drinker isn't going to be satisfied with scooping weak whiskey off the top, is he now? He puts his reed pipe all the way down and sucks up the sediment. But it's heady stuff. Of course there's going be collateral damage."

"Have you run all this by UNESCO?"

"Oh, they know. Trust me, they know."

They paid another short homage to the silence but keeping quiet was always a challenge to a man like Civilai.

"I didn't notice Judge Pimples and Cousin Monolingual come back," he said.

"Me neither. They're probably sampling the nightlife of Phonsavan."

"That should keep them occupied for a good fifteen minutes."

"You never can tell. Sin is all around."

"That's one of the topics the major and I were talking about tonight. It looks like we arrived in Vientiane a few years too late. We missed the Gomorrah period."

"I thought the point was to engage a retired US army major in a debate about the breakdown of American culture. To explain to him your theories of why they lost in Vietnam and go into great detail about how most of the millions of dollars they pumped into Laos went straight into the pockets of the fat royalists."

"I did all that."

"And?"

"He agreed."

"With everything?"

"Pretty well."

"What a spoilsport."

"Exactly. So we had nothing left to talk about other than booze and sex."

"Was that the moment that you called over Auntie Bpoo and dismissed Peach?"

"She's only seventeen, Siri. There's probably a law against two old men talking dirty in front of a minor. Auntie Bpoo was certainly a safer choice, and knowledgeable. Honestly, little brother. I had no idea. Potter used to fly into Vientiane from Saigon to witness perversions unknown in the western world. Freak shows that—were there a section for it—would have made their way into the *Guinness Book of Records*. Honestly, I doubt I could smoke twenty cigarettes at the same time . . . in my mouth."

"All this time together and I had no idea you were interested in sex."

"It's contagious, Siri. Major Potter is obsessed. He went into great detail. I even caught Bpoo blushing once or twice."

"I don't recall seeing either of you walk away in disgust."

"It was an education, Siri. Seventy-four and I'm still learning. I can't wait to go home and tell Madame Noy."

Siri laughed.

"I'm sure she'll be delighted. What does Potter's wife say about all this?"

"Currently between wives. He's had three at last count."

"Why doesn't that surprise me?"

"And he puts away the drink, my word he does. He had his own personal bottle. He has a few swigs of whiskey then a cup of coffee to keep himself coherent. Never seen anything like it. I thought you and I could knock it back, little brother, but he makes us look like amateurs."

"Practice, Civilai. That's all it takes."

Siri refilled their glasses.

"So, apart from the hotspots of Vientiane, you didn't learn anything from him?" Siri asked.

"I almost got a secret or two out of him. He hinted he'd found out some dirt about this mission. Said it wasn't all as clear cut as it seemed. Said we Lao should keep our eyes open for a traitor. By then Johnny was doing most of the talking. But the manager came in and told us we had ten minutes before the generator went off and that shut the major up. I plan to have another go at him tomorrow. There's nothing I like better than a dollop of scandal. I've found there are very few people on the planet who don't have skeletons in their closet."

"I certainly do."

"Goes with the job, I supp—"

The distant sound of chopper blades churned through the silence of the night. It seemed to bounce off the darkness all around, disorienting them. They didn't know where to look.

"Sounds like Judge Haeng and the boys coming home after a night of raging at the post office," Civilai said.

"It's a dangerous night to be flying," Siri decided. "Surely they could have parked the helicopter behind the bar and taken a donkey home. They could even have walked it in half an hour."

The sound became deafening and the chopper loomed over the roof behind them, kicking off concrete slates and sending a shower of rubble onto the two drinkers. They covered their glasses with their hands. The pilot had obviously not seen the building until the last second. The craft's spotlight was angled down at the ground and as it rocked it splashed white light clumsily all around like water from a bucket. At one stage, Siri and Civilai were highlighted cabaret performers. They waved. The chopper angled in to the dirt yard, kicking up dust and landing on one wheel. For a second they thought it might crash onto its side but instead it flipped onto the other wheel, rocked, then settled. The engine growled, the rotors began to slow, and the dust churned in the air in the bright light until the beam was extinguished. The only light now was from the lamp on the rattan table which had miraculously stayed lit.

"Do you suppose it's friendly?" Civilai shouted.

One, then two, then three flashlight beams came to life inside the chopper. Heads appeared as the hatch slid open and the metal steps were unfolded to the dirt. Two figures stepped down, lit occasionally as they moved in front of the beams. Siri recognized the shapes of Sergeant Johnson and Second Secretary Gordon bowed against the downdraft. They reached their hands toward the hatch and an arm appeared. They both took hold of it and guided a man in white down the steps. All of the flashlights were now directed upon this character, the star of the spectacle. He was a physically irrelevant man in his late fifties with long but thinning blond hair combed over a round pate. He wore white shoes to complement the crisp white double-breasted suit, buttoned to hold back a rampant red tie. The trousers were flared. When he reached the ground, his long wispy hair rose and danced in the draft like deep-sea anemones. With Johnson and Gordon propping him up on either side he was rushed toward the hotel entrance. Seeing Siri and Civilai seated there on the veranda, the new guest shrugged off his escorts, approached the two old men and said something with feeling. He then grabbed for their hands which he shook enthusiastically, turning slightly toward a short Chinese-looking woman. In the dim light all they could see of her was crimson lips inside a black pageboy frame. She had no eyes or nose that they could make out but she did possess a splendid-looking camera. There was a flash and before the dots had cleared from their eyes, the stranger had vanished inside the building. In his wake they saw Judge Haeng, Vinai, and Rhyme from *Time*. It was a colorful but very brief carnival which left Siri and Civilai breathless.

The helicopter engine huffed a last breath. Then all was calm again save the ticking of a tired old Mi8 and the slowing whirr of its blades.

"Who was that white-suited stranger?" Civilai asked.

"*L'Empereur est arrivé*," Siri told him.

They walked over to the helicopter where the two young pilots were doing what had to be done to put the beast to bed. They held small penlights between their teeth as they fiddled with the engine.

"What happened here?" Siri asked.

The youngest one answered. To Siri he looked barely old enough to ride a two-wheeled bicycle.

"The senator was supposed to stay overnight in Vientiane, Comrade," he said. "They were going to fly him up tomorrow. But the flight control people said, given the conditions, it might be better if he flew directly up here. The military met his flight at Wattai and transferred him up to the landing strip in Phonsavan. We picked him up there."

"What conditions?" Civilai asked.

"The smoke, Comrade. There's a blanket of smoke all across the Special Zone."

"Slash and burn?"

"We lose two or three months a year of flying time to it up here. The smoke just hangs around the mountains. Combined with the mist it's like flying through soup. You can't even make out the landmarks and, to tell the truth, none of us are that good at instrument flying. Tonight you've got the smoke and the mist and no moon. All we had to do was hop over from town, a couple of minutes. Even so, we almost ran into the hotel. We didn't want to take off at all but the judge insisted. It was hairy, I don't mind telling you, Comrade. And they've only just started burning. In a day or two you won't see a hand in front of your face. I doubt we'll be flying anywhere else for a while."

Siri and Civilai returned to their seats.

"Don't you think that's odd?" Siri asked.

"What?"

"It's August."

"And?"

"Who's slashing and burning in August? The point of it is to wait for the dry season and burn off the top growth in time to plant. I know the wet season seems to have finished early this year but the vegetation's still damp. All they'd get now is a lot of smoke."

"And you believe. . . ?"

"I just wonder whether it might not have anything to do with agriculture. We're surrounded by territory still occupied by anti-government guerrilla forces. They could be burning the land for any number of reasons."

"Perhaps they were getting nervous about the PL air force with its new fighters. I heard a lot of air activity this evening. I'd wager they've evacuated the airfield so they wouldn't be stranded here. That's probably worth setting light to a few mountains for."

"You're right."

"I'm always right. If we had television I'd be the one who wins all the quiz shows. I'd have a new washing machine every week."

They drank for a while, considering.

"Where do you suppose they'll put him?" Civilai asked.

"Who? *L'Empereur*? Wherever he goes it won't take him long to realize he's not at the Oriental any more. I hear the Thais have running water without streptococci."

"Beds without crabs and creaks and odd smells? Sounds like heaven."

"He'll be miserable. He'll stay awake all night, get his photo shoot done at dawn's crack, and be out of here before the smoke gets so bad he's trapped. We might not even get a chance to sit down with him over a few beers and have a laugh together about the domino theory."

"Shame."

11

DROP ADDERS

Senator Ulysses Vogal the Third was up with the unseen sun, although "up" suggests it was preceded by a "down" and the gentleman hadn't dared lay his precious body on a mattress with such an obvious history. He'd spent the night in a chair wrapped in a blanket he'd brought with him watching the minutes crawl by on his luminous watch face. His personal assistant was a Chinese-American called Ethel Chin who could trace her Chinese-American ancestry back four generations, long enough to have lost the Chinese language entirely. She'd ordered room service for the senator but he'd taken one look at it and decided he'd make do with a cup of coffee and a cookie. He had work to do. By seven he was out in the forecourt of the Friendship overseeing the digging of a pit deep enough to bury the Sikorsky tailplane. They were inside the safety zone but the senator stood well back from the hole. They lowered the wreckage into it and sprinkled a thin layer of dirt on top. And there, Ethel Chin and Rhyme from *Time* took several pictures of the senator on his knees unearthing the wreckage. This was followed by several more pictures of the senator standing beside the excavated tailplane beaming like a fisherman. Then came a series with Senator Vogal listening earnestly to a group of communist natives: a tribe consisting of Daeng, Dtui, Geung, Phosy, and Commander Lit. They sat around the great white-bell-bottomed leader listening to his words of wisdom in return for an appearance in *Time* magazine. Rhyme promised to send them each a copy. Perhaps the editor wouldn't notice that all of the listeners had their feet pointing directly at the American elder, or even that he'd know how disrespectful it was considered.

And Siri had been right. It wasn't even breakfast time and the senator was out of his sweat-stained khakis and back in his white suit sitting on the uncomfortable bench of the Mi8 with his overnight bag between his legs. He was a man eager to be anywhere else. His smile was all used up and he had nothing left on his face but anxiety. Everyone else stood in the morning mist waiting for the chopper to lift off. But the craft was silent. The rotors immobile. Vogal yelled at Ethel Chin who in turn yelled at Peach. The interpreter nodded and walked to a spot below the cockpit window where she called to the pilot.

"The senator couldn't help noticing that you aren't flying," she said. "Any problem?"

The young captain had been on the radio.

"They won't give us clearance to fly," he said. "They say the smoke's really heavy over the mountains today. It's on both sides of us, north and south. They aren't prepared to risk it. They say we should stay here till the air clears. Hope for a bit of wind. See what it's like later."

Peach nodded and walked casually to the hatch of the helicopter. She passed on the message with a Lao smile. The onlookers could see the senator's reaction over her shoulder. It was loud and heated and certainly impolite. Peach stood her ground with her arms folded. But even before the tirade had run its course she turned her back and walked away from the helicopter. The senator yelled. She ignored him.

"Five dollars says she quits," said Civilai.

"You haven't got five dollars," Siri reminded him.

The old pair were at the back of the crowd of onlookers with pre-breakfast coffees in their hands and post-whisky-night hang-overs in their heads. They'd deliberately missed the photo session and planned to miss the take-off, but the helicopter remained. The senator seemed suddenly aware that he was being watched and climbed down the steps of the chopper. He performed what some later speculated might have been a polite Lao *nop* to the onlookers, although others suggested he'd merely been catching mosquitoes. He then walked to Peach who was leaning against a tree. He talked more quietly to her now. His head was bowed and his right hand rested upon his heart. Peach shrugged and the senator enveloped her in a hug the major would have been proud of.

"They're doing it," said Mr. Geung with a look of horror on his face. This unintentionally raised a laugh from the viewers.

"In a way," Dtui told him. "It's called a hug."

"It's love."

"I very much doubt that," Dtui smiled. "But don't let that stop you hugging your friend Tukda."

Geung turned the colour of a retired United States army major.

"I . . . I don't. I. . . ."

"It's OK, hon. You don't have to discuss it if you don't want to. I won't pry." She lowered her voice. "But you know if you need to talk about anything—I mean anything at all—you can trust me."

"Nnnnnothing to say."

"Right. No problem."

The crash site was due south of the Friendship Hotel but they would have to carve a large arc east or west to avoid the military assault. Either course would have flown them directly into the smog. PL air force regulations prohibited flying even short distances in smoky conditions so both helicopters were grounded. The pilots were billeted in the headman's house in Phonsavan until further notice. But all was not lost. Toua, the friendly hotel manager, rode his pony into town and returned ahead of two trucks, each with its own driver and porter. There was a dirt road which would transport the teams to within a kilometer of Ban Hoong. From there they could trek across the hills. Toua trusted the Americans would be able to make a small donation for petrol and something for the hard-working porters and drivers who had very little work to feed their families. Potter assured them it wouldn't be a problem.

The senator, already exhausted from the physical and emotional efforts of the morning, and wallowing in the trauma of being trapped in a disadvantaged area, opted not to travel to the search site with the MIA teams. He and Ethel Chin would, he said, wait at the Friendship until the smoke cleared. As there was no wind at all, the likelihood of such an event was remote. Out of what he called courtesy, General Suvan said he'd remain at the hotel also. Although Judge Haeng volunteered to stay behind to keep them company, the general insisted he'd be needed at the crash site.

The further the trucks drove into the hills, the more the teams began to taste the smoke in the air. Now and then black flakes fluttered past them like charred snow and Siri could feel a growl deep in his throat that he knew would soon turn into a cough. The twenty-minute helicopter ride translated to over an hour on the old trucks. As they climbed into the mountains, deep ruts left over from the heavy rains were gouged along the clay road but the wet season landslides had been cleared. Sawn logs from fallen giants lay to either side of them, awaiting collection. As none of the team members knew the terrain, they had to put their faith in the local knowledge of the truck drivers. When they pulled off the road in the middle of nowhere and announced that this was the starting point of the walk to Ban Hoong, the passengers weren't in a position to argue.

"Are you sure you're up for this?" Siri asked Daeng.

"I swear if you ask me that one more time, Siri, I'll file for divorce," she said. "Every day I walk a hundred kilometers from the noodle pot to the tables and back and you say nothing. What's so different here?"

"Oh, nothing much," Siri nodded, "unless you count the fast flowing rivers, cliffs, jagged rocks, poisonous spiders, tigers, enemy snipers and unexploded bombs, none of which I noticed last time I was in the noodle shop. And, Daeng, I tell you, I've seen it too many times in movies. The injured member of the group lags behind. 'You go ahead,' he cries. 'I'll catch up with you later.' But he knows he's doomed so he uses three of his last four bullets to slow down the pursuing Indians and saves the last one for himself. But they overpower him and cut him to ribbons with hatchets before he has a chance to end his own misery."

"And you see this happening to me?" Daeng asked, unloading the packs from the truck.

"If it can happen to John Wayne. . . ."

"And he had rheumatism in this film of yours?"

"Rheumatism, arrow wound, it all amounts to the same thing."

"Have you and Civilai ever calculated how many years of your lives you've wasted watching films?"

Siri reached for his broken heart.

"Civilai!" he called to his friend on the next truck. "Daeng thinks we've wasted our lives watching films. What should I do?"

"You're in good shape for an old man," Civilai shouted. "You'll always be able to find a new wife."

"Watch your back, comrade," Daeng shouted. "We'll be passing along narrow mountain ledges with sheer drops. I wouldn't want you to have an accident."

"Oh, did I hear a threat?" Civilai laughed. "You'll have to get up very early in the morning to get the better of me, comrade noodle-seller."

"We'll see, old man."

Despite Siri's warnings and his unspoken concerns about his own health, the hike was comparatively easy. The path was well used and it wound over gentle hills, avoiding some of the higher peaks. Even so, Civilai maintained a safe distance from Madame Daeng. The teams walked in a long single conga line along the narrow trail. Ugly walked at heel beside Siri like a pedigree show dog. The porters carried the heavier bags and the pace was that of a nature hike for elderly ladies rather than a route march. The only sound, apart from the footfalls of heavy boots, came from Judge Haeng who had remembered his fictitious leg injury and now grunted and grumbled and leaned heavily on a tree branch. Siri pointed out to Daeng that a month earlier it had been the other leg causing so much grief. The whole expedition was tired of hearing the judge's jungle survival story, even as translated by a very sarcastic Auntie Bpoo, today glamorous in a yellow pant suit.

"Can't we shut him up somehow?" Siri asked.

They were walking through a narrow valley full of odd-looking trees with thick foliage.

"Judge Haeng," Daeng called from the back of the procession. "Excuse me. Sorry to interrupt."

The judge looked back over his shoulder.

"What is it, Madame Daeng?" he said. The voices echoed against the karst cliff walls on either side of them.

"You have a reputation of being a man with extensive knowledge of the jungles up here in the north."

"There are those who would say that I am something of an expert," he smiled. "A good communist is like a tree. He stands firm but knows how to bend in a strong wind. He is fertile but gladly gives up his nuts to less fortunate creatures. Why do you ask?"

"We were just wondering about these trees we're passing under right now," she said. "I haven't spent much time in the north but I do believe we have something similar in the south. There we call them *ngoo dtok*."

Siri noticed that as she spoke his wife was surreptitiously unbuckling her leather belt and sliding it from the lugs of her canvas army trousers. "Would you happen to know if these are the same?" she continued.

"I have heard them called that," the judge lied. "I won't bore you with their Latin names or the names attributed by local botanists, but, yes, I believe these are *ngoo dtok*."

"Then it's just as well we aren't in the south," said Daeng, who had just plucked the tree's name from the air. "Because down in Champasak the *ngoo dtok* is the home of the infamous drop adder. I hope that isn't the case here."

"The what, comrade?"

"The drop adder, Judge. The trees are full of them. They're deadly venomous snakes camouflaged the colour of branches."

The local porters began to look up at the overhanging foliage with trepidation. "There is no known antidote to their venom. One bite from a drop adder and it's all over, a long, slow, excruciatingly painful death."

She had her belt rolled in her hand and was taking aim at Civilai four bodies ahead of her.

"They wait for their prey to walk beneath the tree," she continued, "and they focus on a vulnerable spot, a neck, a wrist . . . a bald head. They are remarkably accurate. You step beneath their branch and . . . hiss!"

She launched her belt into the air where it began to uncurl and came down square on Civilai's left shoulder—writhing. He shouted his surprise and beat off the fake drop adder, but the porter directly behind him screamed the heavens down. He ran in a blind panic away from the trees and rid himself of the cumbersome packs by tossing them to one side.

The sound of the explosion was amplified in the gully and the force of it blew the escaping porter clean off his feet and into the rocks. Several of those nearest to the blast were knocked backward. Siri and Daeng felt a whoosh of air and, like the others, hung there in a void of shocked silence. Everyone looked around wondering what had happened. All they could see was a charred nest of a crater gouged out of the grass where one pack had hit the ground. The porter, bleeding from the forehead, rolled on to his back and coughed. Dr. Yamaguchi and Dtui went to attend to him. Siri turned to his wife.

"Well done, old girl," he said.

"It's never quite had that effect before," she admitted.

"Will somebody tell me what the hell just happened?" Major Potter called out. Peach's translation arrived a few seconds later.

"Any idea whose pack that was?" Siri asked.

The porters had merely grabbed all the heavier bags from the trucks to justify a wage so nobody had an immediate answer. The team members looked around for their own bags in order to eliminate whose was missing. It was the major himself who came up empty. He stood with his hands on his head.

"It looks like it was Potter's bag," Peach told them.

There was a crowd gathered now around the smoldering hole in the ground. Not a trace remained of whatever had exploded there.

"Does the major remember what was in his pack?" Phosy asked Peach.

The old soldier was standing in the shade of one of the drop-adder trees looking crestfallen. Peach walked over to join him. Civilai returned Daeng's belt with an ironic smile.

"Victory to me, I'd say," he told her.

Daeng wasn't inclined to disagree, especially with Judge Haeng marching angrily in their direction, once more forgetting his limp.

"Do you see? Do you see?" he said. "More evidence that age does not necessarily equal maturity. Have I not told you on numerous occasions that these childish practical jokes will ultimately lead to disaster?"

"On this occasion it might just have saved a life," Phosy interrupted. "If the porter hadn't thrown off the pack he'd be headless by now. There was something in it that could have blown at any minute."

Peach stood beside Potter who was unconsciously running his hand through his short white hair. There was an unmistakably guilty look on his face.

"Major," she said. "What was that?"

"I don't get it," he said. "There's no way. I made sure like I always do. Double checked."

"Was there something explosive in your pack?"

"Technically, no."

"But in reality?"

"It couldn't have been the dynamite."

"Major Potter. There was dynamite in your backpack?"

"Well, yeah. But it was completely harmless."

12

THE DEAD MAN'S FIELD

It was morning break and the smoky air felt more unsociable with every hour that passed. They'd set up a tarpaulin shelter between the trees, more from habit than necessity. They hadn't yet seen the sun that day. Patches of smog wafted past like wispy black hearses. In the distance the morning mist was trapped beneath one endless bank of clouds. The team felt like the filling in a dirty soufflé. The Lao contingent, minus Judge Haeng and Cousin Vinai, sat in a circle drinking coffee from a thermos and eating some version of NASA space rations wrapped in plastic. They were sure that whatever the snack lacked in taste would be more than made up for if they ever needed to re-enter the earth's atmosphere in a hurry.

"So," Civilai asked. "Have I got this straight? The major had five sticks of dynamite in his pack and was surprised that they blew up?"

"He swears they weren't wearing their detonation caps," Auntie Bpoo told him. "Says they were as safe as celery sticks."

"Except celery doesn't blow people's heads off," said Dtui.

"He was in the ordnance corps for the first five years of his career," Phosy told her. "You'd think he'd know how to make a stick of dynamite safe."

"He's a drunk," Daeng reminded him. "He knocks back half a bottle of whiskey at dinner then goes back to his room and swigs the other half. Then he sits on his bed and disarms explosives for half an hour before collapsing on the bed. Does that scenario make anyone else here feel nervous?"

"I don't know." Siri shook his head. "He's a professional. Wouldn't he have double-checked everything when he woke up this morning?"

"He's a professional who was drummed out of the service before retirement age," said Commander Lit.

"What?"

"It's true," Lit nodded. "We did a background check on him. He's only fifty-seven. He had several years ahead of him. The Americans don't exactly fire their ranking officers. They urge them to step away from the career. It appears his superiors were a little upset about his alcohol and sex addictions. He had the choice of leaving for undisclosed health reasons or facing a dishonorable discharge."

"He's only fifty-seven?" Dtui was shocked. "I was sure he was older than you, Dr. Siri."

"Ah, but I'm not a slave to sex and alcohol," Siri told her.

"That's right," Madame Daeng agreed. "The doctor could give up alcohol any time he wanted." She noticed everyone staring at her. "What? He could."

"Meanwhile, back to the major," said Civilai with a timely intervention. "If the man's such a liability, what's he doing handling explosives?"

"And what's he doing heading this mission?" Dtui added.

"Probably they have the same system as us," Phosy suggested.

"A reward for thirty years' faithful service. An all-expenses-paid trip. The name of a senior officer on the list of personnel?"

"Plus he's had experience in the region," Lit added. "He spent six years in Vietnam. They knew him at the US consulate here. I believe he'd worked with the chargé in Ho Chi Minh City."

"Perhaps they didn't expect him to be this hands-on," Civilai suggested. "They imagined him and General Suvan stretched out on beach chairs together waiting for us to come back from the dig with parts."

"I don't believe that for one minute," said Siri. "The consulate people have been stuck in Vientiane for three years. This is their first chance to get up-country and see what's happening. I think they'd choose their personnel very carefully. There has to be a good reason for Potter being here."

"To blow us all to hell, by the looks of it," said Bpoo. And with no invitation, she launched into a poem.

> The bomb on wheels
>> Congeals above the road, the street
>> His gases sweet
> Rise up   and rot the shield
> A deadly leak
>> Bergs creak and roll
>> And never healed
> Our houses drowned
>> Profound too late

"Interesting," said Civilai.

Unable to comment further, everyone else washed out their mugs, collected their plastic wrappers and headed back to join the Americans. They'd spent the first hour marking out fifty-meter grids across the supposed crash site with pink nylon string. They only had the second-hand word from a sorceress that this was where the craft had crashed. Even though the villagers had led them confidently to this valley just to the east of the village, they'd encountered no debris. Still they persevered.

Mr. Geung was walking a little too close to Dtui as they reached their allotted square.

"What is it, pal?" she said, turning to him.

"I. . . ."

"Yes?"

"I . . . wrote a letter. I wwwwant you to check it."

Dtui was surprised, given the fact that just a month before, Mr. Geung couldn't write. Or perhaps it was fairer to say he could write little more than his name, the names of Dtui and Siri, Daeng, Malee and Foremost ice cream which he was particularly fond of. Hardly enough material with which to compose a letter. Despite the fact that they'd been teaching him for three years, his reading was marginally better.

"Who's it to?" she asked.

"A friend."

"Anyone I know?"

"Yes." He smiled, reached into his back pocket and produced a wad of lined pages rolled into a cone. He handed it to her with some hesitation. Dtui unrolled the cone. The pages were all full. On the first line of the first sheet was the word "Tukda." He'd obviously been practicing. This was followed by what looked like line after line of suet balls. He'd filled every page with them, every space. On the very last page was his name, beautifully written.

"OK?" he asked.

"Do you think she'll know what they are?"

"Th . . . th . . . they're hearts."

"Ah, of course. I knew that."

Dtui turned back to the beginning and looked again. Sure enough, some of the dumplings did resemble hearts. She grabbed hold of her friend and pulled him to her.

"Hug," said Geung, with his arms straight down at his sides. "Is it good?"

"Can your friend Tukda read?"

"No."

"She'll love it."

He pulled away.

"Are you c . . . crying?"

"It's the smoke, honey. The smoke."

It was four thirty on day three and they'd found nothing. Fourteen people had been scouring the earth for the best part of the day and they'd found not a shard of metal, not a bullet, not a tooth. Not a damned thing. They'd walked the grids with their machetes and grass hackers then covered them again on their knees. They'd had to trust the word of Ar the headman who swore that area had never been bombed and no villagers, buffalo or dogs within a twenty kilometer radius had ever been blown up. Even so, the teams were reluctant to dig too deeply into the hard earth. Auntie Bpoo, not a paid member of the team, had spent most of her time in a hammock watching Siri, waiting for his untimely death. She assured him that once his time came she'd know how to deal with it. He hoped it wouldn't come during one of her snoozes.

At one stage, Siri had found himself foraging beside Second Secretary Gordon. The American had a working knowledge of the Thai language which was close enough to Lao to make a conversation possible. Siri had begun with personal questions because he knew the visitors liked to have their ice broken. Gordon was single, a career diplomat with sights on an ambassadorship some day. He'd been posted in Ho Chi Minh City—then still called Saigon— for four years during the war. He was born in the year of the horse, a fact that seemed to be very important to him, as was learning that Siri was a dragon. At last, Siri got around to the point.

"Did you get a chance to read Captain Boyd's service record?" he asked.

Gordon hesitated.

"Yes."

"Were there other blips in the pilot's past?" he asked. "Was he a habitual drug and alcohol user?"

"From what I could tell there was just that one occasion," Gordon told him. "I'm not even sure he liked to drink that much."

"And no other disciplinary problems?"

"He didn't have one black mark on his record."

"But the Air America people covered up the true events of his disappearance that night. They could very well have ignored other such lapses."

"You know, Doctor? Despite its obvious CIA and government connections, Air America was a company. They had regulations and standards. If any of their pilots screwed up they had no problems about kicking them out. There was always a supply of young men in search of adventure to replace them."

"So what happened? What happened that was so drastic that our perfect airman suddenly lost control?"

"I have no idea."

"Do you have access to the interview documents?"

"The people Air America interviewed after the crash?"

"Yes."

"They have a copy at the embassy in Vientiane. I didn't get to look at it in any detail. I do remember they spent a long time talking to the Filipino mechanic and one of the pilots, a Raven. That's what they called the crazy forward air command guys. The pilots who flew in and guided the bombing raids. They were the three getting stoned together that night. The Raven got killed in action a few weeks after Boyd disappeared."

"Is there any way of getting a copy of the interviews up here?"

"That looks less likely with every passing hour. They don't have a fax at the post office and we can't have it flown here, for obvious reasons."

"Do you know if anyone on this mission has read the complete report?"

"Major Potter went through it in detail before we left. He could probably tell you what the witnesses said."

Siri's instincts were kicking in. Something told him the current search wouldn't yield any clues to Boyd's disappearance. But there was something odd going on. He could really use a little super-natural intervention on this one. Since his arrival in Xiang Khouang, Siri had become aware that there'd been very little contact from the spirit world. In many respects it was a blessing. Before his departure his dreams had been overcrowded with disgruntled Khmer souls stuck to his subconscious like moths on drying paint. They'd exhausted him to the point that his waking hours were more restful than sleep. Here in the north he'd slept nights and had no recollections of supernatural nocturnal encounters. He still wore his white stone talisman on a string of plaited hair around his neck but it was starting to feel more like an ornament than a force field against the malevolent *phibob*. Even his angel mother had missed the flight. For almost a year, the old lady with lips red with betel nut had followed him around, offering warn-ings and unfathomable advice. If Auntie Bpoo's prediction was accurate, he really could use a little spiritual backup. Instead, he had to emulate his long-time hero, Inspector Maigret of the Paris Sûreté, and use his brain. There was never a useful ghost around when you most needed one.

He abandoned his search for relics he knew for certain they'd never find, and went in search of Inspector Phosy. After a brief consultation they walked together over the ridge to Ban Hoong where everyone seemed to be going about their business. Rice huskers husked, grain pounders pounded, and chicken pluckers plucked in their time-frozen warp. The headman's son was still sitting in the middle of the central square with his collection of insects. He currently had three in active service buzzing around his hat at the end of their tethers. The peak of the cap provided a perfect landing platform. While Siri and Ugly stood watching him with the same fascinated expressions on their weathered faces, Phosy gathered together the village elders for an impromptu meeting.

"We're working at the place you led us to," Phosy told them. "We were wondering whether anyone in the village has ever come across wreckage from the crash there."

The elders huddled and Phosy sat on the bench provided for them. The answer was no.

"Then, apart from the tailplane falling through your roof, you have no other physical evidence that the craft came down where your sorceress said it did," Phosy continued.

The answer was no.

"How old was your sorceress?"

"Ninety-two," came the reply.

"And she was in control of her faculties?"

"No, she was as mad as a loon," came the reply.

"And what did this mad old woman say when everyone awoke in the morning?"

"Nothing," came the reply. "She was unconscious after hitting her head on a branch. She didn't wake up for three days."

"And when she came round, what did she say then?"

"She said the sky dragon had crashed into the moon and sent it bursting into the jungle to the east."

"And she was certain of the location?"

"Yes."

"Did you notice the charred jungle and the smell of smoke when you passed in that direction?"

"No," they said.

"And you didn't think that was odd?"

"Yes."

"But you didn't question her word?"

"She'd been our sorceress for sixty years. She'd birthed many of us. It would have been disrespectful to doubt her word. She'd never once lied to us."

Siri wandered into the meeting hut. He and Phosy consulted.

"Did she develop any peculiar conditions in her later life?" Phosy asked them. "Anything you noticed that was unlike her?"

They huddled again.

"There was one thing," they said.

The teams were gathering their equipment and preparing for the hike back to the trucks when Siri and Phosy marched jauntily out of the jungle.

"Of course you can both afford to be smiling," said Judge Haeng. "We're all here digging and scratching like peasants while you two run off into the woods together. Don't think we didn't notice. If you don't want your per diem docked you'd better have a good excuse."

"Would it help that we've found the real helicopter crash site?" Siri asked.

"Where?" said Madame Daeng.

"How?" asked Civilai.

Peach passed on the news to the Americans and they gathered around. Phosy told of the ninety-two-year-old sorceress who'd pointed to the crash site and the fact that in her twilight years she'd started to confuse words, particularly opposites. She would say no but mean yes. Say left but mean right.

"It's a condition called Gerstmann syndrome," Siri told them. "It's particularly pronounced when talking about directions. The speaker isn't confused. She honestly sees a mirror image of an event taking place in a different location. In this case it appears she saw the moon explode in the east. She'd watched the helicopter crash and seen the trees burst into flames. When she came out of her coma she was convinced the event took place right here but in fact it all happened to the west of the village. We went to look in the opposite direction and found the site just two kilometers away."

"But that's ridiculous," said Haeng. "Two kilometers from the village and nobody there noticed it?"

"What the villagers found there was a large area burned to a crisp. They assumed it was set alight by one of the fleeing Hmong groups to prepare the land for planting. That wouldn't have been at all surprising in this region, given the number of villages that have been forcibly relocated. There are burnt out areas all through these hills. And this doesn't look like a crash site. There was no obvious debris—just a black, treeless patch of earth. The villagers are afraid of the place. It's been ten years since the crash but nothing grows there. They call it the dead man's field."

After the translation Sergeant Johnson spoke excitedly to the interpreter.

"That would suggest the explosion was fierce and the resulting fire gave off excessive heat," said Peach. "If that was so, the helicopter must have been carrying something volatile, probably a high explosive. A normal helicopter crash wouldn't have caused so much devastation. The sergeant wants to know if there was a crater."

"There's a pond," said Siri. "A large pond with no pond life at all. We wondered whether it could have been a crater. The odd thing is that it's right at the front edge of the clearing. You'd expect a crater to be at the center."

"But how can you be so certain it was the helicopter crash site?" Judge Haeng asked.

"Something went down there," said Siri, upending his cloth shoulder bag and emptying a small mound of objects onto the ground. Everyone gathered around. "We were only there for half an hour but we found these."

In the pile they recognized a petrol cap, melted but in one piece, various bolts and screws all slightly deformed, and what could have once been the trigger of a pistol. The largest sliver of metal was no bigger than a thumb. There was nothing to identify helicopter H32 but the discovery certainly buoyed the mood of the searchers. Were it not for the thickening of the air and the murkiness of the late afternoon, they would gladly have headed to the dead man's field right then. But as they walked back to the trucks they talked excitedly of plans for the following day.

The porter who had been caught in the morning blast was bruised but had made a remarkable recovery. He told them it wasn't the first time he'd been blown up and probably wouldn't be the last. Judge Haeng had insisted Madame Daeng apologize for her practical joke and assure all the porters that there was no such thing as a drop adder. Even so, they walked with their eyes pointed heavenward for the entire journey and were relieved to reach the trucks. The drivers were woken up and the convoy headed back to Phonsavan along the rough dirt tracks.

Siri and Phosy had arranged to sit on the flat bed of one of the vehicles with Major Potter. He had been uncharacteristically quiet for much of the day. Auntie Bpoo served as translator. To the major's surprise, and subsequent delight, the transvestite not only translated his words using a fair impersonation of his voice, but also mimicked his mannerisms. The show obviously improved the old soldier's mood. Siri and Phosy asked what exactly had caused the explosion that morning.

"I've been trying to work that out all day," said Bpoo as Potter. "I've never seen anything like it."

"Is there any way you might have accidently armed the dynamite when you were . . . tired last night?" Siri asked.

"I'd have to be more than tired to do a damned fool thing like that," the major said. "I could be knock-down drunk and still I'd have respect for the tools of my trade. Any of you guys work with dynamite before?"

Phosy had. He knew that unarmed dynamite was unlikely to explode from a small knock unless it was old and unstable. The type of explosives they used in the military had come a long way since Mr. Nobel blew up his family and friends while he was inventing the stuff.

"And did you recheck your bag before we left this morning?" Siri asked.

"No," said the major. "I'd put the dynamite in a pocket of my pack the day before and I'd had no cause to use it. But it was under my bed all night and the chargers were in a different bag. None of them is missing. Look, I know what you guys are thinking," he said. "I like a drink now and then. You've got it into your heads that I got shitfaced and did something stupid."

Neither Phosy nor Siri indicated that they thought otherwise. Bpoo, as Potter, continued.

"But let me tell you this. I've been plenty drunk often enough. But it wouldn't happen that I lost that instinct for personal survival. The dynamite was fresh and safe. That pack exploded 'cause someone wanted it to."

"You think it was sabotage?" said Siri.

"I tell you, I'm real sorry this happened, but it had nothing to do with incompetence. In thirty years I never made a mistake. Not once. Now, if you don't mind, I'd like to change the subject to weird sex."

The Lao were shocked. They wondered whether they'd misheard the translation. Siri turned to Auntie Bpoo.

"What did he say?"

"I'm sorry, he said he wants to change the subject to, you know, sex," she told him.

"He did not."

"Yes, he . . . OK, but I bet he'd join in soon enough if we started," Bpoo smiled. "He's got some great stories."

Siri laughed.

"Bpoo, you're an interpreter. You can't just make it up as you go along. Just tell us what he's actually saying, will you?"

"You may recall I'm not an interpreter at all. I'm a fortune-teller, local celebrity and bon vivant. And I'm excruciatingly bored with all this dynamite talk. Get little miss teen dream over if you want a serious job done. Life's too short for being morose."

The major was feeling left out. He interrupted Bpoo and they locked into a serious discussion before she grabbed hold of his hand and started to read his palm. She was lost to the world of interpretation.

13

LIPSTICK AND TOO TIGHT
UNDERWEAR

Had there been a sun visible, they would have seen it setting just as they arrived at the Friendship. The building was nestled in a thick mist like a blurry uncle in a soft gray armchair. The senator and his secretary were seated on the rattan chairs on the front veranda wearing borrowed mufflers. They were writing flip charts for their next dangerous mission. There were coffee cups in front of them and various files and folders. Siri climbed down from the truck and did an inventory of his aches by cracking all his bones. He marveled at the number of tunes his skeleton had learned to play over recent years. He and Civilai often discussed joining a traditional orchestra as the percussion section. He stood back and observed the teams as they entered the building. There was a lot to be learned from the way people interacted.

Judge Haeng on two sound legs raced across to the senator and bowed low in front of him, offering the kind of *nop* reserved for great-grandmothers of royal blood. This was astounding considering the judge's open hostility to the practice. The senator obviously didn't recognize Haeng despite the judge's fawning of the previous evening. He nodded with a "Who is this guy?" expression on his face. They both looked around hopefully for interpreters but, as none was available, they settled for a four-handed shake and words that neither understood. Haeng was clearly up to something.

As the Americans filed past him, the senator exchanged jokes and pleasantries. Siri noticed Major Potter slide by in the background without acknowledging him at all. As far as he could recall, the two hadn't exchanged a single word. With the Lao, the senator laughed and shouted a newly learned "*Sawatdee krap*" hello, which was actually Thai but as near as damn it. Auntie Bpoo knelt in front of him and kissed his wedding ring. She then licked his finger and winked. Recovering from this, Senator Vogal patted Mr. Geung on the back long enough for Ethel Chin to take a photo then blew a kiss to Madame Daeng who matched his smile and, in southern Lao, told him he was related to a bog lizard. The others were Lao polite and left the VIP feeling that he'd built cultural bridges and mended wounds.

Everyone wore their topcoats to dinner that night. The normally chill air had become even crisper since the sun was no longer allowed through to warm the earth. The dinner tables had been rearranged yet again. Tonight, with the arrival of the emperor, there was now a long head table facing the common masses. His Excellency sat dead center. To his left was General Suvan wearing a blank expression. A stray noodle dangled at the end of his chin. To the senator's right was the vacant seat of Major Potter. Beside that sat Judge Haeng in a strikingly awful pale blue safari suit. He hadn't yet dared move into the major's seat but he eyed it with desire. As always, he attempted to catch the eye of Peach, perhaps believing the suit had rendered him irresistible. As always, she ignored him.

There appeared to be no end to the American rations. This evening's meal was some sort of instant lasagna—tasty but a test for false teeth. There were ever-present bottles of Johnny Red but even Civilai was slowing down on the alcohol input. Too much of a good thing.

"Where's our Major Disaster tonight?" Daeng asked.

"Probably double-checking his dynamite stock," Phosy told her.

"I rather suspect he's avoiding the senator," Siri added. "I know I would if I were in his boots."

"Do you think he's all right?" Dtui asked. "I mean, what if he's had a heart attack? He's normally really fond of his food. I think someone should go and take a look."

Civilai got to his feet.

"*Bravo, mon frère*," said Siri.

"I was just going to the bathroom," said Civilai. "It could be quite a while. My bladder has a mind of its own these days."

"At your age you should be grateful for a mind wherever you can find it," Siri laughed.

Civilai walked through the diners and did a little dance to the Carpenters soundtrack for the benefit of the Americans. They clapped. Most of the guests had gravitated back to their own kind. In fact the only mixed grouping was Auntie Bpoo and Dr. Yamaguchi who were engaged in an intimate discussion on a rear table. She'd finally got him alone and he didn't appear to be too fazed by the attention.

When Civilai returned to the table he seemed somewhat distracted.

"How is he?" Dtui asked.

"What?"

"The major," she reminded him. "You were going to knock on his door."

"Ah, yes. You're right. I was, wasn't I. I . . . damn. I completely forgot."

"Bananas," said Madame Daeng.

"Eh?"

"They're good for the memory."

"Yes. Yes, right," he said, and sat down with no apparent inclination to go back and rectify his lapse. Siri noted his friend had returned from the bathroom a slightly different man to the one who had left them a little while before. Something was wrong.

As a good deal of Johnny Red was called for to wash down the chewy lasagna, everyone drank more than they needed to that evening. After an hour, the major still had not emerged. Dtui went to knock on his door but got no answer. In Siri's mind, something profound was happening. Time appeared to be changing pace, a gallop here, a legless drag there. As they got closer to the dark hours after 9:00 P.M., everyone seemed to drink faster and speak like chipmunks. He felt as if he was the only constant amid all this stop–start action. He was unnaturally alert. The whiskey wasn't having its usual effect. There were times when he felt as if his chair was a meter higher than all those around him. He scanned the dining room and could see everything in great detail. The white talisman vibrated against his chest. He didn't need to turn around to know that Auntie Bpoo was staring at him from the rear table. There was a sudden connection between them as if she were holding a rope, the end of which was tied around his waist, tugging. He wondered whether this was the moment of his demise; perhaps a strip of lasagna had wedged in his throat and choked him. If so, it was a calm death; one observed rather than experienced. He turned to look at Bpoo but she shook her head. "Not yet, Siri. Not yet."

When he turned back to the table, a remarkable thing had happened. It was as if the restaurant had been edited. The film had skipped several dozen frames and jumped from a full, noisy dining room to a room half-empty. He had no recollection of how and when the majority of the guests had left but only a few stragglers remained. The head table was empty now and most of the Americans had gone. Daeng sat beside him and the diehard Lao opposite. He turned to see the empty table where a few seconds before he'd shared a moment with Auntie Bpoo.

"Are you all right?" Daeng asked him.

Her hand was on his. Dtui was laughing at something Phosy had said. Civilai was showing Geung a fork trick. Siri couldn't organize his thoughts. His lungs were heavy as if he'd undergone some physical exertion. His fingers were cold and he had a peculiar scent in his nostrils. What was it? Turnips?

"I think so," Siri told her.

"You've been very quiet," she said.

"Daeng?"

"Yes, my husband?"

"I'm going to ask you an odd question. I don't want you to be surprised."

"It's the lack of odd questions that disorients me."

"I'm serious."

She assumed a serious expression.

"Have I been somewhere?" he asked.

She looked into his watery green eyes and understood he was having a Siri moment.

"You excused yourself for half an hour," she said. "You've just this minute returned."

"You saw me come back? I mean, on foot?"

"As opposed to. . . ?"

"Reappearing out of thin air."

"Is something happening?"

"I've just lost that half hour. One minute I was here enjoying the evening in a crowded room then—cut to now—sober and lost. Did I happen to mention where I was going?"

"No. You headed in the direction of the bathroom. When you didn't come back I assumed you were still having problems with your insides. After a while, Geung went looking for you but you weren't there. You don't remember any of it, do you?"

"I feel as if I've been on a tiring journey. I feel a sense of . . . loss."

"Never a dull moment with you in my life, Dr. Siri."

"Oh for a dull moment."

They had five minutes before the generator shut down for the night; five minutes to shower, shave, clean their teeth, find sleepwear and get under the covers to ward off the bitter night air. Despite this mad rush, the loose generator washers continued to rattle and the electricity did not cut out on the stroke of nine. It gave them an unnecessary seven-minute bonus. Siri could feel the anticipation all around. He lay awake, wheezing, searching his memory for his lost half hour but nothing came. And when the din of the generator finally subsided and the lights all died, there was a massive silence. It was as if they'd reached the end of the story and someone had shut the book on them.

He was awoken by the panicked screams of a bird; one he'd encountered many times in his jungle days. It was brown and unkempt like a feather duster and it had a voice to wake the dead. In all those years he'd never learned its real name, only that any day heralded by the feather-duster bird would be an awful one. And, seconds after the bird's ominous fanfare, there was a frenzied banging at his door. It may have been morning. There was barely enough light to see the shape of his alarm clock and certainly not enough to make out the time.

"What is it?" he called.

The words he heard from beyond the door were in Hmong and they carried a good deal of urgency.

"Yeh Ming, are you awake?"

It was uncanny how many Hmong knew of Siri's connection to the ancient shaman he hosted, and in moments of urgency it was Yeh Ming they called upon, not Siri. Madame Daeng stirred from her deep sleep.

"What do they want?" she asked.

"Help from the ancestor."

"Can't they just take him and let us sleep in?"

"I'm afraid we come as a set."

Siri crawled from beneath the cover and was slapped by the morning cold like a man caught in a snowball ambush. He grabbed his topcoat and jogged to the door. The air smelled of soot. Manager Toua was standing in the shadows beyond the doorway. His face was as pale as crêpe batter.

"Can you come please, Yeh Ming," he said. "There's been a disaster."

Siri had never studied the Hmong language but one day he'd woken up to find himself fluent in it. It was a skill that came and went and he suspected his resident shaman had a hand in flicking on the switch in times of need. He returned for his trousers and slipped into his sandals. By the time he re-emerged through his door the manager had gone. Siri didn't know which direction to head in so he opted for the dining room. As he felt his way along the corridor he became aware of the flicker of paraffin lamplight in the distance. The old parquet rattled underfoot. Toua was on the far side of the dining room beckoning him on toward the far west wing. They arrived at the last door which stood slightly ajar. The manager pointed to the gap and his finger shook. A familiar smell hung at the doorway.

"He always ordered coffee for six thirty," said Toua. "My wife found him."

Siri pushed at the door but it was obstructed by something heavy on the far side. He pushed again. Still he made no impression. He had no choice but to attempt to squeeze through the gap. He wedged in his shoulder and his head followed. His chest was more of a challenge and before it was halfway through he felt totally stuck. But he could see into the room now. The curtains were pulled and the large windows wide open. Dawn was struggling to make an impression on the morning outside. A grubby khaki daylight bathed the room blurred by the ever-present mist. On the ground low to his left were two fat bare legs, toes up, pointing away from the door. He squeezed further and the obstruction gave a little until he was inside and had an unrestricted view of the body that hung suspended from the door handle in a sitting position. Siri was not the type to be easily shocked. He'd seen his fair share of bizarre deaths but he'd never witnessed anything like the sight of Major Potter hung by the neck. A macramé twine was wrapped twice around his throat and tied to the handle. He wore nothing but a pair of woman's knickers, crimson with black lace trim and far too small for him. They cut into his fat like a tourniquet. A post-mortem erection lurched upward from beneath the elastic waistband. His lips were daubed with lipstick and what at first appeared to be an insect on his cheek turned out to be a beauty spot, the type favored by madams at high class brothels.

Although it wasn't necessary, Siri felt for a pulse. There was none. The body was cold and the smell of death was prominent. He took hold of the major's fingers and worked the arm back and forth. He had to make allowance for the low temperature but the rigor mortis suggested the man had been dead for six to eight hours.

"Oh!" came a voice.

He looked up to see Madame Daeng's head peeking through the gap beside the door. She was visibly shocked.

"Now that *is* weird," she said. "Is he. . . ?"

"Very much so."

Dr. Siri and Madame Daeng sat on the edge of the smelly bed and looked at the body hanging from the door handle opposite. They were a couple not renowned for silence but this one lent itself most splendidly to speechlessness. They took in the too-red lipstick and the too-tight underwear. They breathed the whiskey fumes and the scent of vomit diluted with disinfectant.

"Well," said Daeng at last, uncomfortable in the early morning quiet. The foggy mist rolled in through the window and rasped the inside of her throat.

"Well, indeed," agreed her husband.

"This is another fine mess you've gotten us into, Dr. Siri."

"Me? I didn't do it."

"No. Not *it* exactly. *It* you didn't do, I grant you. But the consequences that led to *it*. They've got your fingerprints all over them."

"Madam, judging from the evidence in front of us, I'd say this would have occurred whether we were here or not. And it didn't even have to have happened here. This was a tragedy begging to be let out of the bag."

"Again, you're right. But if you hadn't volunteered yourself, volunteered us all, we'd be at home now beside the Mekhong eating noodles in relative peace. We wouldn't be in this room with this particular body, about to be embroiled in an international scandal. This would be someone else's problem. Someone in good health capable of handling it. But, oh, no. One last adventure before I retire, you say. What can go wrong? you say. Everything's perfectly safe, you say. And look at us now. Five weeks ago we were perfectly content and now we're up to our necks in dung."

"Come on, Daeng. Be fair. What could I have done to avoid it?"

"What could you have done?"

"Yes."

"Torn up the note."

"I think we need to wake up Inspector Phosy," Siri said. "I'll stay with the major. And perhaps you could ask the manager to rouse Second Secretary Gordon and Dr. Yamaguchi."

"Right."

And she was gone.

Siri walked around, being careful not to disturb anything. He knew it wouldn't be long before the room was full of inquisitive people. Once that happened it would be too late to spot any of those anomalies that make a difference to an inquiry. The room was very much like his own in the far wing. There was a strong scent of alcohol with a trace of vomit but there was no evidence that the major had thrown up. At the small carved dressing table he saw the lipstick and an indelible felt-tip pen. The bed was unmade but tidy as if someone had lain there but not slept. An empty whiskey bottle lay on its side on the floor. There was no cap. Beneath the bed was a crate with eight more unopened bottles and four empty slots. Not bad, Siri thought, after only three nights. On the table beside the bed was an open thermos of cold coffee and a used cup.

He only had time for a cursory look into the bathroom. The alcohol and vomit smells were much stronger in there. There was a small pile of clothing below the shower head and what might have been a short rug. They looked as if they'd been doused with water. He heard voices outside the door. He turned around and a shudder ran along his spine. The sight of the dimly lit room gave him a profound attack of déjà vu. He didn't know when or how, but he'd been in this room before—after dark.

Inspector Phosy had barred all but Second Secretary Gordon, Dr. Yamaguchi and Peach, who was needed for her linguistic skills, from entering the room. Peach had taken one look at the corpse and run into the bathroom to throw up. They often forgot how young she was. But she composed herself and, by keeping her gaze fixed out of the window, assured everyone she'd be able to translate. Judge Haeng, who was technically everybody's boss, had barged his way into the room past one of the two old guards they'd posted there. He'd insisted on conducting a search of the major's bags and drawers and even lifted the mattress to see if there was anything concealed beneath. Once satisfied—exactly of what they weren't sure—he'd retired and left them to it. Senator Vogal had made a brief appearance in the doorway, paled visibly and quickly taken Mack Gordon off for a briefing.

Siri and Yamaguchi had unfastened the major from the door handle, a feat made easier by a slip knot device tied into the rope. This should have been the major's escape route; a tug on the loose end and the noose gives way. But, on this occasion, the old soldier hadn't been fast enough. They enlisted the aid of Phosy to lift him onto the bed. He was as heavy as a jeep. As the erection had failed to go away, they covered the body in a sheet for Peach's benefit. All the indicators pointed to death by hanging. There was a clear ligature impression between the chin and the larynx. The face was pale and the eyes protruding. Saliva had dried around the mouth. As for the erotic element to the death, both Siri and the American had seen such a thing before. Siri had witnessed it only once; the death of a deviant neighbour in his Paris apartment. A middle-aged man, dressed in pajamas, had hanged himself from a coat rack in a closet. The rail had given way and he had fallen to the floor, waking everybody up. Yamaguchi, it turned out, had seen post mortem autoerotic accidents on numerous occasions, making them sound as common a pastime in Hawaii as Frisbee. Siri decided Western perverts had too much time on their hands. Although he was convinced that the major had accidentally killed himself, there seemed to be something troubling the American. Yamaguchi retreated to his room to look through a reference book he'd brought along for a little light reading.

Breakfast was laid out on the tables as usual but after the events of the morning few people had an appetite. Sergeant Johnson and Gordon went into town on Toua's ponies to phone the consulate and inform them of events. Judge Haeng, not about to trust his fate to a wild beast, had them send back one of the trucks so he could be driven comfortably into town to pass on the disturbing news to the ministry. At the Friendship, word had spread rapidly and the buzz around the hotel was that this tragedy would surely mark the end of the mission. They knew that as soon as the smoke cleared they'd be on their way back to Vientiane. Only Auntie Bpoo saw the major's demise as "a heroic way for a pervert to go." Other opinion ranged from disgust to pity. Civilai arrived late for breakfast, weighed down with a thunderous hangover and oblivious.

"He what?" he said, after receiving a rushed description of the death.

"I doubt he intended to kill himself," said Siri. "He was involved in a session of autoeroticism." (He'd resorted to French as there was no Lao equivalent for such a concept.) "You do know what that is, I assume?"

"Of course I do," Civilai replied. "It's when you make love to your car. I'm quite fond of my Citroën."

"Civilai!" said Daeng.

"Sorry. Bad time for a joke. Bad joke for the time."

"Tact has never been your forte," said Siri.

"But I very much doubt the major was capable of anything erotic last night," Civilai said. "Sex, even with oneself, is an act of passion. I'm scouring my memory here but I seem to recall it comes at a time of heightened awareness. You become stimulated to the point when you need release. When I saw him he was dead to the world, snoring like a wild boar."

"When you saw him where?"

"In his room. I went there last night."

"You told us you'd forgotten," said Daeng.

"I had to say that. I could hardly announce that the head of the mission was so drunk he couldn't unlace his own boots. That he'd thrown up all over the floor."

"You cleaned him up?"

"And took his boots off."

"How did you get in the room?" Siri asked.

"The door wasn't locked. I knocked and tried the handle."

"Are you sure he was drunk and not ill?"

"Come on, Siri. I know what drunk looks like. He smelled like a whiskey distillery. He looked a lot like you the night Madame Daeng accepted your proposal of marriage."

"That bad?"

"He was slurring so much his tongue kept flopping out of his mouth."

"But it was only, what, seven o'clock when you went to his room," Daeng reminded him. "Seven thirty at the latest. How does a man with Potter's drinking track record manage to get that sloshed in such a hurry?"

"I've never tried it myself," Civilai told her, "but I imagine knocking back a bottle of eighty-proof Scotch whiskey in an hour might just do it. The empty bottle was in his hand."

Siri nodded. "What exactly did you do when you found him?"

Civilai broke the end off a baguette and dipped it in a very cold and runny egg yolk before filling his mouth with it. Siri and Daeng waited patiently until Civilai had washed the mouthful down with coffee.

"He was on the bed on his front, face to his left," Civilai began. "He had the empty bottle in one hand and was reaching for his boot laces with the other. I went over to help him take the boots off and I noticed he had whiskey and sick all down his shirt. Once I'd pulled off his boots I took off his shirt. No mean feat, I can tell you. He'd very obligingly thrown up on the bedside rug rather than the bed cover so I took the rug and the shirt and threw them in the shower, added a little disinfectant from under the sink, and let the water run on them. I may be a kind Samaritan to drunks but I stop short at scrubbing their clothes."

"And you left him there on the bed?" Siri asked.

"It was cold in the room. Both the windows were wide open. So I pulled the quilt over him. He was already snoring by then. I turned out the light, flicked the lock catch on the inside and shut the door. As I say, I can't imagine him coming out of a session like that and feeling amorous."

"Me neither," Siri agreed. "Unless he took some stimulant when he came round. Something got him excited. He was sexually aroused when we found him."

"Perhaps Americans recover faster than us," Civilai suggested. "Out of it one minute. Into it the next."

"It's all wrong somehow, my brother. None of it makes sense."

The senator had been consulting with Dr. Yamaguchi and Rhyme the journalist, and Secretary Gordon. Their thoughts were being

passed on by Peach to General Suvan. Suddenly the group sepa-
rated and Vogal banged a spoon on the table top to get everyone's
attention. Silence took a while.

"My colleagues, brothers and sisters," he began. Peach stood
and took great delight in providing a simultaneous translation. It
obviously threw the senator out of sync to have someone speaking
at the same time as him but, to his credit, he persevered.

"I would like, personally, to express my regrets over the events
of last night," he said. "This is an embarrassment for my fellow
countrymen which I sincerely hope you will not take as an insult.
Major Harold Potter was a great soldier and patriot. Like many of
us who suffer personal traumas in the field of battle, he carried
around his own personal devils. The major's devils defeated him.
As soon as we can, we will return the body to his loved ones. But
I'm certain that Major Potter would have wanted this mission to
succeed. He was a fighter who never gave up in the face of adversity. I know his spirit is looking down at us now and urging us to
honor his memory by returning, not empty-handed, but with news
of the downed pilot. On behalf of the United States senate I urge
you to continue the search. Forge ahead, my Lao friends."

He acknowledged some unheard applause, performed another
silly-looking *nop*, sat down and started eating. The Lao picked at
their food.

"Another one who's accountable to Wall Street," said Civilai.
"The sponsors of today's event are on his back to come up with
results. A little thing like the death of a great soldier and patriot
won't stop him. I bet he's got a speech worked out for each of us,
just in case."

"B . . . but we still get the per diem," said Mr. Geung.

"That's the spirit, Geung," Daeng laughed. "As long as we get
our cut it doesn't matter how many fall around us. It's just a job."

Breakfast was subdued. Nobody knew where to go or what to do so they all sat and muttered. It was a little after eight when they heard the return of first the truck and then the ponies. Gordon gathered the Americans around him at the rear of the dining room. Judge Haeng forced the Lao team out to the veranda where the fog still clung to the eaves and concealed the hotel fence. Siri's cough was constant now as his lungs attempted to filter oxygen from the smoke. The judge glared at him as if this were another deliberate Siri plot to disrupt the meeting.

"Comrades," said Haeng. "I have spoken by telephone to the minister. Like me, he believes we have been afforded a great opportunity. He has instructed us to go on with the mission. He and I both agree that the suicide of the queer major gives us tremendous political leverage. If we also come up with the pilot's bones, we'll be firmly in the driving seat. A good socialist—"

Madame Daeng's hand shot into the air.

"Judge!" she called.

"Yes, Madame Daeng?" he said, annoyed to have been interrupted mid-motto. If the general hadn't been sitting beside him he would probably have ignored her.

"Can I just confirm that you and the minister are still attached to the Ministry of Justice?"

"What kind of ridiculous question is that? Of course we are."

"Well, I don't get it, Judge. The concept of justice, fair play and all that. Letting a man die with dignity."

"A dignified man does not dress up as a girl and garrotte himself. This is an opportunity."

"It's blackmail."

The judge turned to Siri.

"Can't you control your woman?"

Siri laughed.

"This is control, Judge," he said. "You should see her when I let her off the leash. You'd really walk with a limp then."

The laughter was a lot warmer than the morning. Even the general managed a chuckle. Judge Haeng was aware that they were making fun of him. His anger made his acne blink like party lights.

"I want all of you on the trucks in twenty minutes," he barked. "Except you, Siri."

"Oh, good grief. Why not me?"

"The minister wants an autopsy."

Siri scrunched up his nose.

"What? Here?" he asked.

"Unless you'd care to carry the corpse back to Vientiane on your shoulder. Of course."

"And what would we be doing it for?"

"So nobody suspects foul play, of course."

Siri couldn't use the excuse of not having equipment as everyone knew he carried his portable morgue around in a PVC carrier bag.

"Dr. Yamaguchi's probably better at all this than me," he said.

"Good. Because he'll be assisting you."

"Damn. Then I'll need my morgue team; Mr. Geung and Nurse Dtui."

"They're wanted for digging."

"Then I'm not doing it!"

"Sulking again, Siri?"

"No team, no job."

"Siri! You. . . . "

What was he going to do? Fire him?

14

SOME WORDS JUST DIDN'T NEED TRANSLATING

The autopsy was conducted in the old warehouse once used to store stacks of opium. There was still a vague scent of addiction there. The concrete godown had a corrugated roof and was open to the plain on one side. To the rear was a sink and a concrete tub full of old water. They'd lugged a large rectangular table to the center and covered it in plastic. Despite a lot of prodding and coaxing, Ugly insisted on lying beneath it, perhaps to catch scraps. As they didn't bring scrubs, Siri and his team were wearing black plastic garbage bags slit down the back with head and arm holes cut out of them. They'd opted to spare Peach the unpleasantness of watching. She'd protested halfheartedly but seemed relieved to hand the translation duties over to Dtui. At least the nurse was in familiar territory. She may not have known the correct English for a polite dinner party but she could certainly describe the dissection of an inflamed bladder without blinking. There were two others in attendance. Secretary Gordon was there as an observer for legal purposes. And Auntie Bpoo had reminded the judge she was on holiday and had no intention of going out in the truck. She had to keep Siri in her sights.

"Is the major's family OK with this?" Dr. Yamaguchi asked nobody in particular.

"He didn't have anyone close," Gordon told him. He looked up to see whether they were speaking slowly enough for Dtui to keep up. She smiled and raised her thumb. "He had a couple of kids with one of his wives," he continued, "but they don't keep in touch. The army was really the only family he had."

They watched Mr. Geung removing the too-small underwear from the big major, respectfully flipping him this way and that as if he weighed nothing at all.

"Your man knows what he's doing," said Yamaguchi to Siri. Dtui didn't bother to translate.

"He's number one on our team," she said. "I'm number two."

Yamaguchi laughed. He had an easy humor and a dazzling smile. If only they could turn his volume down.

"Nice of you to let Dr. Siri come along," he said.

Siri was too nervous to notice they were talking about him. He'd never performed an autopsy in front of an expert before. He was the first to admit there were large gaps in his proficiency. He was a surgeon by choice and a coroner because nobody else wanted the job. He told Yamaguchi he could step in with comments whenever he wanted, and began with the external examination. He made observations about the general condition of the body, the ravages of alcoholism, odd bruising here and there, and, last but most certainly not least, attention turned to the penis—modest but at attention. Siri had noted the pathologist's questioning look in that direction when they'd first encountered the body. As the American had experience in dealing with autoerotic accidents, Siri asked whether this was a normal phenomenon.

"I have seen post-mortem erections," Yamaguchi said. He spoke slowly and Dtui enjoyed translating for him. "But only on two occasions were they the result of sexual stimulation," he continued. "At one time we were called to a house where a rather large man had died while making love to his very slight wife. She hadn't the strength to remove him and he was still erect so it was rather like uncoupling a train carriage."

Auntie Bpoo, sitting on a recliner with her back to the autopsy, was able to help with the imagery whenever Dtui got lost.

"The other occasion was an autoerotic incident not unlike this," Yamaguchi continued. "The only difference was that the cord had broken and the victim fell onto his face. So you would notice that in both cases the victims were face down. The erection was maintained because the blood followed the rules of gravity and then congealed. I was confused when I saw the major this morning because he'd died suspended in a sitting position. The blood should have drained away from his organ, not into it. I needed to check with my manual as to whether this was physically likely but the situation wasn't covered. I'd need to consult with a urologist to be certain but I really don't see how this was possible."

Siri knew the Americans would very much like to learn that the death of their major was not the result of perversion. He respected Yamaguchi for his experience but he didn't know the man personally. Siri lived in a world where doctors were constantly encouraged by the authorities to see things that did not exist or to overlook things that might be an embarrassment to the Party. He saw no reason why the imperialist West should be any different.

"So you're saying you don't think he died in the position we found him?" Dtui asked.

"I'm always learning new things," Yamaguchi told her. "There will always be mysteries and anomalies."

It was a diplomatic answer, given that this wasn't his autopsy. But the response gave Siri more fodder for thought. He'd also been confused by one or two things. He lifted the major's chins to get a better look at the ligature marks. The band of bruising formed an attractive macramé necklace high on his throat. The hands were clenched and there were no fingernail marks around the wound which might indicate the victim had fought to free himself. Mr. Geung and Yamaguchi helped him roll the body onto its stomach. There was surprisingly little hypostasis on the back of the thighs, perhaps because the major was suspended when he died. Or so it had appeared. So far, everything had been predictable. That was until Siri traced the ligature marks to the back of the neck. He leaned to one side to follow the bruising then stood back. Yamaguchi, seeing the look of surprise on Siri's face, stepped up to the table. He tilted his head to one side, looked up at Siri and shook his head.

"What? What is it?" Dtui asked.

"Come and have a look," Siri told her.

Dtui focused all her skills of observation on the bruising but nothing came to her.

"Think of where he was found," Siri said.

"He was behind the door hanging by the neck from the doorknob," said Dtui, "so he . . . he was hanging. That's it. If he died from hanging the bruise would climb up like an inverse Y," she said.

"Whereas?"

"Whereas this goes flat around his neck like a necklace. But that means. . . ."

"It means Yamaguchi was right. Major Potter didn't die in this position and he didn't die from the hanging. I'd say he was strangled, probably while he was lying on his stomach under the quilt. That's why there are no fingernail marks as he tried to loosen the garrotte."

Yamaguchi was explaining exactly the same hypothesis to Secretary Gordon who looked every bit as surprised as Dtui.

"What about the erotic . . . bit?" Dtui asked.

"The erection? I don't know. He'd had a lot to drink so it might have even been the result of a full bladder. If he was face down it's more likely that it occurred on the bed in his sleep."

"So someone must have set this whole thing up."

"It's the only logical explanation. Drugged him, I wouldn't wonder."

"Why?"

"The first thought that comes to me is that if the US embassy believed their representative had died in extremely embarrassing circumstances they'd want it covered up. The Americans would be on the defensive and our people would be in a very strong negotiating position. If it was straightforward murder, we'd get the blame and the old brown sandal would be on the other foot."

"Doc? The explosive."

"I was just thinking the same thing."

"If he'd been blown up by his own dynamite they'd blame his drinking habit. It wouldn't be quite as embarrassing as this but bad enough. Drunk in charge of explosives."

"Someone wanted him dead and embarrassed. The first attempt didn't work so he or she resorted to this."

They looked up to see Yamaguchi and Gordon staring at them across the body. Dtui and Siri stared back. There was a long silence.

"What do we do?" Dtui asked.

"We either keep our suspicions to ourselves and mobilize our morgue squad to come up with a concrete plan," said Siri, "or we share our suspicions now with the Americans."

"Perhaps they haven't worked it out."

"Look at them, Dtui. How many years of education do you suppose they have between them? They've got it, all right, and if I was one of them I'd be certain *we* did it. Holding back makes us look more guilty."

"It does all point to us," Dtui agreed.

Ignoring the corpse, Siri, Dtui, Mr. Geung, Auntie Bpoo, Yamaguchi and Gordon sat on fold-up chairs overlooking the plain and went through the case step by step. Of course the Americans had come to the same conclusions. Together, they made two rather quick decisions. Firstly, not to perform a full autopsy on the major. He'd been victimized enough. His name was tainted and somehow they'd have to find a way to clear it. They decided to wrap the body, find a cool spot for it and hope that the smog cleared soon so they could send him home.

Secondly, and this was risky, they agreed not to tell anyone other than Inspector Phosy about their findings. They didn't want to alert the killer that they'd seen through the deception. Siri would secretly tell Civilai and Daeng but that subclause didn't need to be included in the oral contract. Someone had gone to a good deal of trouble to kill the major. It was somebody who would not draw attention by being seen around the hotel. As they were surrounded by exploding countryside, the only access was through the front of the Friendship and past the dining room. So the perpetrator was either one of the staff or a member of the teams. They drew up a list of suspects. The hotel had a permanent staff of four, including the manager and his wife, plus three day workers who walked up from the town to prepare the meals for the guests. The two old guards could barely lift their muskets but nobody was being left off the list. Not even the truck porters who were supposed to have gone home before dark. Any one of them could have hidden in the grounds. The major weighed over a hundred kilos and his body was dragged from the bed to the door and lifted off the ground. The murderer was either somebody extremely strong or this had been a team effort. If the latter was true, nobody could be excluded.

Siri drew up a mental list of anyone in the Lao team he couldn't personally guarantee with total certainty. He came up with four. Reluctantly he had Commander Lit in fourth place. Siri had known him briefly and believed him to be hard working and intelligent. But he was a loyal cadre of the security division and a very serious party member who would not question Politburo orders. Auntie Bpoo would have been delighted to hear that he had her at number three on his list. He knew nothing about her background, especially why it was she spoke fluent English. At number two was Cousin Vinai who had come on the mission under false pretences. And in the top spot was Judge Haeng. Siri knew, of course, that the judge wouldn't have the spunk to commit the crime himself but he would certainly have been able to recruit a killer. Haeng was a devious character with a number of agendas and he'd been acting suspiciously since they arrived. He'd insisted on searching the major's room that morning and not told anyone why. There was also the added bonus that Siri just plain didn't like him.

There was something about the sophistication of the crime that suggested this wasn't some local killer with a grudge against Americans. Sinister groundwork had been laid and they agreed that motives beyond the political should be investigated. In order to do so, they needed to fill in some of the gaps that existed in their information about the mission. There were still questions as to what possessed the missing pilot to go to pieces on the night he disappeared, and then the matter of Potter's comment to Civilai that this MIA venture wasn't as clear-cut as it seemed. Secretary Gordon took one of the ponies back into Phonsavan. He had a close friend at the embassy who could copy the documentation they had concerning the mission. He promised they'd find a way of getting the information up-country if it was humanly possible.

The depleted MIA teams had already left for the crash site. General Suvan slept in his room and was hopefully not dead. Senator Vogal was going through papers on the veranda with Ethel Chin. The hotel staff members were attending to their duties. Dtui decided it would be a useful ploy for her to stroll into the kitchen and engage them in idle girl talk. There was a lot to be learned from gossip. Her departure and the mysterious absence of Auntie Bpoo left Siri and Yamaguchi with no means of communication other than the experience that comes from a joint hundred years of medicine. Bpoo never seemed to be around when there was physical labour to be done. Geung helped them carry the body to the rear of the complex where they laid it in a huge cluster-bomb casing lined with straw and natural tobacco leaves. The other half of the casing completed the sarcophagus. They cleaned up their impromptu morgue and shook hands.

Siri, Ugly and Mr. Geung took advantage of Auntie Bpoo's disappearance and walked unchaperoned to Phonsavan. The sooty air had become even more solid. The exercise didn't help Siri's breathing but there was no available transportation. Geung wasn't suited to the cold. His nose and eyes had been running from the moment he'd arrived. They were a sorry-looking pair. They passed the airfield, currently the second largest in Laos. Until two days before it had been home to a large fleet of Russian Antonovs and Migs. The logic of this placement was brought into question for three months every year when the fires began and the site was cleared.

The new town of Phonsavan was a ramshackle place of hurriedly erected wooden shops and slow-moving building sites where more permanent structures were being assembled, it seemed, one brick a day. Once the decision was made to abandon the old ruined town of Xiang Khouang and move the capital to the village of Phonsavan, a wait-and-see attitude had pervaded. Would people come to live here or would they, through nostalgia, return to what had once been a beautiful town? The reconstruction had begun in 1973 and was progressing apparently without planning. It was as if anyone turning up with a wheelbarrow of wood and roof tiles could erect himself a hut anywhere he fancied. There was variety but not colour. Like Vientiane, the dust had turned everything into a sepia photograph. It coated the walls and the strays who slept on the unpaved streets and powdered what humble plants grew in the gardens. Even the ramshackle market lacked the gay colours of blood and fruit and vegetables that should have been the art and craft of a village center. A modest collection of rare animals hung by their necks like criminals.

Siri and Geung were on the main street just approaching the little post office when it exploded. To be more accurate, there was a loud bang and the communication tower toppled onto the building, bringing down half the roof. Second Secretary Gordon had just walked into the car park and had been about to climb back onto the pony when it shied away and galloped off into the street. Gordon looked around in astonishment and immediately ran back through the door. Siri and Geung rushed in past the front gate, climbed the steps and hurried in after him. The side of the roof that had collapsed was opposite the counter where just the one postal worker stood looking dazed but unhurt.

"Anybody else in here?" Siri asked.

"Just me," said the official.

Gordon stood staring at the telephone booth from which he'd just emerged. Another thirty seconds and he would now be as crumpled as the tall stool upon which he'd sat to make his calls. He looked up at Siri.

"Shit," he said.

Some words just didn't need translating.

Siri and Geung were walking back to the Friendship after helping with the cleanup at the post office. It was a miracle that nobody had been killed. There was usually a long queue for the single telephone line but the MIA team had been monopolizing the place so the locals kept away. Second Secretary Gordon had been counting his blessings as he rode the pony back.

"I'm sorry you didn't get a chance to talk to your friend," said Siri to Mr. Geung.

"Lucky I don't wwwwalk so fast," Geung smiled.

"Your legs saved our lives, Mr. Geung."

Geung found that incredibly funny and laughed all the way to the intersection. Their shoes were gray-red from the dust and Siri wheezed as he spoke. The smoky horizon seemed to be closing in on them from all sides. Siri weighed up this latest attack in relation to everything else that had happened. He'd been using Geung as his sounding board.

"Do you suppose it's all tied together?" Siri asked.

"I—"

"I mean the explosion yesterday and the one today?"

"I—"

"And Potter's murder. Do you suppose it's a deliberate attack on the Americans? If it isn't coordinated it's one hell of a coincidence."

"I saw—"

"And what would the point of it be? To cause friction between us? To protest against the MIA mission? Did you want to say something?"

"I saw it."

"Saw what, friend?"

"S . . . s . . . somebody climb in the window."

He still had the giggles.

"The major's window?"

"Yes."

"When?"

Siri stopped and turned to Geung.

"Llllast night," Geung chuckled.

"Who? Who did you see?"

"Stop it. You're making me laugh."

"Geung. Tell me who you saw."

"You."

15

A CRASH COURSE IN CRASHES

The trek to the new helicopter crash site had been uneventful for the MIA teams. Nothing exploded. No adders dropped. No time was wasted. They'd passed briefly through the Ban Hoong village then headed directly for the dead man's field. Of the villagers, only headman Ar's son Bok bothered to go with them. He followed from a safe distance with four or five jars and bottles in his arms. Two tethered beetles flew from his cap like the antenna of a nervous ant.

The teams reached the edge of a clearing that stretched before them like a lake of dark rust. It was true that very little had grown there. Plants had tried but they now poked brown and lifeless from the ground. Trees once tall and proud were now cigar butts. If the spirits of the land had really chosen this as their garden, they were truly awful gardeners. The teams crunched to the far edge of the clearing where they found the pond. It wasn't the type of natural spring you'd dip into on a hot day. It looked polluted. There was something eerie about the whole place.

"This isn't just a crash site," Peach told them. She'd been talking to Sergeant Johnson. "He's seen numerous crash sites. A lot of forest gets burned but the jungle's a hungry place. Three months later and it's reclaimed the burned land and hidden the evidence of the crash. By then you'd only find wreckage by accident. It's been ten years since Boyd went down and still nothing's been able to grow. He thinks there was something on that helicopter with the power to destroy nature completely. Not even Agent Orange would have this effect."

The sergeant walked to the edge of the pond and spoke as if to the spirits.

"In all my years of active duty, I've never seen anything like it. There's only one thing for certain. If the chopper really did come down here, whoever was flying it is in pieces so small we'll need someone with a microscope."

Everyone shared these feelings and nobody had a theory as to why the crater was at the edge rather than the center of the site. But there was still a strong urge to begin the search. There was a belief that they'd be able to find something to identify the helicopter. They laid out a plastic groundsheet beside the pond and by ten it was piled with shrapnel, shreds of PVC, petrol caps and wire from the surrounding jungle. There were no identifying marks but they were sure there was a workshop somewhere that would be able to recognize the materials and pinpoint the type of machine they'd come from. Technology had advanced to the stage that a single bolt might yield the make of a helicopter. They hoped. All they were missing was a pilot.

One unavoidable reality was that someone would have to get wet. The crater was the hub of the explosion and it was likely that debris had been blasted into the ground there. The pond was repulsive but, even so, Sergeant Johnson was the first to volunteer to go in. Commander Lit's hand then shot up almost immediately. He wasn't about to be out-volunteered by an American. And Inspector

Phosy became the third member of the pond detail if only because he was bored with picking up screws. He was in a hurry to find something substantial so they could all go home. Something was niggling him about the major's death and he wanted to take another look around at the hotel. A quick resolution to the pilot hunt would make that possible. A skull would be nice, preferably wearing a helmet with H32 written on it.

At its deepest, the pond went down four meters and was thirty across. Diving to its depths was like swimming through hair oil. The three brave divers, stripped down to their underwear, would take a breath, grovel through the mud below until their lungs hurt, then return to the surface with their spoils. Lit was by far the most competent. He could remain underwater so long, one of his dives equalled two of Phosy's. At one point the two were resting on the bank together wrapped in blankets against the cold.

"You swim very well," Phosy told him.

"Grew up on a river. I was the one they always sent out to catch lunch."

"You're from Huaphan?"

"That's right."

"I'm surprised we didn't run into each other up there."

"I spent most of my army life in Vietnam. I just returned to Xam Neua a year ago."

"Why do you suppose Dr. Siri included your name on his list?"

"Hard to say. We'd worked together on a case up in Vieng Xai. I suppose something about me impressed him."

"I dare say."

They sat for a while and admired the fog bank rolling over the far ridge.

"My wife was in Vieng Xai with Dr. Siri," Phosy said.

"I know. That's where I met her."

"Right. You know, I was just wondering. . . . She mentioned a security officer she'd met up there. Someone who'd made advances toward her."

"She did?"

"Yes. You wouldn't happen to know him?"

"Well, that depends."

"It does? On what?"

"On your definition of "making advances." If that includes a proposal of marriage, then the security officer in question would be me."

"A proposal. Yes."

"Then it was definitely me."

"Good. Just wondered."

"Right."

Sergeant Johnson noticed a new enthusiasm in the diving after that point. Inspector Phosy seemed to have found a new lease on life and a new pair of lungs. He was spending far more time underwater and returning with much heavier chunks of wreckage. The sergeant was a good swimmer but he couldn't match these two Lao. But at one point, neither returned to the surface. The water was far too murky to see the bottom of the pond so Johnson trod water and waited . . . and waited. He looked up at Rhyme who'd been taking photos of the dive. He too was concerned about the missing men. Not even river dolphins could stay under that length of time. Johnson duck-dived down to the mud. At first he found nobody but after a long frenzied search he bumped onto first one, then the other diver. They were hunched over and pulling at something large buried in the mud. He joined them. His hands found the edge of some sort of machinery, but not even his added strength was able to budge it. The three men burst to the surface gasping for air.

After a prolonged discussion over who had first laid hands on the object, the divers agreed that they should attach a rope to it and get everyone to join forces to pull it to the surface. Rhyme from *Time* loved it—the ultimate iconic peace photo. An Iwo Jima flag-raising for the seventies. Lao and Americans pulling together. Men and women, soldiers and laymen, young and old. Judge Haeng, inspired by the camera, was at the front of the rope with his shirt off. Rhyme snapped about sixty frames. This was his bread and butter. Sweat, mud and camaraderie in the jungles of Indochina. He already had his tie picked out for the Pulitzer dinner.

Centimeter by centimeter they heaved and their catch edged its way up the slimy embankment. At last it surfaced, a lump of machinery with no obvious markings. It soon became clear why it had been so hard to dislodge. It was held back by some sort of anchor. A steel cable was attached to the machine and seemed to pull from the other direction. The team won the first round. They had their catch on the ground in front of them but the cable still stretched back into the water. They abandoned the rope and pulled directly on the steel line which seemed to have no end. It curled around their feet as the pulling grew easier, and they issued a disappointed groan when all they found at the cable's end was the cable's end.

"I was rather hoping for a fish," said Civilai.

Sergeant Johnson knelt beside the machine and explained what they'd found. He was obviously the helicopter expert in the American team.

"It's a winch," he told them. "It's certainly from a helicopter. It's normally attached just above the side hatch. It's controlled by the flight mechanic. Originally, its main purpose was for sea rescues. They'd lower the cable with a harness on the end and pick up shipwreck survivors. But they found it worked pretty good on rescue missions in the jungle too. Picking up downed pilots in spots where there was too much vegetation to land."

The depression of the early morning had been eased just a fraction. They had a significant souvenir, confirmation that a helicopter had come down here and, as a bonus, a registration stamp inside the equipment that could be tied to a specific craft. They decided that they needed no more wreckage and would spend the remainder of the day looking for human remains.

While the others were unwrapping their packed lunches, Phosy noticed Madame Daeng kneeling beside the winch. He put on his shirt as he walked over to her.

"See something?" he asked.

"Not really," she said.

"Come on, get it off your chest."

"I was just wondering how easily these things come unraveled." She noticed his smile. "You were wondering the same thing, weren't you?"

"And you weren't alone," came Peach's voice from behind them.

The interpreter was standing with John Johnson.

"The sergeant was just telling me his thoughts on that same subject," she said.

"If the whole thing was blown to smithereens," Johnson said, "the cable might have been dislodged from the winch. But apart from a bit of charring, the unit looks in pretty good shape. The winch is hardly touched."

"So does that mean what I think it means?" Daeng asked.

"The cable was down when the chopper exploded," said Johnson.

"And how common is it for a helicopter to fly with its cable down?" Phosy asked.

"It doesn't happen," Peach translated. "It's against regulations and just plain dangerous."

They all exchanged knowing looks.

"Peach, do you think the sergeant might be persuaded to give us all a crash course in . . . well, crashes?" Daeng asked.

"I think he'd be delighted."

They invited Civilai to join them and sat together eating their space lunches. Judge Haeng and his cousin slept under a tree. Sergeant Johnson was a very knowledgeable man. They'd covered the most obvious reason for a helicopter crashing in war time—being shot down. But because very few missions were flown at night, anti-aircraft batteries weren't manned after dark. On the night Boyd crashed there was reportedly a full moon. It was possible an infantryman with insomnia might have shot him down with a lucky bullet but very unlikely.

If the pilot was drunk and stoned as reported, he could easily have passed out and lost control of his ship. Most of the professional advice garnered for the report pointed to this as the most likely cause. The only problem here was that the team was certain they'd found the crash site yet they hadn't turned up so much as a toenail in evidence. It was obvious that the craft had exploded above the ground, probably at the tree line. This fact was dubiously corroborated by the sorceress eyewitness who claimed to have seen the explosion. There was one hell of a bang sending helicopter parts far and wide, but something other than a mere engine fire had destroyed the surrounding jungle. This brought them to the cable.

"Could he have been so out of his mind he let down the cable just for the hell of it?" Madame Daeng asked.

Johnson explained that the controls for the cable were in the cabin beside the hatch. The pilot would have to leave the cockpit and climb down to the body of the helicopter to operate the winch from there.

"Helicopters aren't exactly gliders," he said. "They're very temperamental. You can't just take your hands off the controls and float. You abandon the joy stick and the craft will likely toss you all over the place. You wouldn't make it to the hatch."

The Lao considered this news.

"OK, my turn," said Civilai. He hadn't spoken for a while and he would probably have asked a question just for the pleasure of hearing his own voice. But he had a serious query. "Let us imagine for a second that our young pilot had neither been shot nor overcome by drugs. Let's imagine he was merely on a joy ride, enjoying the moonlight and the beautiful mountains of Xiang Khouang province. What un-extraordinary disasters might befall him?"

Peach and the sergeant went through the options together.

"The two most common reasons for coming down are running out of fuel and a mechanical fault. But Boyd's chopper would have been checked by his mechanic, Sebastian, and refueled the moment they arrived in Long Cheng that afternoon. That was standard practice."

"Any chance of sabotage?" Phosy asked. "A fight with the mechanic?"

"Unlikely. First, the mechanic usually flies with the pilot so that would be more like a suicide mission. Second, they were pretty good friends. It was the mechanic he'd chosen to get drunk with that night. Third, all the aircraft were double-checked by the head flight mechanic, an ex-pilot called Leon. I knew him when he was still with the marines. He was a bit of a deadbeat socially. I heard he lost his flying license for inappropriate behaviour. I was surprised to hear he was in Laos. But he'd been a good flyer and he was serious at his job. He wouldn't have let anything untoward go by. Once they were checked, the helicopters were guarded all night."

"And the guard let a drunk climb into a helicopter and fly it away?" asked Madame Daeng.

"He would have known Boyd was the pilot of H32. There weren't that many American pilots in Spook City at any one time. Most of the planes were flown by Hmong pilots. And most of the guards were around twelve years of age so he wasn't about to stop a hundred and ninety pounds of muscle from getting into his own chopper."

"So, a mechanical fault?" Phosy asked.

"A mechanical fault is more likely than sabotage. There are a million things that could go wrong in a war-battered chopper. They've been shot at, flown badly and overloaded. That's why every helicopter pilot flies with his own mechanic."

"So if the pilot was up there by himself and something went wrong, he wouldn't know what to do," said Lit.

"Some do. A lot of pilots are pretty good mechanics too."

"What about Boyd?"

"I don't know."

"So, what happens when you're dropping out of the sky in a big metal box?" Civilai asked. "I assume an ejector seat's out of the question?"

"The pilot might have a chance to operate the autorotate," Johnson told Peach. "What that means is that you disengage the rotor from the engine and control the rate of descent by changing the pitch of the free-turning blades. It's quite possible to land a craft on autorotate without any damage at all. A few of us back home have done it without causing any injuries. That's why I was asking how long the gap was from when Boyd's engine cut out to when the village woman heard the explosion. Depending on his altitude when the engine died, those extra few seconds could mean that the pilot controlled his dive rather than just drop."

Phosy asked, "What are the chances of him getting out alive in thick bush even if he did autorotate?"

"You'd have to pick an open spot and aim for it. It was night. The jungle was dense. His chopper exploded so he probably collided with the trees."

"But how long would he have had before the crash?"

"Judging from the woman's description, I don't know, about thirty seconds?"

"Could he have bailed out before the chopper blew up?" Daeng asked.

"You know, they used to put chutes in helicopters in the early days," Johnson told her. "But they turned out to be more messy than helpful. A lot of guys got tangled up in the blades. Most fliers I know don't even bother to bring one along."

"So, back to autorotate," said Civilai. "Once you've disengaged the rotors you presumably know the trajectory of the fall. Am I right?"

"You'd be traveling at about a forty-five degree angle. But, yes, you'd be kind of swaying down in a straight line. You'd be at a ground speed of about sixty to seventy knots."

"More control than say just letting go of the joy stick when you're flying normally?"

"Yes."

"And how long does it take to release the steel cable from the spool?"

"Pretty slow if it's working through the pneumatics. But there's a release catch you can use if that doesn't work. The cogs disengage and the cable drops at its own pace."

"And how long would that take to be fully extended?"

"No more than ten seconds."

"Civilai, what's your point here?" Daeng asked.

"Just playing the odds, Daeng, old girl," he said. "I'm a young helicopter pilot. I've just engaged autorotate. I'm slicing toward the trees with a full gas tank. I have nowhere to land. I know in thirty seconds I'll be blown to hell. As I'm quite fond of myself, I'd rather not let that happen so I climb down into the fuselage, release the cable, grab hold of the harness and jump."

"And what damned good would that do you?"

"Push the odds more in my favor, comrade. I'm traveling forward at sixty knots at the end of my thirty-meter cable. That means I hit the trees a few seconds before the helicopter which, as that would be an isosceles triangle, is thirty meters away by the time it explodes. Due to the trajectory and speed the force of the explosion sends its whatever volatile substance ahead of it. Hence the crater being at the edge rather than the center of the crash site. A sixty–forty chance of the pilot not being blown up. *Voilà*. Mathematics was my favorite subject at school. What does our American think of that?"

When Peach passed this fantasy on, Johnson laughed until his belly hurt.

"You'd be flying into trees at eighty miles an hour," he said. "You've dropped to the end of a steel cable in ten seconds. If the harness hasn't crushed your ribs you break your head on a tree."

"Tree tops being basically soft leaves," said Civilai, determined to rescue his hypothesis.

Johnson asked for the old Politburo man's telephone number. He told him he had friends in Hollywood who'd really be interested in a man with such a vivid imagination. To his surprise, Civilai took out a pencil and started to write it down. He was interrupted by Phosy who shot to his feet and looked around as if he'd scented an ambush.

"Damn," he said, and rushed off at full speed into the jungle.

"See? Now you've upset Phosy," said Daeng.

"What do you suppose that was about?" Civilai asked.

* * *

By the time the search continued after lunch, the objectives had changed. More of them were hunting with the hope of not finding any human remains. Civilai's fanciful theory that the pilot might have enacted a daring escape had secretly sparked more hope in the others. Madame Daeng knew nothing of the character or dreams of the young pilot but her sense of adventure left her willing him alive. Nobody knew what had happened to Inspector Phosy. Someone suggested he might have come down with diarrhea after eating too many NASA lunch modules. But when he returned at three, he looked none the worse for wear. He had headman Ar in tow. The old man called his son's name and the boy emerged from his hiding place in the undergrowth. He walked over to his father and grinned at the policeman. Phosy called for everyone to gather around as he had an announcement to make. He asked Peach if she'd be so kind as to help with the translation. He put his arm around the boy's shoulder. Bok shrugged him off.

"As some of you already know," Phosy said, "this is Bok. He's headman Ar's son. Bok cannot speak and he's a little slow to understand. But he's very talented. He hunts well and he knows all the secrets of the jungle. His speciality is catching insects, as you can see. I asked his father when he first developed this fascination with lassoing little creatures and it appears it was somewhere around the time the sorceress witnessed the dragon crash into the moon. She believed Bok's sudden change was another manifestation of the disaster that happened that night. Apart from his insect fetish, Bok also started to draw pictures. In the beginning he drew them in the sand but his father bought him some paper and crayons and Bok became an artist. Another miracle. Before that the boy just used to sit in front of his hut day and night, staring off into the distance. Suddenly he could walk and the strength returned to his fingers. He was a different person. He couldn't yet speak but his father believes it's just a question of time. So what really happened to stimulate Bok's mind?"

Phosy pulled an old Thai Mekhong Whiskey calendar from his pack. On the front page was a colour photograph of a young girl in a bikini. The audience looked on in dismay. Was the boy's mind turned by half-naked women holding glasses of whiskey? Fortunately not. The inspector turned over the calendar to show that the backs of the photographs were blank and someone had made sketches on the large white sheets. He flipped them over one by one. The illustrations, without exception, were of what looked like a large monster. It had big feet and hands like table tennis bats. All of this might have been attributed to an inability to draw. But attention had been given to small details like the flowers on the monster's shirt and blood spurting from the mouth. And the main feature of each picture was a string leading from the monster's hand. It reached up into the sky and at its end was a bizarre flying creature with one huge eye.

"Very nice story of rehabilitation," said Judge Haeng. "Very heart-warming. Now perhaps you'd like to rejoin the search. We've been covering for you for two hours."

"No, I feel a point coming on," said Civilai.

"The point is," said Phosy, "there's no ground in any of these pictures. The monster is flying. For ten years, Bok has been training insects so he can fly like the monster. Where did a boy with no schooling or life experience pick up a concept like that? Why would he ever believe he could be carried away by insects?"

"By being at ground level and watching a man fly down at the end of a string," said Daeng.

"It's the only thing that makes sense," said Phosy. "From Bok's point of view the helicopter was as small as an insect. There was a full moon so he could see it clearly. And to him, the man was a monster. Civilai was right. Boyd did come down at the end of the cable."

"Oh my goodness." Judge Haeng laughed and looked around apologetically at the Americans. "What rubbish. Surely this isn't what we pay you for: the psychological analysis of mental retards."

"It sounds plausible to me," said Madame Daeng.

"Of course it does, madam," said Haeng. "And we all know that you studied for five years at law school. So . . . no wait, it was primary school, wasn't it? I seem to recall you didn't even make it to high school. And if you had, you'd know that such a farcical theory is inadmissible. It's missing the two key ingredients known as empirical evidence and logic. Giants being transported by hornets won't get you far in a court of law. Am I correct in assuming you don't have any concrete evidence of this, Inspector?"

"No . . . sir," said Phosy.

"Just as I thought. Now perhaps—"

"No, I mean, no you aren't correct. The evidence has been in front of us all the time but we didn't look."

He turned to Bok and said something in Phuan. Bok looked at his father who nodded. Slowly and gently, Bok removed his cap. The exhausted beetles were both resting on the peak. Phosy took the once yellow cap and held it up to the audience.

"I don't know if you can read it from where you're standing," said Phosy, "but the lettering on the cap says UNC. At the orientation they told us that Boyd played college football for the University of North Carolina."

"The boy might very easily have found it at the secondhand market," said Haeng.

"Together with atomic submarines and Elvis Presley wigs," mumbled Civilai.

Phosy turned over the cap. Sewn inside the lining was a label.

"Peach, could you read this for us?" Phosy asked.

She took hold of the cap and smiled.

"It's printed with the name "BOYD BOWRY, 1960." If Bok found this in the market, he got real lucky."

The discovery caused elation in all but the judge. He continued to argue that the hat, like the tailplane, could have been blown away in the explosion and found at a later date. He wasn't able to explain how it escaped the flames. It didn't irrevocably prove that the pilot had survived the crash but Sergeant Johnson apologized to Civilai for doubting his hypothesis. He promised to buy him a beer and the Hollywood deal was still on. As they walked back to the trucks, there was just the one remaining mystery to be solved.

"Since when could you read English?" Civilai asked Phosy.

The policeman smiled.

"I may be an old dog," he said, "but Dtui's been teaching me some tricks. I can't have a wife who's smarter than me, can I now? English this year. Russian next. By the end of the seventies I'll be a chief inspector at Interpol."

16

THE MAN WHO MISTOOK HIS WIFE'S HAND FOR A NAPKIN

Toua, the manager of the Friendship Hotel, greeted the returning trucks by running down the front steps and waving his arms frantically.

"The senator. The senator," he shouted.

"What about him?" asked Lit, jumping down from the flatbed before the truck had come to a complete stop.

"Somebody shot him," called Siri, who was sitting at the rattan table on the veranda with what looked like a can of Budweiser beer in his hand. He was looking remarkably cool, considering. Ugly was looking even cooler in the chair opposite.

"Is he dead?" called Phosy.

"No. But he sustained an injury which might end his career."

"Where was he shot?" asked Lit.

Everyone had climbed from the truck. One group surrounded Toua, who was acting out the shooting quite dramatically, and the other stood in front of Siri.

"He lost the tip of the index finger of his right hand," Siri told him. "He may never shake again."

"I don't consider it fitting to take this so lightly, Doctor," said Judge Haeng, who ran inside with the Americans.

"Where is he?" asked Phosy.

"Dining room, basking in sympathy. I dare say he could use some more."

"This is getting out of control." Phosy shook his head.

"And you haven't heard the half of it," Siri told him. "Go do your investigating and I'll tell you the rest when you get back."

Civilai and Daeng opted to join Siri at his table. Ugly eyed them both and decided to let them sit there.

"I didn't do it," Siri told them.

"I didn't think for a minute you did," said Daeng patting his hand.

"I wanted to," he confessed. "I've had to put up with his whining all afternoon. There's never a gun around when you need one."

"How's his finger?"

"He'll live. He bled like a geyser though. Quite impressive."

"Do you think that was the plan?" Civilai asked. "Just to wing him?"

Siri sipped his beer and Civilai looked around for service. He could barely see the inn door. The murky sky had brought on the dusk an hour early. The generator clunked and rattled and gurgled in the distance and a small pale bulb came to life above their heads.

"I went to the Russian Circus once," Siri said. "Saw a man shoot the tassel off a woman's bra. She didn't even flinch. But in the real world I can't say I've ever seen a sniper good enough to pick off a joint."

"So they were. . . ?"

"Aiming at his heart? Quite possibly."

"He let you treat his wound?" Daeng asked.

"Reluctantly. Yamaguchi argued that he was better at cutting them off than stitching them on."

"Where was the hit?" Civilai asked.

"Just here," said Siri, pointing to a scrubbed area beyond the table.

"And I assume they didn't catch the shooter."

"No."

They stared out at the dark shadows that lingered between the bushes.

"So, it probably isn't wise to be sitting here under a lamp," said Civilai.

"Buffalo dung never lands twice on the same mushroom," Daeng reminded him.

"Of course."

Civilai called out for one of the hotel staff without much hope he'd be heard. But a small, rugby-ball-shaped girl in overalls ran out to the balcony. He ordered three beers.

"Did you find the bullet?" Daeng asked.

Siri leaned back and pointed to a hole in the stucco with decorative cracks.

"It's probably in there," he said.

"You didn't have an urge to dig it out?" Daeng asked.

"Phosy would only sulk and ask me who the policeman was in this outfit."

"And the senator's finger?"

"Probably in there with the bullet."

The evening meal, ever different, was this night a sort of grand jury with food. The tables had been pushed together and all those who hadn't been killed or shot at and those not under the delusion that they'd be next, sat around it. On the menu was spam with local cabbage, and clam chowder out of cans with sticky rice. The liquid accompaniment was Johnny Red on the rocks and tepid Coca-Cola. Those opting for room service included the senator and Ethel Chin, General Suvan, Judge Haeng and his cousin. Also absent was Rhyme from *Time* who was using his bathroom as a darkroom and had to do his exposures while there was still electricity. Dr. Yamaguchi sat once more with Auntie Bpoo at a separate table. The astounded gossip about them was rampant.

Once he'd skipped lightly and incompletely over the autopsy findings, Siri was happy to give details of the communication tower explosion in Phonsavan and his theories on the slash and burn. At the post office he'd met the regional governor. The man had no idea why there were so many fires lit around the town. Like Siri, he was certain it had nothing to do with agriculture. All the planes had left the airfield so there was no danger of an attack there, and as far as he knew all the rebels were focusing their resources on the defence of the base at Phu Bia. But with the felling of the post office tower, and now the attempt on the life of Senator Vogal, Siri had become more concerned that the target might just be the Friendship Hotel itself, and more specifically, the American contingent.

"Can't we just put them on a bus and send them somewhere outside the smoke?" Dtui asked.

"I'm afraid that's not possible," Commander Lit told her. He gave her a warm smile that Phosy didn't fail to notice. "Given the current unrest, none of the roads are completely secured," he said. "None of the truck drivers in Phonsavan would agree to drive us out of the region, no matter how much we offered them. Army convoys are the only things moving. Despite the fact that we aren't that well protected here, the Americans will be much safer at this place than on the road. And we aren't certain there's really a threat."

"What are you talking about?" Phosy asked. "Someone shot a United States senator."

"Right," said Lit. "But as you pointed out, the bullet turned out to be musket shot. We have two musketeers right here at the hotel. There's a possibility that one of the old guards tripped over his own sandal and dropped his weapon. Muskets aren't the sniper's weapon of choice. And the explosion in Phonsavan would seem to be more an act of sabotage than an attempt on the diplomat's life. If they'd wanted to kill Comrade Gordon they could have done so on the road into town."

If Lit and the others were to learn that Major Potter's death was also murder, Siri knew they'd be more inclined to believe that this was an attempt to cull the American population. Siri had briefed Phosy about the autopsy but he wasn't at liberty to tell everyone. There was a very strong likelihood that the murderer was in their midst and Siri and Phosy knew that capture would be easier if the perpetrator believed he or she was getting away with it. There was, however, a consensus at the dinner table that security was wanting at the Friendship and they would attempt to recruit new guards, professional soldiers from the local garrison, as soon as possible the following day.

Attention turned to the successes in the field. For the benefit of those left behind that morning, Civilai gave a colorful rendition of the day's events. Both sides agreed that there was a great deal that didn't make sense. Secretary Gordon told the group that all the documentation related to this mission was already at the consulate in Vientiane. The pouches would be taken on a Swedish forestry helicopter via Luang Prabang to Muang Kham, thus avoiding the smog. From there they'd be put on the local bus to Phonsavan which currently traveled with an armed escort. Gordon had no idea how long this process would take but there were better than even odds that they'd arrive before the teams departed. The weather report from the capital was that the smog had shrouded a fifty kilometer radius around Phonsavan and there was no wind forecast. They could be there for a very long time. Fires were still burning and to Siri it really looked as if a thick curtain of intrigue was being deliberately pulled around the hotel.

As the whiskey took hold, the full-table discussion crumbled into smaller groupings. Phosy had taken the opportunity to continue his discussion with Sergeant Johnson. Peach acted as their translator with Dtui making up the four. At one stage during their conversation Dtui was absolutely astounded when her husband reached across the plastic tablecloth and took hold of her hand. She thought he'd mistaken it for a napkin but he kept hold of it. It happened right there in public for everyone to see. Even Commander Lit noticed. She put it down as a small miracle right up there with his remembering her birthday—which he didn't.

"I still don't get it," Phosy said. "The sergeant here learned to fly with his dad in their family business. He got his license when he was seventeen. He graduated from high school with A grades in all the sciences . . . and the marines wouldn't let him be a pilot?"

"That's pretty much it," said Peach.

"Why not?" Dtui asked Johnson directly. He laughed.

"For the same reason they wouldn't let me be a quarterback," said the sergeant. "Some things are reserved for white boys."

"He couldn't be a pilot because he was black?" Dtui asked.

"I've applied to the marine air corps every six months and been knocked back each time," Johnson told the interpreter. "I guess I should think myself lucky they let me be a chief mechanic. It took me eight years to work my way up to that lofty position. When the war ended and they weren't desperate for mechanics any longer they had me in uniform guarding a half-empty consulate in Vientiane. But it could be worse. I could be dumb *and* black."

"You must be angry," Dtui said.

"Things are getting better," said the marine. "Hell, I wouldn't be surprised if my son makes it to copilot by the time he's fifty."

"How old is he now?"

"Four."

They were disturbed by the sound of Rhyme the journalist yahooing like a cowboy as he walked in the door of the restaurant. Under his arm he had a thick folder. He grabbed the first glass he came to and quaffed it. The owner didn't seem to mind.

"Ladies and gentlemen," he said. "I bring you the magic of aerial photography. The wonder of journalism. The genius of man."

He took out one large photographic print from the folder and held it up, walking around the table like the round-announcing girls at boxing matches, complete with the sexy walk and blown kisses. The Lao assumed he was drunk with whiskey but it turned out he was merely drunk with the glory of discovery. The buzz of Peach's translation accompanied his announcement.

"It was the first day of the mission," he said. "And our last period of visibility. As we floated over the picturesque landscape from Spook City to Ban Hoong, our fearless photojournalist leaned bravely out of the hatch behind Sergeant Johnson here and recorded our descent to the merciless terrain that had claimed our young pilot. We followed the crack carved through the thick jungle by the Ban Hoong stream. And there, no more than three miles from the village, was where the ghost of our pilot stopped to rest and clean the blood from his mouth."

"How could you know that?" Yamaguchi asked.

"Because, respected sir, he had the foresight to tell us so."

Rhyme dropped his first print onto the table in front of the doctor, reached into his back pocket and pulled out a large magnifying glass. This he handed to Yamaguchi.

"Perhaps you could tell our audience tonight exactly what it is you see there at the bend in the river."

Yamaguchi squinted through the glass and pumped it back and forth in search of a focus.

"A pile of rocks on a sand bank?" he said.

"A pile of rocks. Yes, sirree. A pile of rocks. But look what happens when you zoom in to that pile of rocks."

Rhyme dropped a second print in front of the doctor. It was a blow-up of the rocks.

"My goodness," said Yamaguchi.

"Your goodness indeed. What is it you see there now, sir?"

"The rocks have been arranged to spell out a word."

"And that word is. . . ?"

"BOWRY."

"I thank you for your cooperation, sir."

And the journalist took a bow. Everyone left their seats to get a look at the photograph. There was no doubt. Boyd Bowry had survived the crash. Sergeant Johnson shook Civilai by the hand. Mr. Geung bounced up and down. The elation of the hunt had control of them all . . . all but Commander Lit.

"I'm afraid I can't let you keep those photographs," said Lit via Peach.

"What are you talking about?" Rhyme asked. "They're my pictures."

"The close-ups you can keep," Lit told him. "But I'll have to take all the aerial photographs. You didn't have clearance to photograph from the air and I'm afraid there are security issues I have to take responsibility for. If I'd been on your helicopter I would have stopped you taking them."

"He's serious, isn't he?" Rhyme asked.

"Sure is," said Peach.

"Geung, are you certain it was Dr. Siri you saw climb through the window last night?" asked Madame Daeng.

She and Dtui had taken the morgue assistant back to the doctor's room and they were sitting either side of him on the bed. Siri was on the chair opposite. He'd spent much of the day considering what Mr. Geung had told him. His friend was incapable of telling a lie. If he said he'd seen the doctor climb into Major Potter's room, then it was true. Geung clearly didn't sense the gravity of the situation. In fact he thought it was a splendid game.

"There's only wuh . . . wuh . . . one Dr. Siri," he sang to a popular Thai radio jingle.

"When was this exactly?" Dtui asked. It was not the most sensible question to a man with an abstract grasp of time.

"You asked me to to to look for the doctor in the t-toilet," he said.

"But when you came back you said you hadn't seen him," said Dtui.

"You you asked if he was in the t-t-toilet."

"You're right. I did."

"And I said he wasn't."

"That's true. Where else did you look?"

"Everywhere."

"And you went out the back and saw him there?" Daeng asked.

"Yes. I said, 'Doctor! Doctor!' but you didn't hhhhhear me. And you got in the window."

"Did you look inside?" Dtui asked.

"Yes."

"What did you see?"

"Dr. Siri sit sitting on the bed and talking."

"Did you see who he was talking to?"

"No."

"Did anyone answer?"

"No."

"Did you see anyone else in there?" Siri asked.

"No. Too dddark."

"What did you do then?" Daeng asked.

"Come back."

"Why didn't you tell us you'd seen him?" asked Dtui.

"Be . . . cause Dr. Siri was being nnnnaughty," he whispered. "I didn't want to tell on him."

"So what the hell was I doing in there?" Siri asked himself.

"And why don't you remember?" Dtui asked.

"I should turn myself in."

"Don't be ridiculous," Daeng told him. "You get out of breath lifting a chicken wing. You did not strangle a hundred-kilogram man to death and drag him across the room."

"How can you be so sure?" he said. "A lot of peculiar things have been happening to me recently. I may be capable of anything."

"Not murder, my love."

"I'll have to tell Phosy."

"Yes, I think you will. But he'll say exactly the same thing. And you really don't need to tell the Americans."

"I told Second Secretary Gordon I'd share everything."

"Not this, Siri. Trust me."

"Then I need to go and see someone."

"Now?"

"Yes."

* * *

Siri took their flashlight and walked along the corridor and around to the rear of the main building. The light attracted one of the old guards who insisted on following close behind. When he arrived at the rearmost cabin, Siri turned to the old man and said, "I'll be all right now, thank you."

But the guard didn't leave. He merely took a step back and held on to a toothless smile. A faint yellow glow was seeping through the crack around the door. Siri sighed and knocked. Auntie Bpoo opened the door. To the doctor's horror, she was wearing a flowing black negligee and high-heeled shoes.

"What kept you?" Bpoo asked.

Before walking past her and into the room, Siri looked back over his shoulder to see that the guard's smile now occupied most of his face like a tunnel. Farewell to Yeh Ming's reputation in the northeast. The small cabin was lit by seven red candles around the headboard of the bed.

"What do you know?" Siri asked as soon as Bpoo had closed the door.

"I know that one day Mount Aconcagua and the Himalayas will be the only land masses visible above the oceans."

"About last night."

"Oh, that."

She went to sit on the bed and crossed her legs slowly. If she hadn't been a fifty-year-old man it would have been an evocative gesture. She patted the mattress beside her. Siri put his hands on his hips.

"Given your proximity to the end of your life, I wasn't about to let you go wandering around alone in the middle of the night."

"You followed me?"

"Of course I did. I crouched in the shadows like a sleek black panther."

"What did you see?"

"You were in some sort of a trance. First you climbed in the sleazy major's window, then poor lovestruck Mr. Geung arrived and peeked in and went away, then you garrotted the American and climbed out again."

"I. . . ? You saw me. . . ?"

"Only joking, sweetheart. I didn't see any such thing. No idea what you were doing. It was all rather dull, really. You were in there for half an hour."

"You didn't go and take a look through the window?"

"You can't be serious. You expect me to tramp through a turnip plot in my eighty-thousand-*kip* cocktail shoes? Be real, Dr. Siri."

"Bpoo. I don't remember any of it. Do you think there was some supernatural connection?"

"You're the shaman. Not me."

"You have contact with the spirit world."

"They only call me when your phone's off the hook."

"Come on. I'm serious. What do you think happened last night? Something drew me to that room."

"Rooms are just slabs of concrete and plaster and tacky faux-wood paneling. They have no particular life or afterlife of their own. If you were summoned it would have been by a spirit. A particularly pushy one."

"The major's?"

"Well, no offence to the departed, but I didn't get the impression he had a particularly awesome aura. No, it would have been somebody else."

"How can I find out?"

"The spirit wanted you there for a reason. Something happened in that room, something significant. I would begin my investigation there."

"You think the room's haunted."

Bpoo laughed.

"Ghosts have much better things to do than haunt, Siri."

"Like what?"

"Like going into the trainee nurses' shower room and watching them undress. Spirits are perverts just like the rest of us. If it makes you feel better, you weren't the only one with an interest in that room last night."

"What do you mean?"

"I'd seen somebody else go in that room earlier. But he used the door."

"Who?"

Siri returned to his room with the guard chuckling a few meters behind him. The doctor shone his flashlight on the bed to be sure it was Madame Daeng sleeping there then climbed beneath the covers.

"Is that perfume I smell?" she asked.

"Yes. I was in Bpoo's room."

"It's nice. I'll have to ask her where she got it."

"Daeng."

"Yes, my husband?"

"I think Judge Haeng might have killed Major Potter."

"That's just wishful thinking."

He breathed heavily.

"I'm not so sure. Bpoo saw him go into Potter's room earlier that night."

17

THE STREAM TEAM

It transpired that very few of the team members had managed a particularly restful night of sleep. For want of something to do, most had arrived in dribs and drabs long before the morning meal was served. They all went first to the large picture windows and looked out at a view that ended four meters beyond. A murky sky pressed down on the Friendship Hotel. A pocket of gloom was closing in on them. For those privy to the fact that the major's death was not a suicide, the feeling permeated that an unidentifiable danger was squeezing them into a corner. The smoggy mist and a lack of oxygen gave the place the feel of an Andean mountain village. Breath was no longer taken for granted. Even those with no hereditary respiratory problems were wheezing. Headaches abounded. At breakfast there were baggy eyes and long canine yawns and heads nodding over empty place mats.

Siri and Daeng arrived just as the sausages and spicy salad left the kitchen on large trays. Before the couple could take a seat, Second Secretary Gordon called Siri over to his table where Dr. Yamaguchi and Auntie Bpoo were already seated. Siri had naturally told his wife about the autopsy but the Americans weren't to know that and they did have an agreement to keep a lid on the findings. So Daeng sat with Mr. Geung who was deep in some impossible conversation with John Johnson.

"The embassy documents have arrived," said Gordon.

"Already?" said Siri. "How's that possible?"

"Army convoy in transit to Phu Bia. They traveled overnight. Dropped off the documents at the local battalion. Their courier brought them up early today. And, four armed guards arrived this morning at the behest of your judge."

The thought of more weapons around in the hands of bush soldiers hardly put Siri's mind at ease. But the arrival of the files was a positive and they needed an excuse for Yamaguchi and Gordon to stay at the hotel that day to go through the documents. As everything was in English, Siri and Phosy wouldn't be much help. But they came up with a plan that would pass the inspection of Judge Haeng. The Americans would claim to be putting together the paperwork to ship Major Potter's body back to the US. For this purpose they could commandeer Nurse Dtui for her Lao translation skills of medical terms. In actual fact, Dtui would be summarizing the findings from the files to pass on to Siri and the others when they returned.

Most of the remaining team members shared Commander Lit's theory that the bombing of the post office was a cowardly act of terrorism, and the shooting of the senator was most likely an accident. And well, yes, he was only a senator. Potter had killed himself. So only the morgue team and those present at the autopsy were aware of the actual danger. The decision was taken, therefore, that everyone else should go to visit the site of the stones at the bend in the river—an excursion of sorts. Missing were the same characters who'd opted for room service breakfast and, as Judge Haeng was amongst the absentees, the atmosphere was more relaxed than normal. There was an unreal party mood, a general buzz of excitement as they closed in on the missing airman. The fashion statement of the day was made by Auntie Bpoo in combat boots, flak jacket and cherry red hotpants. To the contractor's displeasure, they only needed the one truck to go to the site. The truck dropped off the stream team one kilometer further along the potholed road than usual. With their maps and compasses, the aerial photographs, improvised face masks and plenty of water, they headed off into the smoky jungle.

They reached the stream a lot sooner than they'd expected. They'd only been trekking for half an hour and the sudden giggly sound of the icy water tickling the rocks surprised all of them. But the map indicated just the one stream and it was a good sized watercourse. The photograph Rhyme had taken gave them only a rough estimate of the distance of the stone message from Ban Hoong. They were approximately in the right place but didn't know whether to head south or north. They decided to head upstream for an hour. If they found nothing they'd turn around and follow the stream all the way to the village. Siri noticed Bpoo nod so he felt confident they'd made the correct call. Only twenty minutes south they came to a bend in the river and a broad sandbank which disappeared into the mist.

"This looks promising," said Rhyme, running to the head of the convoy. "Now all we need is . . . aha!" He was the first to spot the blurry dark gray boulders at the far side of the clearing and he jogged across to them. The team followed. Rhyme already had two of his cameras primed. He flipped open the dust caps and began to snap away at the rocks. The word BOWRY was spelled out neatly in boulders approximately the size of bicycle wheels.

"The pilot couldn't have been hurt at all," Civilai told his friends proudly. "Some of those boulders must weigh a hundred kilograms. They would have taken some shifting."

"I'd need a dozen elephants and a long chain," said Siri. "And I haven't just fallen out of a helicopter."

The source of the large stones was at the river's edge where they'd been smoothed by the constant passage of water and coated with a black moss. They'd been rolled across the clearing to a point where they contrasted with the white sand and on a clear day would have been easily visible from the air. It must have taken considerable effort.

"Almost a miracle that they weren't spotted by anyone else," said Daeng. "The rescue flights. Trips back and forth to Spook City."

"No more a miracle than escaping from a falling helicopter, madam," said Civilai.

They sat beside the idyllic stream, a picture framed in fog, and drank tea from a thermos. It reminded Siri of a scene in an exotic calendar on the wall of some French matron. "Natives in the harsh jungle."

"How do you think he survived out here?" Phosy asked.

"He was a marine," said Daeng. "They train them for jungle warfare."

"I doubt he'd ever come across anything like this in his training," Siri told them.

Rhyme had almost all the pictures he needed. He called for just one more team photo, everyone lined up behind the rocks. They clambered to the far side and took up a pose like the grand explorers of the Tibetan highlands with the body of the slain yeti at their feet. The photographer stood as far back as he dared, aware that the smoke would make his pictures appear out of focus.

"I say, you," Rhyme called out. "Would you mind standing up?"

The journalist was talking to Phosy who was on his knees reaching between the rocks. Peach translated but the distraction had already spoiled a very nice photograph. Now others were leaning over Phosy and watching as, from the narrow gap, he pulled a large plastic envelope fastened with bright yellow tape. Even Rhyme abandoned his post and went to look at the prize. Phosy didn't wait for a consensus, he used his fake Swiss army knife to slice open the tape at the top of the envelope and tipped out the contents onto one of the rocks. It was an English language newspaper. He passed it to the American sergeant.

"It's the *Bangkok Post*," Johnson told them.

"What on earth's that doing here?" Civilai asked nobody in particular. "What's the date?"

The question was met by a low whistle from Johnson.

"Well, this is weird," said the American. "This newspaper is dated June second, 1978. A little over two months ago."

"Ah," Civilai laughed. "I remember something like this in France. *Poisson d'Avril*—April Fish. I can't recall the exact date but it's the day you play a joke on people just for fun. Our Politburo has something similar but theirs is every day of the year. Next thing you know somebody with a camera jumps out of the bushes and shouts, 'Surprise! April Fish!'"

"It's August," Daeng reminded him.

"And I don't see anyone laughing," added Siri. "But I'd wager somebody's playing a trick on all of us."

"It's possible the newspaper isn't related to the rocks," Commander Lit suggested.

"You mean like some local was sitting on a boulder reading a newspaper and it started raining so he put it in a plastic bag and stuck it down beside the rocks so he could finish it once he'd learned English?" Phosy said without looking at the security man.

"Actually, I meant that someone wanted us to find the newspaper so they left it in a place they knew we'd search," said Lit in the direction of the same bank of fog.

"As opposed to leaving it in front of the hotel?"

"And have the old guards burn it to keep themselves warm. Good idea."

"I do wish Dtui was here," Daeng laughed. "Men can be so predictable."

"I'm not predictable," said Siri.

"I knew you'd say that."

The Americans had split up the newspaper and were going through it page by page. Peach translated.

"An Australian journalist swam to Laos in scuba gear to rescue his Lao girlfriend," she said.

"US abolishes import quota on Thai textiles," read Johnson.

"A beauty competition for fat women," said Bpoo. "What a civilized country."

"OK," said Peach. She'd picked up the sheet Randal Rhyme had just put down. He apparently missed the reference. "Laos gets a mention here in the editorial. I think this might be relevant."

"Rumor has it that the Communist Lao government is in bed with her old nemesis, the USA," she read. "Despite a massive push to establish cooperatives nationwide, the People's Democratic Republic has found itself with a shortfall of 113,000 tons of rice as a result of last year's drought. And who should step in to find that mere nine million dollars but Uncle Sam himself. What's nine million compared to the fifty million they were pumping in per year during the war? On Wednesday, the Senate appropriations committee, under its new chairman, Senator Walter

Bowry of South Carolina, approved a budget to help out one of the poorest countries in the world. It was, as the senator told a press conference with a straight face, "for humanitarian purposes." The good gentleman went on to add that, "despite twenty years of hostility, the US bears no personal animosity toward the Pathet Lao." Right. We at the *Post* doubt the congressman has any ill feelings at all considering the fact the gentleman's family amassed a sizeable fortune from exports from the region during the second Indochinese war. We doubt it would do him any harm at all if that channel was reopened through this new détente.

"'I am pleased to be in a position to assist the country in its hour of need in an official capacity,' he told reporters. Good on you, senator. And we hope such a magnanimous gesture doesn't damage your political standing given the anti-communist feelings in Washington. Let's hope that nine million oiling will grease the wheels for the Lao to agree to the demands of the powerful MIA lobby. Wouldn't that make Senator Bowry one popular gentleman on both sides of the globe."

The teams sat around on the rocks and lobbed views and opinions back and forth. If this editorial were factually correct—and Rhyme pointed out that the *Post* was known to make things up every now and then, particularly when attacking communism—then two aspects of it were particularly relevant. Firstly, they'd underestimated the power of Boyd's father, now the chair of the appropriations committee. If he'd been influential in releasing the funds for Laos, he had a vested interest in making sure things went well here. Then there was the fact that the senator had connections in the region and had apparently done very well financially during the Vietnam War. But, more importantly, and most baffling, if the budget was approved back before June 2, the photographs of the downed pilot and his tailplane must have arrived after that decision was taken. And, if that was so, the senator hadn't put pressure on his committee because his son was a downed pilot. To the Lao, that kind of nepotism would have been easy to understand. But that last point made no sense to anybody.

"It might just be that the photos arrived earlier and they held back the announcement till after the committee's decision," said Civilai, ever aware of the subterfuge of government.

"Not possible," said Johnson. "The incoming mail at the embassy is time and date stamped."

"Then we would have to assume that the photographs were sent in response to the announcement," said Siri.

"And what would be the point of that?" asked Rhyme.

"I have no idea."

"What I'd like to know"—Johnson shook his head—"is what the congressman was importing from here that made him so goddamned rich. And I bet you it wasn't coconuts."

"All right." Phosy clapped his hands as if he were frustrated with the direction the discussion was going. "Let's come back to whoever it was who left the newspaper here. I suggest we take a hike back to the Phuan village. See if they remember seeing anyone around who shouldn't have been here. Any objections?" He turned specifically to Commander Lit, who merely smiled.

Before they left the sand bank, the teams combed the tree line and the rocks but found no other confusing evidence. As they walked, the debate continued. Were the boulders laid out by a young pilot hoping for a rescue, or were they a recent creation? Were the person who left the newspaper and the rock-speller one and the same? And if Boyd didn't spell out his own name after the crash, what became of him? Was he captured by the PL? Killed? Did he succumb to the many dangers of the jungle? Die from hypothermia?

"They flew a hundred hours of search and rescue looking for him," Johnson said. "I can't believe in all that time nobody spotted a name written on the sand. They train the boys to leave messages. It's what the rescue pilots look for. With all the slash and burn going on, they wouldn't have looked twice at a burned-out stretch of ground like the dead man's field with no visible wreckage, but something like this. . . ."

"So what is the message?" Daeng asked. "If they left the rocks there for us, what are they telling us? That Boyd didn't make it, or that he did?"

"Perhaps if we find the messenger we can understand the message," said Phosy.

When they finally reached Ban Hoong, the team members were happy to take off their boots and relax in the village. Much of their march north had been along the bed of the brook, closed in on both sides by the unkempt jungle. They stretched out their damp socks on the rocks with little hope that the blurry cheese ball of a sun might dry them off. Even at midday there was a chill in the air. The sky was a dark sheet of ash. A chorus of chesty coughs rose from the riverbank like toad calls.

Siri and Phosy took a moment to play with Bok then sat with his father and the elders. As was customary, they drank some herbal brew and stared around appreciatively at mother nature before getting to the point.

"How did you know when to take your dragon's tail to Spook City?" Phosy asked. Ar acted as spokesman.

"The sorceress told us before she died that there would be a sign," he said.

"Did she tell you a date? Make a map?"

"No," Ar and the elders laughed. "She was blind by then. She said one day the dragon's daughter would come and ask for her father's tail back and we'd have to return it."

"And she did?"

"Two moons ago. She arrived in the village one afternoon. Just walked in out of the jungle with her bodyguards as if from nowhere. She looked like us, dressed like us, but she spoke a strange language. There was a girl here then who could speak Lao—she's gone now, went to find work in the city—but even she had trouble understanding what the woman was saying. She was beautiful. Her face had been painted by the gods. She asked if we had any wreckage from an explosion. When we told her about the dragon's tail she asked to see it. When we took her to the meeting hall we could see in her eyes how happy she was. We knew she was the dragon's daughter."

Phosy could tell from the headman's expression that he didn't buy in to all this dragon hooey. He was merely keeping the old men happy.

"Did the dragon's daughter stay overnight?" Phosy asked.

"No, brother."

"Did she have a camera?"

"I didn't see one."

"Did you ever leave her alone with the dragon's tail?"

"Of course. It was only right. She needed some time to honor her father. Before she left she told us that someone would come from the government. That we should tell them about the tail. But we'd promised our sorceress we'd deliver it in person. So when the cadre came by in her stiff uniform and told us about your visit, we loaded the tail onto a litter and set off for Long Cheng. We left it a bit late. We only had two weeks to get there."

Phosy and Siri consulted.

"Do you know of a place upstream where there are dark rocks on a sand bank?" Phosy asked.

"Of course."

"Some of the rocks form a word . . . a shape."

"The rocks move all the time. The river swells and pushes them here and there."

"So if someone made a shape with the rocks this year. . . ?"

"It would probably be moved along by the next rainy season."

"Comrade Ar, apart from the dragon's daughter, do you remember seeing anyone out of place? Anyone who really shouldn't be here?"

Ar laughed.

"Brother Phosy, that would be us."

"So, who do you think she was?" Daeng asked. "The dragon's daughter?"

They were all in the rear of the truck bumping along the trail back to Phonsavan. Not even five and the truck had its headlights on.

"Well, if this was two moons ago, it could technically have been after the budget announcement and before the photos were sent to Bangkok," Siri told her, his words arriving in an asthmatic squeak.

"It wouldn't surprise me if she had an instamatic stuffed down her bra," said Civilai.

"Takes a picture of the tailplane," said Siri, "moves the rocks, secretes the newspaper. She's undoubtedly the person who's orchestrating this whole prisoner-of-war story."

"So you're convinced it's fabricated?" Daeng asked.

"Of course it is. Who on earth would want to keep an American pilot locked up for ten years? This mystery woman would have to be someone who knew of Boyd and his connection to the senator. It would have to be someone who'd met Boyd during the war."

"Or it could be Boyd himself," said Daeng.

"Good, now you're into the spirit of things," said Civilai. "A pilot survives for ten years, unseen in the jungles of Laos. Then one day a copy of the newspaper drops out of the sky and he reads about his father's good fortune. Where's he going to find a copy of the *Bangkok Post*?"

"Thailand." Siri and Daeng said it at the same time.

"Ha," said Civilai. "I see it. You're just attempting to muscle in on my Hollywood deal. Boyd abseils from a crashing helicopter then walks sixty kilometers to Thailand through hostile enemy-controlled territory."

"This isn't all enemy territory," Daeng reminded him. "He'd be just as likely to meet an ally. There were plenty of friendly villagers around who'd be happy to help out a nice young American boy."

"If that were so, why wouldn't he get himself returned to his base?"

"Embarrassment for trashing one of their choppers?" Daeng suggested.

"Or, perhaps he didn't want to go back," said Siri.

"A deserter?" said Civilai in mock horror. "I thought he was supposed to be a model soldier. No black marks."

"Something was troubling him that night," said Siri. "Something made him act out of character. Perhaps he was afraid to go back."

"What if the crash wasn't an accident?" said Daeng. "What if somebody wanted him dead?"

"All right." Civilai put up his hands. "I give up. I'll go sixty–forty with you. No more. But I want first billing on the credits and 'Based on an original idea by Civilai Songsawat' somewhere up there on the screen." They shook hands to seal the deal.

Only Lit didn't join in the laughter.

"You're all missing the obvious," he said.

"And what would that be?" Phosy asked.

"That you're all so intrigued by the fantastic you aren't seeing the simple. If you could look beyond the dragons and their relatives and the exploding moon and blind sorceresses you'd see it too. Your sweet little Phuan village is the hub of all this intrigue. How about this? Your pilot crashes but he survives. The villagers capture him, take pictures of him and the helicopter tail, and wait for an opportunity to cash in on their good fortune."

"For ten years?" Phosy laughed.

"And how exactly are they cashing in?" Daeng asked.

"You wait, madam. I bet you a silver bangle they'll miraculously discover his remains. The pilot's father, in gratitude, will reward them handsomely. Or they'll suddenly remember there's a grave site and they'll charge to take you there. Just you wait."

Everyone wanted to argue, Phosy in particular, but nobody did. Thus far, it was no less logical than any other theory.

18

A US REPUBLICAN SENATOR IN A LOCKED ROOM

They'd washed off the dust of the day and were changing for dinner. Dtui noticed that her husband had been even more subdued than usual since their return to the Friendship. He'd told her about the events of their field trip but with no real enthusiasm.

"Is something wrong?" she asked.

"Not really."

"Phosy?"

"I . . . he said you were strong-willed."

"Who?"

"Your security commander fellow."

"He did? When?"

"When Daeng explained you were working with the Americans today."

"Well, that's a compliment, isn't it?"

"I suppose so. If you don't take it to mean stubborn, as in, 'If she hadn't been so stubborn she could have had me instead.'"

Dtui smiled to herself.

"Oh. But he didn't actually utter those words?"

"It was unstated."

Dtui *nopp*ed a thank you to the heavens.

"Inspector Phosy, you're jealous."

"I am not . . . of him? Huh. Just. . . ."

"What?"

"Why didn't you tell me it was him?"

"What was him?"

"That he was the one you met in Vieng Xai."

"It didn't occur to me. Didn't seem that important."

Phosy was doing a bold job of keeping his emotions in check. He smiled till cracks appeared in his cheeks.

"Not important? He asked you to marry him."

"Oh, comrade policeman," she giggled. "If I had to point out every man who's ever proposed to me we'd never make it through a day. Now, shall we go?"

She stood, opened the door and sniffed his flushed cheek as he passed her.

The dinners which had begun four days earlier as such jolly affairs had taken on the air of refueling stops. Although still available, the Johnny Red was not flowing nearly as freely and the diners were more concerned about the quality of the air than that of the food. Officially, Civilai was still not in the inner circle of those who attended the autopsy but of course, like Madame Daeng, he had been told all about it. Siri was waiting for an opportunity to introduce them into the group without betraying the trust of the Americans. So it was decided that this evening Civilai, with Peach as his interpreter, would do what he did best. Hard as it may have been to believe, especially for those who only knew him outside the Politburo, the old man was a diplomat of the first order. He could schmooze with the best of them; dally with dictators and tango with tyrants. He could make despots in the most constricting ideological girdles take a breath. He had been granted an audience with Senator Vogal. As the senator had hardly left his room since what he was liberally calling "the assassination attempt," it was no surprise that Ethel Chin had ordered room service. Civilai would be joining them for an after-meal tête-à-tête.

For the others the meal experience was accomplished barely half an hour after it began. Siri and Bpoo, Dtui and Phosy accompanied Dr. Yamaguchi to the room of Secretary Gordon. Ugly took up a guard position outside the door. Inside they upended the bed to lean against the wall and used all the available floor space to spread out their paperwork. Mr. Geung was given the very special role of lookout. He stood between the curtain and the window pane and if anyone came near he would cough loudly. Originally they had told him to whistle but that and nuclear physics were two skills he hadn't yet mastered. Auntie Bpoo went into the bathroom and didn't come out for a very long time.

"All right, what do we have?" Siri asked. His voice had developed an embedded growl like that of a street dog attempting to speak human.

The main points had already been listed during the long day of research. All Dtui needed to do was read from her notes then check with the Americans to see if they had reactions to the Lao comments. Meanwhile, Yamaguchi and Gordon continued to work their ways through the unread files.

"First," Dtui said, "were the documents that had been sent to the US embassy in Bangkok. They explained the rationale for the initial MIA joint action. Not surprisingly, the letter from the senate committee said that the approval of the rice budget would be totally dependent on the Lao agreeing to this mission. No MIA, no rice. But, as you've since discovered, at that stage they hadn't finalized the name of a flier to go after. They acknowledged that most of the missing airmen had been lost in Vietnam but saw Laos as a back door for getting permission for similar actions with the Socialist Party of Vietnam. When Boyd's name came up there was obviously talk of a conflict of interest given the relationship with the senator, but I get the feeling they didn't have that many downed pilots to choose from. Certainly none with empirical evidence like a photo. They needed success so they selected Boyd. We've got his CV. He was a smart lad. Clean service record with the marines. Selected for 'special missions' by Air America."

"Any idea what that means?" Siri asked.

"The classified stuff didn't make it into the reports. But there was some evidence. Gordon and Yamaguchi noticed discrepancies in Boyd's flight records. The pilots were paid by the mission. They got ten dollars an hour, which is about what I get a month, so most pilots kept very detailed logs. But not Boyd. His first year was normal, every hour accounted for. But by the second year these empty blocks started to appear. Whole weeks where he didn't claim any flying time at all."

"Could he have been on vacation?" Phosy asked.

"Nope. His vacation time was clearly marked on his time sheets. Plus there was no record of him traveling out of the region. People on vacation don't hang around in a war zone. This was all unexplained dead time. So we assumed 'special missions' meant he was doing something secret for the CIA. That's why Gordon would like to ask your permission to bring in Sergeant Johnson. He thinks we need some inside military information and he believes the sergeant can be trusted."

Siri had his window. He agreed to Johnson in exchange for Civilai, and, with a little push, Madame Daeng was included in the package.

"All we have left is the background report from Air America," Dtui continued. "That mostly talks about the loss of the helicopter. The mystery of how it could just vanish completely. There were comments about Boyd's state of mind from other pilots back in the base at Udon in Thailand. They all seemed to like him. Said he was a good flier. For the first year he was one of the boys, joined in, friendly. But some commented that for the last three months he'd started to act strangely. Some said he'd become paranoid. He used to be a two-drink-a-night man. Said he didn't like booze that much. But toward the end he was matching them drink for drink and all these odd rants started. He'd say how they shouldn't be surprised if he found a deadly cobra in his bunk. Or if he was shot down by friendly fire some day. He said 'they' were after him."

"Did he say who 'they' were?" Siri asked.

"No. The other pilots assumed it was . . . us, the enemy."

"All right," said Phosy. "What's—"

He was interrupted by heavy coughing from behind the curtain. The conspirators lowered their voices.

"What is it, hon?" Dtui asked.

"I . . . I swallowed a bug," said Mr. Geung. "Sorry."

When she'd stopped laughing, Dtui continued with her notes.

"That brings us to the interviews," she said. "We have incomplete transcripts for the interviews with Nino Sebastian, the Filipino flight mechanic, and David Leon, the senior flight person at Spook City. They were the last two to see Boyd alive, unless you count the bear. There were two interviews with Sebastian; one by the AA investigator shortly after the crash, and another sponsored by Congressman Bowry and conducted by a private detective in the Philippines. That interview ran out to forty sheets. The congressman released only twelve of those to the MIA committee. Six of those twelve are marked on the file as 'On loan to Major

Potter.' As you might imagine, the six we're left with don't say very much. We learn that Boyd and Sebastian had flown together on around forty occasions. That afternoon they'd flown the chopper directly up from Udon in Thailand with cargo that was labeled 'Refugee Supplies' due for Ban Song. Then we cut sixteen pages to Sebastian stoned and drunk in a bear cage wondering where his pilot's gone."

"But what that *does* tell us is that both the pilot and the mechanic were out of control," said Phosy. "Hence the crash. Doesn't sound like foul play to me."

"According to the regulations, AA flight crews weren't allowed to drink or mess with intoxicants up-country," Dtui told him. "Somebody there got our boy stoned. That could be construed as foul play."

"What about the AA interview?" Siri asked.

"Six pages in total. All but one signed out to Major Potter. That one page suggests that Sebastian was cut up about not having done enough to save his young friend's life. He didn't say who supplied the LSD. He blamed himself for getting dragged into the drink session and for not saying no to the drugs. Plus the fact he'd left open the bear cage and next morning the hung-over beast attacked four locals before they could subdue it."

"Nothing worse than a bear with a sore head," Siri nodded.

"AA agreed with Sebastian's appraisal of himself and fired him. He scratched around Thailand doing odd mechanic work before heading back to the Philippines with his savings. He and his family opened a service station and café. He stayed there till his death."

"When did he die?" Phosy asked.

"Three weeks ago," said Dtui. "There was a sticker attached to the front of the interview sheet."

"Cause?"

"He drowned. There was a storm drain at the bottom of his property. They found him face down in the water."

"You said there was another interview?" Siri asked.

"David Leon. Senior flight mechanic at Long Cheng. He was one of the witnesses who heard the explosion. Talked about Mike Wolff, the pilot who'd been drinking with Boyd and Sebastian that night. Explained that Wolff was shot down a couple of weeks later. They'd recovered his body. Ten page interview. Four pages released to Major Potter. Leon had been a fighter pilot in Vietnam but lost his licence, and the reason for that isn't anywhere in the files."

"But there was no interview organized by the congressman for this man?" Siri asked.

"No. Leon had been hired directly by the embassy in Vientiane to work with the Ravens—the forward air command. The embassy conducted the interview. There was just the one. Why?"

"I don't know. Boyd's father hires a private detective in the Philippines to interview one mechanic—forty pages worth—but isn't interested enough to interview the only other witness there that night. Doesn't that strike you as odd?"

"Perhaps he died before they could interview him," Dtui suggested.

"He's dead too?" Siri asked.

"Yes."

"When?"

"About the same time as Sebastian. In fact there was a couple of days between the two deaths."

"He didn't fall into a storm drain, by any chance?"

"No. He had a heart attack in a go-go bar in Thailand."

"Oh." Siri gasped and coughed. "This is far too much of a coincidence for my liking. No wonder Major Potter found something smelly here."

"I think the fact that we didn't find any of those released papers in the major's belongings is relevant," said Phosy. "Whoever killed him helped himself to those."

"It also makes you wonder whether Judge Haeng was looking for them too," said Siri.

"You think Justice might be involved in all this?" Daeng asked.

"I don't know. Haeng was looking for something he didn't find. He'd been in Potter's room earlier. And he's been acting like the Americans' own private little Pekinese all week. He's up to something."

"You think he's being nice to them so he can have them killed one by one without being suspected?" Daeng asked.

"No. I believe the killer of Major Potter was a completely different animal to whoever took a potshot at the senator."

Phosy agreed.

"You think we have two different assassins?" Daeng asked.

"Maybe three if you include the post office tower explosion."

It was time to bring Dr. Yamaguchi and Gordon into the discussion.

*

Meanwhile, deep in the west wing, Civilai had chuckled and hmm'd and ahah'd through thirty minutes of Senator Vogal eulogizing himself to heaven and back. Ethel Chin was always at the senator's side. From this close proximity it was clear why she had joined the senator in isolation. The stress of events at the Friendship, or perhaps just the unpleasantness of being in such a nasty place, had brought her lower face out in hives. She'd pasted a layer of make-up over it but the damage to her skin was plain to see. She sat at the desk purportedly reading a book but with such lack of commitment as to look up with a laugh at all the senator's jokes. Not a minute into the meeting, Civilai had become the American's best friend. The senator had already shared two tearful "not even my family knows this" moments.

On the rare occasion that Civilai was allowed a few seconds to respond to a question, he did so with a respect and humility that made Peach's nostrils flare. After exactly twenty-eight minutes, there came a knock on the door and Rhyme entered with his flash unit attached to a cumbersome hunk of equipment and he took several photos of the elder statesmen in conversation. Ironically, in the photos, the senator appeared to be listening intently to Civilai's thoughts. Rhyme's departure was clearly designed to be the end of the dialogue. Vogal stood at the door bidding farewell and nodding at Civilai who remained seated. Peach stood then sat down again. Ethel Chin rolled her eyes. Reluctantly, the senator closed the door, locked it, and returned to his perch on the end of the bed, making a pointed study of his wristwatch. It wasn't as if he had somewhere to go. Civilai decided it was time to probe.

"Peach," he smiled, "ask the senator what type of family it takes to produce such a noble and intelligent son."

"Do I have to?"

"Please."

The senator beamed when he heard the question and settled happily into the role of interviewee.

"All my people are in tea," he said. "Importing originally from Ceylon. My family are the business brains. My Uncle Edwin and I were the black sheep. We had our hearts set on public service. Money just didn't seem too important to me. My focus was on removing evil from the world and replacing it—and I know this sounds corny—but replacing it with a little love and humility. I believe we owe it to the world, not just to take, but. . . ."

This drivel went on for another two minutes before the subject eventually found its way home.

"It was my Uncle Edwin who introduced me to the foreign service and for that I shall be eternally indebted to him. God rest his soul. He was a great man."

"So you were in the foreign service?" Civilai asked. "I knew it. I just knew it."

"How?"

"Your confidence. Your way with words. The way that the common people just naturally relate to you."

Peach's eyes had rolled so many times they should technically have been on the other side of the room by now. But Civilai urged her onward.

"It's true," said the senator. "I do feel a great deal of love from the little people. I guess that's what spurred me forward when times were hard."

"We could have used skills like yours in this region."

"Oh, I was here, of course."

"You were?"

"Didn't you know?"

"No."

"Goodness me, yes. I was in Vietnam during the war. If I hadn't been so valuable at the embassy I would have enlisted. As it turned out I took over the role of my Uncle Edwin. I was in Saigon for two years. Just a small administrative position."

"He was in Saigon for two years," said Dtui, reading her notes about Major Potter. "He was the military attaché there. It seems he did a lot of the hiring and firing of advisors. Pretty powerful. But it appears his drinking habit started over there too. Looks like he couldn't handle the pressure."

"Wasn't Sergeant Johnson in Saigon?" Daeng asked.

Dtui went back over her notes on the original CVs.

"He was there from sixty-five to sixty-eight."

"And Major Potter?"

"Sixty-six to sixty-eight."

"If they knew each other they didn't say," said Daeng.

"I imagine the place was overcrowded with men in uniform," said Siri. "It's possible they didn't run into each other."

"Another coincidence, though," said Phosy.

"And if Potter was doing all the hiring and firing, and Johnson was applying for a pilot position, you'd think they'd at least have heard of each other," Siri added.

Auntie Bpoo emerged from the bathroom at last and Siri noticed Dr. Yamaguchi squeeze her hand as she passed. No accounting for taste.

"That's it for Potter," said Dtui. "We just have a few words about Senator Bowry. It seems the war was good to him, too. He'd been struggling with a little family import business, teak furniture from Asia mostly. A lot from Thailand. Then in the late sixties I guess the teak business took off. Made a lot of money. He invested his profits in real estate and the next thing you know he's stinking rich. He used his money to get into politics."

"That was certainly a meteoric rise from embassy clerk to senator in the space of ten years," said Civilai. "How did you achieve that?"

"Not a clerk, exactly—senior administrator, more like. I admit I had some pull. And those were war years. Crazy times."

"*He means all the good guys were dead*," Peach added outside the confines of her translation. She'd learned a thing or two from Auntie Bpoo. Civilai didn't react.

"A man of a certain . . . stature could rise through the ranks back then," Vogal continued. "It's not so easy now. I had an excellent track record, clearly defined political goals and a respected family name."

"*And shit loads of money and a pretty wife*," Peach contributed. She was losing control. It was time for Civilai to go on the offensive.

"So, you were a senior administrator at the embassy. . . ?"

"I was dealing mostly with the movement of personnel." The senator remembered his watch. It was barely eight.

"Of course, Saigon." Civilai nodded knowingly. "I imagine everything was open and above board there. No shady dealings whatsoever."

"We did our best to maintain a certain transparency, it's true."

"Not like in Laos then."

"What do you mean?"

"I'm afraid you Americans weren't quite as transparent over here. In fact, I'm tempted to say your money was responsible for buying and selling several coalition governments that didn't suit your fancy."

A US Republican senator in a locked room. Civilai felt a warm glow. The senator's smile was as fake as a Giaconda with blonde highlights. He took up a tone of syrupy condescension.

"Oh, Mr. Civilai," he said. "You have to remember that you were in an information cocoon here in the wilds of Laos. You couldn't possibly know just how much good the US was doing for your country. It's common knowledge to anyone outside of Red Indochina that the vast majority of our budget for Laos was spent on aid."

Civilai laughed, which caused the senator's brow to rise and his wispy comb-over to flop across his field of vision.

"The vast majority of your budget went on B-52s and ordnance," said Civilai.

"A common misapprehension," said Vogal without missing a beat. "But with all due respect, Mr. Civilai, you can't honestly believe your own propaganda machine."

"Then let's look at the statistics. Perhaps we can believe the US embassy budget release for the fiscal year 1970, just as an example. I have a copy in my room if you'd care to see it."

"How could. . . ?"

"Your total expenditure in Laos for that year was $284 million. . . ."

"It—"

". . . $162 million of which was tagged as military assistance. Only $50 million—which a cursory calculation tells me is around eighteen per cent of your total budget—was assigned to aid."

The senator cast a desultory gaze at Ethel Chin who returned to her novel.

"That's still a considerable humanitarian effort in anybody's book, sir," he said.

"Except in your book," Civilai continued. "Humanitarian aid included feeding the Royal Lao Army and several thousand irregulars. What little remained was pumped into a refugee program that wouldn't have been necessary if you hadn't bombed a third of the population out of their homes."

"Don't be ridiculous. The refugees in Laos were fleeing communism. They were escaping the atrocities that you people inflicted upon them."

"There are members of the US senate who'd disagree with that view."

"What are you talking about?"

"In 1969, the findings of a US subcommittee headed by Senator Edward Kennedy were that some four-hundred-thousand refugees in Laos were dispossessed as a direct result of US bombing."

"Sir, Kennedy is a Democrat with undisguised communist leanings. He couldn't . . . and besides. . . ." The senator had found himself backed into a broom closet of an argument but he didn't get where he was today by conceding defeat. "Look, my wound is causing me some concern here," he said with a wince. "I need to take my medication and get some sleep. I do honestly hope we have an opportunity to continue this fascinating discussion at some future date. It's been a delight, sir, an absolute delight."

"You were amazing," said Peach.

"Yes, I get that a lot," Civilai replied. They were walking along the corridor in the direction of the dining room. One of the new guards from in front of Vogal's door was marching along behind them.

"How do you remember all those facts and figures?"

"I don't."

"But you . . . you made them up?"

"I think I hit the general ballpark, as you folks say. But the nice thing about facts is that you can toss them in here and there merely to win arguments. It doesn't matter if they're accurate. Just look confident and hope your opponent doesn't have a photographic memory for figures. I didn't lie exactly. The Kennedy thing was true."

"See why I want to be on your side?"

"Even in our information cocoon?"

"Sure. It feels a lot warmer in here."

19

SUPER NAPALM

You could taste the soot. It was so thick in the air it was like waking up in a house fire—a bitterly cold house fire. Siri sat on the edge of the bed, his head in his hands, wheezing for breath. The room was blacker than the soot it contained, as black as the inside of a sarcophagus. And all felt odd. His instincts told him that everything was in the wrong place—a mirror image of his actual room. The window was open but he was certain they'd shut it before retiring. There was no breeze or light through the loosely pulled curtains, just a mellower shade of black that showed the general shape of the window and drew very faint outlines here and there around the room. He kicked something with his heel. Between his legs an object protruded from beneath the bed. He reached down. A crate.

His heart raced. He looked behind him at the figure sleeping there. A black shape, of course. Not Madame Daeng, of course. Not his own rightful place or dimension—of course. Why, in his own dimension, would he be sharing a bed with a dead major?

And there was another shadow almost as out-of-focus as himself. On its hands and knees it was, searching for something across the room. All Siri got was a grand view of its backside, or perhaps a front view of its headless shoulders. Black against black. How could he know for sure? His heart gently fluttered back to its rightful place as he recognized his role in another nightmare. It had been a while. He knew whatever happened here would not affect his physical being. Not unless his subconscious became so wracked in horror that it caused its live self to hold its breath. Not unless his heart burst in shock. He'd seen the results of both. So he sat calmly and waited.

The figure on the ground edged its way across the parquet. And the shadow slowly gathered into contours and the figure achieved a shape. It was an elderly man. Stocky. Well dressed. There was something familiar about him. He was moving away so there was no sight of his face. His fingers seemed to be clawing at the ground as if he were peeling old varnish from the wooden tiles. Siri called, "Do I know you?"

And just as the figure began to turn, to show its face, a cold hand grabbed Siri by the back of his neck. His heart felt like it had been kicked off a steep ledge. He let out a squeal so shrill he doubted it could have come from his own lips. He slapped away the hand and leapt to his feet. The figure on the ground melted into the shadows. The doctor couldn't catch his breath. He paced back and forth looking for a rhythm that might start up his lungs.

The major said, "Siri?"

Then spoke again with a different voice.

"Siri?"

"Daeng?"

Madame Daeng climbed from the bed and felt for her husband in the darkness. When she found him she massaged his stalled lungs and calmed him with her words.

"Shh. Shh. It's a dream, my love."

He found a breath. He gulped it greedily. He could taste the soot. It was so thick in the air it was like waking up in a house fire—a bitterly cold house fire.

There was a good deal of throat clearing over breakfast. Officially, it was the day they were due to go home—the fifth day. The morning meal today was the last meal on the agenda. From here on the US pantry was bare. They still had no evidence that Boyd was dead or alive. With no team leader, a general who was confined to his bed to conserve oxygen, and a senator who had armed guards stationed at his front door and rear window and daren't leave his room, nobody really knew who was in charge. Of course, Judge Haeng thought it was himself. He decided there was little point in going outside into the smoke. Instead, he announced that this would be a good day to bag and label all the souvenirs they'd brought back from the crash site. He also insisted the Lao team members begin work on their individual reports. They should be careful to comment on their American counterparts, including any personal knowledge that may have been gleaned during social moments. Siri and his team had about as much intention of writing spy reports as tying themselves by the bootlaces to the rockets at the fertility festival. But they did grab several sacks of wreckage and set up a "by appointment only" group in Siri's room.

With the addition of Sergeant Johnson, Madame Daeng and Comrade Civilai, the insiders now outnumbered the outsiders at a ratio of five to four. The odds were getting a little ridiculous. The newcomers were briefed in their respective languages. The expanded group discussed matters sitting cross-legged on the floor, all but Secretary Gordon who had trouble getting and remaining in that position. He was allowed a chair. Mr. Geung was stationed behind the curtain. Sergeant Johnson was the star turn, accompanied by Auntie Bpoo on the translation. They wanted to know what circumstances might prompt gaps in a pilot's flight record. Unnerved by the size of the group, Johnson was reluctant at first to give away what might be considered state secrets. It was only when Civilai assured him that everything the Americans believed to be secret was documented in great detail at the ministry of defence that he relented.

"I wasn't ever with Air America," he said. "But you hear things. There was a lot of crossover between different departments. A lot of people passing through town and the military aren't renowned for keeping its collective mouth shut. Give a guy in uniform a couple of shots of bourbon and he's your best pal. We heard about one base up at Tahkli in Thailand. It's a fenced-off compound inside a regular military base. It's where they parked the U2 spy plane. It's also the home of a lot of clandestine ops. All the customers up there wear civilian clothes. Now, when I say clandestine, I don't mean one small secret part of a big CIA master plan. I mean a hell of a lot of little secrets instigated by this ambassador or that general or one or other of the section heads—none of whom have the first idea what the guy in the next office is up to. Hell, I've heard about two identical operations set up by different departments run on the same day. Guys were tripping over each other."

"Now, the reason this place comes to mind, is that some of the pilots I have in mind had that same odd thing going with their time records. They'd put in their sheets at the end of the month and there'd be four days unmarked here, a week there. But they never claimed holidays or sick days. None of the brass ever queried it. One of our fighter pilots called it the Tahkli lottery. If you got lucky and didn't get yourself killed, you'd come back with a whole heap of money in your pocket."

"And some didn't come back?" asked Auntie Bpoo.

"You'd never know," Johnson told her. "If anyone was MIA it was always swung around somehow to look like a regular mission gone wrong. You won't find the name of any active US military personnel MIA in Laos unless they got lost. There was a lot of clumsy border misidentification, if you know what I mean. Guess you can't always trust all that expensive cockpit equipment."

"So, do you think Boyd might have been deployed on special ops by Air America?" Phosy asked.

"Why not? Air America was CIA."

"But how would we ever be able to find out what he was involved in?" Dtui asked.

"Ask him," said Civilai, ever hopeful.

"All right," said Yamaguchi. "It's the thing about the flight mechanic that worries me. Boyd returns quite unexpectedly from the grave and within a month his mechanic meets a mysterious end."

"Not to mention the chief mechanic from Long Cheng," Siri added. "He died within days of Sebastian. Then there was the pilot Wolff who'd drunk with them on their last night together. Odd that all the American witnesses to that last flight are now out of the reckoning."

"Except for Boyd," Civilai smiled.

"You think your pilot's running around killing everyone, Civilai?" Siri asked.

"Why not? Revenge for getting him addicted to drugs. He's probably been in an opium den for the last ten years."

"See, this is something I've never really understood about the transfer of Leon from Saigon to Long Cheng," said Johnson. "If he was involved in 'inappropriate behavior' serious enough to have his flying license pulled, what was he still doing in the service? I remember he was using drugs back then, he wasn't the only one. He got a couple of warnings. So inappropriate behaviour could have been a euphemism for losing control of his habit, or dealing. But if you're caught at either it's a dishonorable discharge. You're out. You don't get transferred to an inactive post somewhere else in the war. Not even Air America would take you on."

"So how do you think he got here?" Gordon asked.

"Well, either he didn't actually do anything wrong and it was just a ruse to get him out of Nam and into this specific role in Laos for some reason, or he did do it and he had mighty big friends in high places who found him an easy well-paid job up here."

"Which makes you wonder whether all this is about drugs," said Dtui.

"Oh, I very much doubt they'd need clandestine operations for drug dealing," said Civilai. "It was hardly a secret the CIA were buying up all the Hmong opium and selling it as heroin on the streets of Saigon. They had regular scheduled flights from Long Cheng to Vietnam full of the stuff. The pilots used to land upside down just from the fumes."

"All right, so not drugs," said Yamaguchi. "What else could he have been involved in?"

"I'm afraid war gives you a lot of scope for profiteering," said Madame Daeng. "There's no end to the possibilities."

"Then let's start with something we know," said Gordon. "Boyd was carrying something he shouldn't have been that night."

He held up a sheet of typed foolscap.

"This is the official manifest for Boyd's cargo when he left Udon," he said. "Pretty standard stuff for those milk runs: rice, blankets, nails, canned food. But here, tucked away at the end is twenty ten-gallon containers of cooking oil. It was all destined for the refugee camp at Sam Tong."

"You think there's something suspicious about it?" Siri asked.

"I do. Air America flights stopped doing overnights in Long Cheng in sixty-seven. They had their own dorm in Sam Tong right next to the refugee camp. If all he had on board was refugee supplies, what was he doing parked at Spook City drinking with his buddies with a full aircraft?"

"And I can't recall anyone mentioning cooking oil in any of the in-service courses I took on incendiaries," said Johnson. "And I can't see two hundred gallons of Crisco permanently destroying two acres of jungle, nor lighting up the night sky with fireworks."

"Then what *did* they talk about on that course of yours?" Siri asked.

"A lot of stuff. Magnesium can be nasty," said Johnson. "I've seen a whole village burned down with one canister. I guess most commonly used would be the defoliants: Agent Orange, napalm. They can both do untold damage."

"Aren't there any rules for . . . I don't know, fair war?" Dtui asked.

"Not for this kind," Johnson told her. "You can put together any cocktail of benzene, polystyrene and gasoline and rain it down wherever you please and you haven't broken any international regulations. Nobody cares, except maybe the kids that took shelter under the trees when they saw the bombers pass over. I thought I'd seen it all. But I haven't ever witnessed anything that leaves a permanent scar on the landscape like that no-man's-land at Ban Hoong. Napalm just burns the leaves off. Whatever Boyd was carrying destroyed the trees, permanently."

"How would you send down something like napalm?" Daeng asked. "I mean, I doubt you'd just fly over in a helicopter, take off the caps and sprinkle it."

"It's usually fed into a canister," said Johnson. "The canister explodes on contact with the ground. Dropped from altitude.

So you'd need an airplane. Nothing less than a Skyhawk. But I guess if you had a crop-dusting attachment you could do the sprinkle thing on a defined target if there were no anti-aircraft batteries."

"Were there Skyhawks flying out of the secret ops compound at Tahkli?" Daeng asked.

"Everything with wings flew in and out of there at some point."

"Bpoo," said Siri, "ask the sergeant if he remembers the day he navigated us from Long Cheng to Ban Hoong. He had the hatch open the entire time and the journalist was there beside him. Did he notice whether the man photographed the entire trip or just the flight down along the Ban Hoong stream?"

Johnson remembered it well.

"The guy was clicking away the whole time," he said. "Must have used up half a dozen films just on tree tops."

"What are you thinking, Siri?" Daeng asked.

"Well, apart from whoever it is setting light to all the mountains round about, there hasn't been a great deal of slash and burn in Xiang Khouang over the past ten years. I'm just thinking out loud. If there happened to be any stretches of land devoid of vegetation around here, there's every chance that it's a result of the same type of super napalm that laid waste to the dead man's field. If nothing has regrown there after ten years, the area should be visible from the air. A bald patch on an otherwise hairy landscape."

"It's worth a try," said Daeng.

"Commander Lit has all the photographs he confiscated from Rhyme in his room," said Phosy.

"I could probably get a look at them," said Dtui. "I'm sure he'll—"

"No!" said Phosy. "That's all right. I'll go and see him."

"If you're sure," said Dtui.

"I'm sure. I take it nobody has any objection to me sharing the super napalm theory with him?"

To his displeasure, nobody objected.

The only two men to have proposed—marriage that is—to Nurse Dtui sat icily together at the foot of the security commander's bed with forty black and white photographs between them. Both men wondered why the journalist had used up so much of his valuable film photographing the tops of trees, and why, given that he had taken so many more interesting snaps, he should have gone to the trouble of developing these first. Neither man voiced these questions because he didn't want the other to think he might not be the urn of all knowledge. Man has carried this burden since that first slimy walk up the bank in search of vertebrae. Instead, they kept to incontrovertible facts and steered away from feelings.

"These two photographs are interesting," said Lit. "I calculated from the sequence numbers on the negatives that they were taken some twenty minutes out of Long Cheng."

"Very astute," said Phosy.

"Thank you. You'll notice that this picture shows the beginning of a clearing. But it's too long and straight. Some of the trees on either side have grown over but you can clearly see this barren strip. It extends right off the photograph in both directions. Nothing seems to be growing there at all. It's very similar to the area around the helicopter crash site. And take a look in the next photograph." He handed Phosy a magnifying glass. "There are a number of craters visible."

"The chances of this being a natural phenomenon are—"

"Almost nil."

"Nil."

"Almost."

"How far are we from this area?"

Lit nodded, walked to the desk and gathered the edges of a large map draped over it. Phosy noted there was something . . . feminine in the man's walk. Lit laid the map on top of the photographs.

"Here's this hotel," he said. He traced the arc that followed the chopper route. "The clearing in the photograph would be . . . here. That would make it the skirt of Phu Kum mountain."

"Was there a base there in the sixties? An armory?"

"Not a thing."

"But, all these craters. Who'd want to bomb and clear a deserted area of land?"

"Your guess is as good as mine," said Lit, reluctantly.

"I have to go there," said Phosy, leaping to his feet.

"I . . . can't let you do that."

"You can't let me do what?"

"Go off into a restricted zone without a pass."

"We're already in a restricted zone."

"But you're here accompanied by a representative of the security division."

"You."

"Exactly."

"So, if I wanted to go take a look at this area around Phu Kum. . . ."

"You'd have to go with a representative of the security division."

"You."

"Exactly."

"I see. Would I have to fill out forms and queue up at the office of domestic security?"

"No. Just ask."

"Ask?"

"Politely."

Phosy sighed. "Would you be kind enough to accompany me to Phu Kum mountain?"

"Absolutely no problem."

"How do we get there?"

"According to the map, the road only takes us to a spot ten kilometers from the mountain."

"Ten kilometers isn't that much of a hike."

"Not for me, certainly."

"Me neither. And the Phonsavan trucks are parked out front. It looks like nobody told the drivers we've run out of spending money."

"There's always a way."

"I know that."

Toua the hotel manager was beside himself with worry. There was one last package of space rations that might get all his guests through lunch, but nothing Western to offer the foreigners for their evening meal. The American consulate had planned the meals meticulously for every day of the mission. According to the schedule, on day five they were on the choppers and heading south before midday. Job done.

"So, give everyone local food," said Daeng.

She and Siri were standing in the kitchen with the staff looking at all the empty shelves.

"But they're Americans," said Toua's wife. "They don't have the system for our food."

"This is an emergency," Daeng reminded her. "I bet they'll eat ethnic Lao food rather than starve to death. Just repackage it. Put in lashings of ketchup and leave out the chilies."

"The market's a bit low on edibles," said Toua.

"What have they got?"

"Webbed duck feet in batter, buffalo skin, dried squirrel, snake, porcupine, ant eggs."

"All right. Buy whatever they've got that doesn't stink to high heaven. It's all fixable. Trust me. I'm an expert. What have you got in the way of seasoning and herbs?"

One of the kitchen girls walked behind the huge zinc soup pots and threw open the pantry door. Daeng stood in the doorway and breathed in the sweet smell of spices. She assessed the stock. There were tubs of lemon grass and galangal and dried mushrooms. No shortage of garlic. But three large sacks stuffed into a far corner drew her attention and an idea took root.

"Siri, come here," she called.

Siri abandoned the sesame crackers and joined his wife at the larder door.

"You know the kitchen's more your thing than mine," he said.

"Ah, there's cooking and there's cooking up," she reminded him. "Look what we have here."

"Oh dear."

"You remember Civilai's throwaway line just now that in order to know what's really going on here we'd need to put microphones in all the rooms?"

"He has a lot of faith in surveillance techniques."

"Well, what if everyone just stood up and confessed? Do you recall those stories about the OSS?"

"Certainly. They were the boogie men they used to frighten children with before they invented the CIA."

"Then you'll recall their secret truth drug."

Siri laughed.

"Geneva probably has some sanction against its use," he said.

"Come on. At the very least it'll be a way to forget we have no oxygen."

"I'm all for it. But, Mata Hari, how do you plan to administer it? Hypodermic?"

"No problem whatsoever."

She called over one of the Hmong.

"Little sister," she said. "Do you have any fat here?"

"Fat, auntie?"

"Butter? Lard?"

"We have goat's butter . . . and cheese."

"Perfect. Sugar?"

"Oh yes. We have a twenty-liter tub full."

"That should be enough."

With the girls despatched to Phonsavan market and Madame Daeng in control of the kitchen, Siri took the opportunity to speak with the manager. Auntie Bpoo sat on a wooden chair inside the kitchen entrance like a mafia bodyguard.

"I wanted to ask you about the room the major died in," said Siri.

"I've let nobody in since, I swear."

"I know."

"I have both the keys and the windows are locked."

"Yes, good. But that's not what I'm curious about. I was wondering whether anyone else has ever died in there."

"What kind of hotel do you think I'm running here? Isn't one death enough for you?"

"More than enough, yes."

It was always difficult for Siri to broach the subject of the supernatural with strangers. But Toua was a Hmong and he was apparently already acquainted with Siri's alter ego.

"You know about Yeh Ming?" he asked.

"Of course. Who doesn't?"

"Good. Well, Yeh Ming has sensed something in that room and it has nothing to do with the American's death."

"This place has been through a lot. Who's to know what happened here before my wife and I took over?"

"Quite. So in the time you've been here you haven't had any . . . notable guests, nobody out of the ordinary?"

Toua paused before saying "no," and in that short void Siri recognized a falsehood.

"You can't lie to Yeh Ming," he said.

"I'm not . . . it's just. . . ."

"This is important."

"They told me not to tell anyone."

"Who are they?"

"Influential people."

"Comrade Toua, in our group we have a judge, a general, an ex-Politburo member and a combined two hundred years of membership of the Communist Party. How much more influential do you need than that?"

Toua filled his cheeks with air then rasped it out between his fat lips.

"My wife will kill me," he said.

"They always threaten—rarely follow through."

"They brought him here before they sent him up to Vieng Xai. He was here for a week."

"Him?"

"Yeah. You know. The king. He was here with a large group of dignitaries. He used that room."

"Did something happen to him there?"

"No. No. They told me to treat him like a VIP. The room was locked and guarded but we fed him well. Everyone was most polite. He even shook my hand on the day he left. Not every day you get to meet royalty."

20

COLLECTING OLD FOOTSTEPS

There was a legend that extended far back beyond the Lan Xang era six hundred years before. One that could be read of in palm-leaf documents as far away as Lanna in Siam. It was the belief that the spirits of the dead may make a plea before passing on to whatever lay beyond. The spirit had the right, so it was told, to return to places once treasured in life, there to collect old footsteps. Once gathered, those footsteps became a memorial of all the happier times on earth. But the Party made it quite clear that such legends were ridiculous. Like the stories of religion and the fables of the ancient tribes it was all balderdash. No self-respecting socialist would be gullible enough to fall for any of them. But where did that leave a man who has seen the spirits of the dead and traveled to the Otherworld of the Hmong?

Siri sat on the major's bed looking at the weathered parquet. He knew now why he'd come to this room on the night of the major's death. The spirit of the king had summoned him here. They'd met, briefly, in life and as far as a man of royal blood and a bloody communist could ever find common ground, they'd developed a mutual respect. They'd shared two bottles of home-brewed rice whiskey and discussed issues as only two wise old men can through to the early morning. Siri had liked the man and, if this invitation to a late night séance was any proof, the king had found a fondness for the doctor. Siri knew the old man would find many a pleasurable footstep in his old fruit orchard in Luang Prabang.

If they'd talked while the king collected his footsteps from this room, Siri had no recollection. He didn't know how he'd died or why he'd chosen to pass through this inn. Perhaps it was the last place he'd been shown respect. Perhaps he'd come to leave a message for the doctor. It was all a mystery. But the only thing for certain was that the last regent of the Kingdom of Laos was gone. Siri was no stranger to death, nor to the afterlife, but his feelings as he looked around the musty room were mixed. He felt sorrow for a friend. But he could not deny a sense of relief, perhaps even elation. In his own mind, this vindicated him from any and all involvement in Potter's murder. He doubted the "locked in conversation with a dead king" alibi would gain him much ground in a court of law, but in his soul he knew he was innocent. A great weight was lifted from his shoulders. Despite the fact they hadn't seen the sun in all its glory for three days, the room seemed brighter. The world offered up new opportunities. This, he decided, was a cause for a toast and a celebration.

The whiskey supply in the kitchen was down to one or two fingers of depth in a few remaining bottles. But below the bed was Major Potter's own personal stash. Siri was sure the old soldier wouldn't begrudge them a taste. He got to his knees and slid out the crate. It was of a good old-fashioned wooden variety but the partitions between the eight remaining bottles were cardboard. It was a snug fit between each one. He prised a bottle out and held it aloft. No common Johnnie Walker this. *Glenfiddich single malt Scotch whiskey, 12 years old* read the shiny silver and gold label. Potter was a connoisseur. Siri wondered whether eleven o'clock might be too early for a celebratory snort. But then he remembered how close he was to the end of his days and could think of no better way to go than with the taste of neat Scotch whiskey on his lips. The crate weighed far more than the bottles so he removed the pillow case from its pillow and started to load them into it, being careful not to clink them together too violently. When he pulled out the fourth bottle, the cardboard partition came away with it and Siri immediately understood. Major Potter hadn't been asking Civilai's help to untie his laces. He'd been pointing to the crate. And disguised as lining for that crate were three large manila envelopes.

As an herb, marijuana adds a certain aromatic charm to cooking. It's particularly compatible with aubergine. If the Americans hadn't made such a fuss about it, marijuana would be dried and diced and in its rightful place in a little bottle on the spice and herbs racks around the world. Fried or boiled it is no more criminally liable than oregano or thyme. But steeped in saturated fat and served in sweet hot water it becomes clear why the director of the United States Federal Bureau of Narcotics once called it: *. . . the most violence-causing drug in the history of mankind which produces in its users insanity, criminality, and death—makes darkies think they're as good as white men and leads to pacifism and communist brainwashing.* Which makes you wonder whether he'd ever tried it.

In fact smoking cannabis gives one a rapid buzz that passes into a short-lived high. Euphoria is fleeting and needs continuous top-ups. Marijuana tea, on the other hand, takes its own sweet time. It could be an hour before the first effects are felt, and they linger. And there is no generic reaction. To each his own. Some may find their latent paranoia bursts to the surface like a submarine short of air. Others may trip over hilarity with every step. And, as Madame Daeng remembered correctly, until they found their own agents employing the stocks for personal use, the OSS did use weed as a truth drug, often with hilarious effects. For some, marijuana opened the floodgates of overacting and loquaciousness.

Daeng had worked for an hour to produce her tea. Although she'd had to be careful not to overfill the tasting teaspoon, she had to admit that she'd produced a most delicious brew—twenty liters of it, judging from the size of the pot. It was served in huge mugs and she advertised it as a local herbal tea with a bit of a pick-you-up. It was the perfect thing to combat the smoke in your lungs. With the two kitchen girls by her side, she delivered the tea personally along with the lunch rations. She was selective about which doors she knocked on. In her rounds she visited General Suvan, Judge Haeng and his cousin Vinai, Peach, Senator Vogal and Ethel Chin, who seemed to spend more time in the senator's room than in her own. Daeng refused to leave them all until they'd tasted her tea. She knew that once it caressed their lips, they'd be unable to resist finishing the cup. They might even come back for more. For good measure she gave a cup to the kitchen staff, the two old musketeers and Mr. Toua and his wife. She drew the line at the young guards newly assigned by the local garrison because they all looked as if they were already on something. The combination of drugs and AK47s was always best avoided.

Exhausted but excited at the thought of what effect, if any, her tea might have, Daeng retired briefly to her room. Siri wasn't there. She assumed he'd gone off with Dtui and Phosy because she hadn't seen any of them during her rounds. Lit and Sergeant Johnson had vanished also. She supposed she'd have to resort to Civilai as backup when observation time arrived. Her legs were troubling her as always and she made the mistake of laying her head on the pillow—just for a second.

It was 1:00 P.M. when she felt the tugging at her foot. She opened her eyes to find the room lit with spotlights and the humble wall designs dancing. Mr. Geung was at the foot of the bed holding on to her ankle. While she was asleep somebody had found a cure for rheumatism. For the first time this trip, her joints were as fluid as those of a ten-year-old Romanian gymnast.

"Everyone's gone mad," said Geung, and gave another tug on her foot.

"I beg your pardon?"

"I don't know what's happened. Everybody's mad."

"Geung, what's happened to your speech?"

"It's the same as ever."

"No, it isn't." She sat up on the bed, which rocked from side to side in an attempt to shake her off. The room was truly beautiful. She yanked her foot from Geung's grasp. "You aren't stammering and stuttering."

"Sorry."

"Geung! What have you done?"

"Nothing."

"Did you drink the tea?"

Daeng was OD'ing on senses: smell, hearing, the taste of her own tongue.

"Yes," said Geung. "One half mug."

Despite the dire seriousness of the situation, Daeng laughed. On the strength of just a few teaspoonfuls of her tea, she was floating. She'd had her share of marijuana in her life but nothing this potent. This was outstanding. And Mr. Geung had drunk half a mug full. What had she done? She laughed until tears rolled down her cheeks.

"You forgot people," said Geung, looking quite serious which only caused Daeng to laugh more.

"What?"

"Some people didn't get tea. Comrade Civilai, Auntie Bpoo, Dr. Harikiri."

"Did you give. . . ." It was just too funny.

"It was good tea. It's not fair to give to some and not to others. The guards liked it."

"You gave it to everybody?"

It was so awful she was afraid she'd wet herself.

"Some had two mugs."

Daeng roared with laughter and fled to the bathroom. What a balls up. Friendly fire. Hoist with their own petards. Scuttled. Buggered. Yet still she laughed. Even more so when the bathroom tap produced nothing but a rude fart. She bounced back into her room on legs that felt like pogo sticks. Geung was still staring at her shape in the thick quilt as if he hadn't noticed it had already released her.

"I'm here," she said. "Let's go."

"Where are we going?"

"To the carnival."

The discovery of Major Potter's hidden documents had its downside. They were all written in English. But, once he'd made that discovery and wished for a translator, the wishful thinking service couldn't have been any better. He looked up at the sound of the knock at the door. He hurried across the room and turned the handle. Auntie Bpoo stood outside with a large mug in each hand.

"It's soon," she said.

"My death?"

"Unless we can prevent it."

"What's that you're holding?"

"Tea. Mr. Geung said it was delicious. I brought one for you."

"Hardly worth the effort if it's just going to end up as postmortem stomach contents."

The doctor paced back to the bed, leaving Bpoo in the doorway.

"I tell you what," he said. "This is really bad timing. I've probably got all these valuable leads and clues and whatnot but I can't read the darned things. Can't we . . . I don't know . . . postpone it or something?"

"I don't think death is that cooperative," said Bpoo. She stepped into the room and closed the door with her rump. Siri, through his bizarre experiences of the past few years had learned not to ignore the signs. If Bpoo said he was going to die—die he would. But he wasn't about to sit down and wait for the ox cart of death to pull up in front of him.

"All right," he said. "So time is of the essence. Put those down and come over here and take a look at these. Tell me what they're all about."

He fanned out the papers and sat on the bed with them. Auntie Bpoo downed anchor halfway across the room.

"Old man," she said. "Don't you want to prepare or something?"

"Prepare what?"

"Yourself. For death."

Siri laughed.

"Well, Bpoo. Let's see. If the Buddhists are right, I'm just on my way to the next incarnation. Unless there's a manual for how to behave correctly as a gnat I'm not sure how I'd prepare for that. If the Catholics are right, nothing short of an asbestos suit and a glass of iced water will help where I'm going. And if the communists are right, you do your best and when you're gone they put up a statue in your honor and the locals dry their laundry on it. So, if I'm going, you're the heir to today's legacy. So come here and translate for me."

Half an hour later Siri and Bpoo walked into the dining room. Fellini was apparently directing a crowd scene there. Like survivors of a natural disaster, the hotel guests had all congregated at a central spot. The tea urn was the focal point. Dr. Yamaguchi was standing on the table dipping his mug into the dregs. Siri recalled Civilai's description of the bodies found in the rice whiskey jars. The pathologist seemed to have no fear for his own life as his bottom wagged from side to side in the air. The senator was standing on a chair orating. His audience was a crowd of Hmong and Civilai who was pretending to translate but was instead making terrible fun of the statesman. Vogal, buoyed on by the cheers and laughter, was in danger of falling off his chair as he waved his arms around and yelled to the heavens. In a corner, Daeng was engaged in a *ramwong* dance of almost imperceptible motion with General Suvan. The music that only they could hear was presumably being played on a cassette tape which had stretched as a result of exposure to heat. Ethel Chin sat alone at a table sobbing miserably into her folded arms. Mr. Geung stood beside her, patting her on the back and saying, "There, there," over and over. Secretary Gordon was charming the manager's wife who blushed and giggled like a teenager.

Siri was just in time to witness Judge Haeng reach in the direction of Peach's breast. She leaned back in time, clenched her fist, and landed an impressive haymaker on the judge's nose. After a few frozen seconds the sound of a crack circuited the room and blood spurted out of the law enforcer's nostrils. He used his right hand to squeeze his nose then made a second attempt, this time at the other breast, with his left. It was Peach's knee this time that floored the judge and, very likely, ended any hope of future generations of Haengs. Journalist Rhyme was in grave danger of making himself blind because he'd become fascinated with the awesome power of his camera's flash unit and uttered an impressed "wow" every time he flashed himself.

This left only Cousin Vinai who had fashioned a sort of noose out of kitchen napkins and was on a ladder attempting, without the benefit of coordination, to suspend it from one of the rafters.

"This is exactly why I didn't let you drink the tea," Siri told Bpoo.

Bpoo turned back for the room but Siri caught her by the arm.

"Where do you think you're going?" he asked.

"We've got two full mugs of this stuff back in the room."

"You aren't going back."

"But look at these people."

"We need to be alert."

"I can be alert and stoned. I"m adaptable."

"Bpoo!"

"Please."

"You're my only hope to stay alive today."

"Oh, great. Play the 'You're my only hope to stay alive' card right now, why don't you? All right. But I'm drinking it when all this is over. Both mugs."

"No problem. Now, we don't exactly know who killed Potter but there are two, perhaps three people we can cross off the list of suspects. That leaves a very small select few to choose from. So I propose we take advantage of their temporary insanity. We'll never have them in a more vulnerable state. We should focus on the weak and wounded."

"Well, there she is," said Bpoo, nodding in the direction of Ethel Chin. Even Geung had abandoned her. She sat alone now with tears streaming down her ruddy blistered cheeks.

"You're right. A stray has wandered from the herd," Siri agreed. "Sharpen your talons."

They sat on either side of the personal assistant. When she looked up to see who had joined her, the crying intensified.

"I'm supposed to be getting married in October," she snorted. "Now look at me. I'm so ugly he'll never talk to me again."

Siri nodded.

"Oh, look at you, deary," said Bpoo. "You were hardly Miss Hong Kong even before your face erupted. Your fiancé's obviously a very charitable chap. Fully sighted, is he?"

Chin howled her misery.

"I suppose he knows you've been rolling in the hay with your boss while you were on these missions. Or did you forget to mention it?"

It was as if the woman were so full of tears she couldn't get them out in time. It was a job well done on Bpoo's part. Intimate thuggery. At such close quarters, Siri was able to get a good look at Chin's face. The makeup was doing a poor job of hiding her sores. In fact, it was probably exacerbating the infection. And then, in a sudden flash of obviousness, it came to him.

"Of course," he said, and slapped the scar tissue on his forehead.

"What's that?" Bpoo asked, still waiting for a pause in the sobs so she could continue her assault.

"Once again, it's taken me several days to see what Inspector Maigret of the Paris Sûreté would have noticed instantly."

"Who?"

"I'm a disgrace to the detective brotherhood."

Bpoo raised her crayoned-on eyebrows.

"Desist from your random scratching and biting," he told her. "We can now go directly for the jugular."

"All right, old man. I'll translate as meanly as I can."

"Good. Then we'll begin with a story. It's the story of the Jesuits." (Bpoo stared. He ignored her.) "Apart from importing their peculiar religion and cheese and braziers to our barbaric land, the Jesuits also introduced firearms. Installing religion was apparently not enough for them. They were expecting us to fight to the death to defend it. The weapon of choice, popular in Europe at the time, was the musket. The locals were a resourceful lot and they learned to reproduce these guns using local materials. As there was no quality control supervisor in attendance, our version of the musket carried the odd idiosyncrasy."

Ethel Chin had dried up. Her red, bloated eyes were now staring angrily at Bpoo, who stared confidently back at them.

"It is incredible," Siri continued, "given the availability of cheap weapons over the past thirty years of warfare, that the country folk still favor their old muskets. But one thing they've all learned is to hold the weapon well away from the face when they fire it. Forgetting to do so is likely to lead to a very nasty powder burn. Someone unfamiliar with this rule, someone who learned their gunmanship from television cowboy shows, for example, would very likely rest their cheek against the barrel."

Chin turned to Siri.

"It's a rash," she spat.

"No. It's not," Siri told her. "And I can prove it's not because microscopic gunpowder deposits remain embedded in the skin for months after. Luckily we have an electron microscope at our lab."

Auntie Bpoo was taking great delight in the translation . . . and the lie.

"And why would I be shooting a musket?" Chin asked with a different type of tears welling up in her eyes.

"To remove suspicion from your employer. The assassination attempt on the senator was orchestrated to remove him from the list of potential suspects in the murder of Major Potter. In this way he was a victim. I doubt he was delighted that you actually made contact. I imagine the plan was to run off into the bushes where you'd secreted your musket and fire a shot perhaps two meters to his right. But, as I say, those muskets can be devils. Lucky you didn't actually kill the blighter."

"This is ridiculous," Chin cried. "It was . . . it was an attack by someone who . . . who hates us. An assassination attempt. Murder? What do you mean murder? Potter killed himself."

Chin was confused. Good. She was temporarily out of her comfortable mind.

"Well, of course you know that isn't true," Siri continued calmly. "You had to think on your feet once the attempt to blow him up failed. I'm assuming one of you snuck into his room during the evening meal and put an old, unstable stick of dynamite amongst his safe ones. Perhaps you armed it too. You can fill in the details for us later. I hate to interrupt a good dénouement. As I said, once that attempt failed, you had to look for a plan B. The major was a lecher, by all accounts. An autoerotic accident would fit nicely. Dead and discredited all in one go. Except you'd both been so sure plan A would work that you weren't really prepared for this new show. You had to ad lib. Intercepting his coffee and putting in the sedatives wouldn't have been that hard. Bit heavy on the drugs, I'd say. Lack of knowledge of how much it takes to knock out a big man so you threw in the whole pack. Am I right? So you go back to check. He's unconscious and all ready for the main act. I noticed you stopped wearing your lipstick after you arrived here."

"Why would anyone need lipstick in the jungle?"

She spoke now without the arrogance they'd become used to.

"Yet you were wearing a very impressive rouge when you first arrived. I wouldn't be at all surprised if we could match your usual shade with that on the major's lips. And then there was the beauty spot."

"Tell your old doctor to stop," Chin pleaded, but Bpoo merely shrugged as if the process were irreversible.

"You were trying to be too clever there," Siri told her. "I don't know what type of relationship you have with the senator—"

"He's a respected United States rep—"

"And I don't really want to know. But I get a creeping feeling at the back of my neck when I imagine you two in the major's room late that night. It's as if you took delight in it. Your victim is unconscious. You strip him. You both drag him to the door and tie him up. I wonder how it is your boss knows so much about tying a noose with an escape knot. It isn't something you learn in the boy scouts. And then the two of you go about the degradation; the underwear, the lipstick, and, as the pièce de résistance, the beauty spot. One detail too many. If a man has a late night hobby of making himself look like a woman, he's going to know better than to use indelible ink."

"It's true," said Bpoo.

"I took the liberty of stealing one of the pens you and the senator have been using on your flow charts. The one we found in the room was the same make and the fingerprints on it were identical."

As he hadn't sampled his wife's tea, it was impossible for Siri to know exactly what was happening in Ethel Chin's mind during all this. But it appeared her logical self was vying for equity. She laughed haughtily and rudely into the face of Bpoo.

"I'm a law graduate, you know?" she said. 'Top five percentile at Yale. That's pretty shit-hot lawyering, don't you think? And you know what? Not one single thing you've told me would get you past a preliminary hearing in a court of law. You tell your coroner here he's got nothing. He can go take a hike."

Both Siri and Bpoo smiled as she passed on this regrettable news.

"I'm a medical graduate, you know?" said Siri. "Bottom ten percentile at Hôtel de Ville hospital in Paris. Not particularly hot, not even lukewarm, I admit. But I do know where to insert a common sewing needle in the spinal cord to cause permanent paralysis."

Bpoo positively squealed with delight before translating.

"Which should serve to remind you of where you are. It's irrelevant whether our evidence will make it through a court of law because we only have the one judge and he's an idiot. And we don't have any laws. And you're in the deep deep wilds of Indochina with no friends, surrounded by hostiles. And you could scream injustice till your lungs popped out and nobody would hear you."

Once she'd passed all this on, Bpoo sighed like a nail puncture in a tractor tyre. She took Siri by the hand.

"If you weren't married. . . ."

But Siri retrieved his hand. He hadn't finished yet.

"I don't know what this is all about," he said. "Not yet. I haven't worked out why you're really here or what your boss's real relationship with Bowrys senior and junior is, but I do know that Potter was on to him back in Ho Chi Minh. I've seen Potter's notes about Vogal abusing his position at the embassy. I've also seen evidence that it was Vogal who got Potter kicked out of the war. There's a copy of a letter from Vogal to the State Department citing Potter's excesses. It recommends he be asked to step down.

I don't doubt Potter was a drunk or that he had issues. But the very fact that he was here heading this mission tells me how driven he was. And he'd have to have friends in high places who shared his convictions or he wouldn't have been offered the position.

"So, the question is, what's everybody doing here? According to the missing pages of Sebastian's interview, there was a briefcase. Captain Boyd kept it with him in the cockpit at all times. He told his mechanic it was his insurance policy. He claimed it contained evidence enough to incriminate all the bad guys. If that briefcase survived the crash I'm sure there are a lot of people who'd like to get their hands on it. Well worth funding an MIA mission for. Well worth the senator flying in to prevent its contents being leaked. Well worth killing a few people for. I bet Potter was delighted to see the senator's name on the shortlist, but it looks like he underestimated just how evil your employer is."

Ethel Chin was crying now because she deserved to be. She was undone. Siri looked across at the wispy-haired senator, still high on his marijuana tea, still entertaining, still oblivious. In no fit state to fight or resist a citizen's arrest. The villains were outnumbered. Inspector Siri saves the day. Solves another one. Hooray for Dr. Siri. And, not for the first time, while he was busy patting himself on the back, basking in his overconfidence, he failed to notice fate creeping up with its teeth bared to bite him on the backside.

21

ORE INSPIRING

They'd been walking for an hour through the type of jungle that Hollywood did so well in papier mâché and polystyrene. The group was low on oxygen and conversation. The mission had begun with Phosy and Lit as reluctant comrades on a trek to Phu Kum mountain. But they'd needed to show the photographs to John Johnson for a third opinion. It would have been a long walk to visit some swidden farm project in the hills. In order to talk to Johnson, they'd had to bring in Dtui. Johnson was fascinated by the photos and pointed out that slash and burn and napalm left tree stumps, sometimes entire charred trees that nobody had the equipment to remove. The area in the photographs showed a bald landscape that no known defoliant could have created. In Johnson's modest opinion, this area had been cleared by the same unknown juice that had cremated the dead man's field. Naturally, he'd insisted on going along. There was no denying him. And this created a further annoyance for Phosy in that Dtui would have to accompany them. The journey would take twice as long if they walked at her pace.

With the Phonsavan driver asleep in a hammock, they'd boarded his truck, released the handbrake, and sailed silently down the incline and through the front gate. The old musketeers saluted as they passed. They were a hundred meters away before they engaged the motor and set off in search of the nearest point to Phu Kum.

"Are you quite sure this is the way?" Phosy asked, not for the first time. They'd parked the truck beside the dirt track and headed off into a dense jungle. Lit chose not to answer. The smoke seemed to be clearing a little and he had a vague outline of the sun to guide him. He had his map and his nose and no Vientiane policeman would distract him from his task. He did, however, allow himself to compliment Nurse Dtui on her stamina, her sense of humor in times of adversity, and her skill in a foreign language. All Phosy could offer to counter this was, "Are you quite sure this is the way?"

When they arrived at the clearing, Phosy's question was answered tenfold. It was as if a celestial hoe had been dragged across the jungle and removed all but a washed-out yellow topsoil. Thirty meters away on the far side the vegetation continued but to the north and the south of them was a barren scar where nothing grew. Dtui confessed that the hairs on the back of her neck were tingling. The men had the same feeling but none of them admitted it.

"Why the hell. . . ?" said Johnson.

"The mountain's off to the left," said Lit. "Assuming it's still there."

And so they headed north, their boots crunching on the dead undergrowth. Their hearts heavy in their chests. Here and there Phosy pointed out tire tracks in the dirt. They came across plastic bags and empty petrol containers. This dead channel through the jungle had been used. After twenty or thirty minutes a fuzzy dark shape appeared ahead of them.

"That's Phu Kum," said Lit.

Dtui patted him on the back and complimented him on his orientation skills. Phosy slapped him a little harder than necessary.

"Yes, well done, comrade," he said.

They arrived at what could only be described as a quarry. Enormous rocks littered the bare landscape. Craters were all around. Ahead, the mountain had been opened up like a spoon through a blancmange.

"Messy," said Dtui.

"We're here," said Phosy. "But I'm not sure what it is we've found."

"Somebody's blown hell out of this mountain, is what we've found," said Johnson. He climbed up onto a heap of rubble and looked back along the devastated trail. "How far are we from the Thai border, here?"

Dtui asked Lit.

"A little over forty kilometers," she said. "Why?"

"I don't know. It just looks like a lot of trouble's been taken here to set up some kind of quick transportation route south from this point. To clear the land this dramatically using conventional methods would take half a year at least. The spooks were always experimenting with different chemicals. I wonder if they really did come up with some super napalm and some enterprising spark had the bright idea to use it to clear jungle. There has to be something in that mountain to make it all worthwhile."

Dtui had broken out the space rations and water. They sat in the shade of a bellyache tree that had held out against the bombs and the napalm and somehow survived. Phosy wasn't interested in eating. He threw back a cup of water and said he had to take a leak. He walked around to the rear of a ridge of dislodged boulders and began to work his way up to the cliff. He was a slave to his curiosity. A man less fit than Phosy might not have made it over the debris. It wasn't an easy climb. But the scramble over the rocks left him barely winded. He knew he could be up and back before the others had finished their lunch. Geology wasn't his strong point but the multicoloured veins in the boulders all around filled him with wonder. It wasn't their beauty that impressed him, rather the fact that these whites and browns and greens had taken thousands of years to form and he was so new compared to. . . .

The bullets peppered the overhang beside him and sent shards of rock into the side of his face. One caught his eye. He recognized the yap yap of an AK47—a second burst and he was on the ground now, his body pressed tight up against the cliff face. There was no cover. The shots were coming from above—far to the right. Blood stung his eyes so he couldn't see the shooter. He tried to make himself as small a target as possible but he knew it would only be a matter of time before one of the 7.62 shells found him. At the end of the second volley, he heard a familiar voice.

"He's one of ours, you idiot," shouted Commander Lit. "Hold your fire." There were a few seconds of silence before the shooter's own voice echoed down from a cave entrance.

"How am I supposed to know that?"

"Because I'm telling you."

Although Phosy couldn't see, he could tell the security commander's voice was coming from not far down the slope. He'd been following the inspector up the mountain.

"And who are you?" asked the shooter.

"Well, soldier, unless you stole that PL uniform you're wearing, I'm your damned commanding officer so—"

"I don't know that."

"No, that's true. You don't. But my duty papers are in my pack here. If you think you can hold back from killing the pair of us, I'll take them out and show you."

"I've got my orders."

"So have I. I'm Commander Lit Keovieng, previously security head in region five. Currently on special duty in Vientiane. The man you just shot at is the inspector of police in Vientiane. If you kill either of us you'll be in front of a firing squad before supper time. Now put down your weapon and get down here and look at these papers before I climb up there and pull you down."

There was another silence.

"They didn't tell me anyone was coming," said the shooter.

"They didn't tell me anyone would be here trying to kill us," said Lit.

"I'll have to radio it in."

"Are you relayed to Phonsavan?"

"Yeah."

"Then tell Captain Chuan that Commander Lit is here from Xam Neua."

"Right. Don't go anywhere."

"I'm going up to look at my colleague, if you don't mind. Wouldn't want him bleeding to death, would we?"

Lit climbed the final twenty meters where he found Phosy bloody but grinning.

"That was madness," Phosy said.

"Nonsense."

Lit removed a cloth from his shoulder bag, spat on it and started to clean Phosy's face.

"You bleed a lot for someone with no wounds," he said.

"Thank you."

"What for?"

"Saving my life."

"I did no such thing."

"Standing down an armed guard. He could just as easily have shot you too. You aren't in uniform. That was a brave thing you did."

"I doubt he could hit a tank from two meters."

"You're probably right, but, thanks."

They were hit by a small avalanche of pebbles from above as the shooter, his weapon now over his shoulder, scrambled from his roost to join them. He was wearing flip-flops so much of his descent was on his backside. He smiled a set of dark brown teeth.

"Comrades," he said, holding out his hand. "No hard feelings, eh?" Phosy shook the hand. The shooter's salute to Lit looked more like a backhander to his own ear.

"Commander," he said. "Just following orders."

"I'm sure you were."

"Truth is, they told me to shoot to kill. But I usually just wound 'em. Then they can limp home and tell their friends not to come. If they're dead, people come looking for 'em, right?"

"Right."

They heard footsteps on gravel and the sentry reached for his weapon.

"Relax soldier," said Lit. "I think that's the rest of our party come to see if we're alive."

"Phosy! Phosy, are you all right?" came Dtui's anxious voice.

"I'm fine," Phosy yelled.

"Lit?"

"I'm fine too," shouted Lit. He shrugged at Phosy. "Thanks for asking."

Dtui, aided over the rocks by Sergeant Johnson, appeared around a huge boulder. When she saw the state of her husband she scrambled alone over the last few meters. She could hardly catch her breath.

"What's he doing here?" the soldier asked when he saw Johnson.

"Prisoner. Don't worry about it," said Lit.

"Who did this to you?" Dtui screamed.

"That was me, comrade," the soldier grinned. "It's not as bad as it looks."

She glared at him, grabbed the cloth from Lit and began her own inspection.

"Always have to be the hero," she mumbled. "Always have to run off on your own to show how clever you are. Can't wait five minutes. Safety in numbers, ever hear of that? Heavens, Phosy, you've got a lump of rock sticking out of your face . . . and you've cracked a tooth. How, pray tell me, is that not as bad as it looks?"

"Could have been a bullet through his skull," said the shooter looking over her shoulder at the wound.

She reached into her pack for her own medical supplies and pointed a bandage at the soldier.

"You," she said, "I'll get to you later."

"Be nice to have the support of a good woman," said the soldier.

"So what exactly is it you're guarding up here so enthusiastically?" Lit asked.

"You don't know, comrade?"

"If I knew I wouldn't ask you, would I?"

"That's true. It's gold, sir."

"Gold?"

"Lots of it."

"We have gold?" Dtui looked up in surprise.

"It's all around," said the sentry. "The mountains in Xiang Khouang are chock full of the stuff. Locals have known about it for centuries but, until the war, nobody knew how to get to it.

No heavy equipment. No roads. Some of the villagers would come up here to do a bit of mining. Trek a week up, a week back. All they could carry on a donkey. But by the time they'd sold it to the Chinese dealers, it barely covered the cost of sticky rice for the journey. Not worth it."

"What do you mean, 'until the war'?" Phosy asked.

The sentry looked at John Johnson.

"American, is he?" he asked.

"Yes."

"Speak Lao, does he?"

"No."

"All right. Well, it was them, you see? The Americans. They got wind of the fact that the mountains of Xiang Khouang were full of gold. So they picked themselves the mountain nearest to Thailand and bombed the shit out of it. As you can see."

Dtui was shocked. She asked John Johnson whether such a thing was possible. He thought about it and laughed.

"No question," he said. "The bombers were just offloading where they were told to. The Raven would lead them to a target, give them the coordinates and they'd drop their load. All you'd need is one Raven on your payroll and he could lead strike after strike on any mountain you had a mind to blow to smithereens. The pilots would have no idea they were bombing a hunk of empty rock. I mean, look at this. There must have been a hundred strikes here."

Once they heard Johnson's opinion, both Phosy and Lit became animated.

"Wolff," said Phosy. "The Raven drinking with Boyd and Leon that night. The pilot was killed a few weeks later. I bet he was the FAC who led the strikes on this mountain."

"And once he'd done his job, they didn't need him any more," said Lit.

"In fact, it would have been better for everyone if they could shut him up permanently," Phosy agreed.

"And who better to make sure his plane had an accident than the chief flight mechanic, Leon?" said Johnson. "That's why he'd been transferred to Long Cheng. To keep an eye on the pilots. You know? I bet he fixed Boyd's chopper that night too. The young pilot was starting to get edgy. He was a liability."

"But what was Boyd's role in all this?" Phosy asked.

"He was the gofer," said Johnson. "He ferried in the super napalm from Thailand. Did all their odd jobs. Might have even dropped the canisters to clear the land. Who knows? Once the mountain was broken and the swathe was cut to the nearest road, they didn't need these guys any more. The fact is Captain Boyd was in it up to his neck and he had to go."

"They'd need a factory on the Thai side," Lit said. "Somewhere to process the ore, extract the gold."

"And some sort of export deal with the Thai junta of the month," said Phosy.

"Teak," said Dtui.

They looked at her.

"Teak furniture," she said. "It's heavy. Comes in crates. You'd just need someone on the payroll at customs in the States to sign it all through without inspection. Exotic wood products from Southeast Asia. There was a war going on. Who'd give a second thought about dining room tables?"

"Bowry senior set the whole thing up," said Johnson. "Business suddenly picked up during the war. He got so rich he bought himself a state. He was importing gold, goddamn it. He had Vogal, his best buddy from high school, based in Saigon altering all the orders and transferring people. He had a disbarred pilot directing things from Spook City. They had an FAC leading the bombing.

Man, they had it all covered. I take back all I said about the CIA. They didn't do this. This was a private deal. They had it worked out. Five or six guys on the inside. A bunch of hired help for the shifting and processing. It was a real neat little operation."

"But Major Potter got suspicious," said Lit.

"So Vogal had him kicked out," said Phosy.

"And suddenly here was Potter on an MIA mission to find the pilot they'd tried to eliminate," said Lit.

"It must have driven Vogal and Bowry senior nuts," Johnson laughed. "What if they really found the boy? It would have all been over for them. They had no choice but to make sure Vogal was here to see that nothing was discovered. He couldn't let anyone meet with young Boyd or find the briefcase."

"And that puts Vogal at the very top of the list of suspects in Potter's murder," said Phosy.

"It sure does," Johnson agreed.

"Oh," said Dtui. A new reality had just hit her. "If Captain Boyd's father was running the show, it would have been his decision. . . ."

"To have his son killed," said Phosy. "That's correct. That's the kind of people we're dealing with here."

The soldier was crouched on his haunches enjoying all the intrigue. He had his own contribution.

"Two villages melted," he said.

Lit looked at him.

"Melted?"

"The pink rain," said the soldier. "When they sprayed it they burned two villages. About ten families in each one. They were well away from the Ho Chi Minh trail. No enemy activity around here. They thought they were safe. No need to evacuate. Then, one day, they were gone. Dissolved. Nothing left of them. My wife's family was in one of the villages. Melted like ice."

The soldier's brown smile belied the horror of what he'd just told them.

"That's what haunted Captain Boyd," said Dtui. "That's what made him turn on his cohorts."

"We've got to get word to the Friendship," said Lit.

"The radio," said Dtui.

"Nah, no good," the sentry told them. "They're all on their way to Phu Bia to have another go at the Hmong. I got through just as they were leaving."

"Then we've got to get back," said Phosy.

He shook the soldier"s hand again.

"I'm sorry about your wife's family," he said. "And thank you for not killing me."

"My pleasure," said the soldier.

As the visitors set off down the mountain he called after them.

"By the way," he said. "Forgot to mention. Captain Chuan said that with all the commotion up at Phu Bia he hadn't been able to release any of his men you asked for. Said he's sorry about that."

The visitors froze and turned back to the sentry.

"Captain Chuan didn't send any guards up to the Friendship Hotel?" said Lit.

"He said he was sorry. Hoped it wouldn't be a problem."

22

WHEN DID WE GET TOO OLD
FOR THIS?

The head of the senator's bodyguard detail—the four men everyone assumed were soldiers—was a Filipino named Emiliano. He'd recently returned from a trip back to Manila where he'd killed Nino Sebastian, and a swing through Pattaya where he'd made Cueball Dave's death look like a heart attack. He was very good at what he did which justified the money they paid him. He spoke only a little Lao and very few words of Thai, which explained why he'd not opened his mouth since their arrival. His team comprised two Thais and a Lao. Mercenaries all. They communicated with their employer in English. They were there not merely for the protection of the man who paid their substantial salaries, but to eradicate obstacles. For four days they'd been setting light to jungle and blowing up communication towers, so they all felt more comfortable back in a milieu for which they were better suited—murder. The killing on the agenda today would not be one for the squeamish. They had an entire dining room full of people to massacre. But they'd done worse.

To its credit, the marijuana tea took the edge off the menace.

Although the hostages were supposed to be sitting cross-legged on the floor, three were now curled up and fast asleep. No amount of shouting would rouse them. Dr. Yamaguchi had a terrible case of the munchies and his crunching of sesame biscuits provided a constant soundtrack for the drama.

Peach, still stoned but coming down, had lost the ability to speak in any language at all and had become quite angry with herself. Secretary Gordon had found that he was now able to sit cross-legged on the floor. He crossed and uncrossed his legs and laughed with amazement whenever he didn't fall onto his side. Everyone had been told to shut up but this was a talkative crowd and there were very few in its midst who really understood the gravity of the situation. Siri and Bpoo sat together at the back assessing the chances of getting out of there alive. Senator Vogal and Ethel Chin had left the room. There were guards at each point of the compass with their AK47s trained on the heads of the hostages. Only one of them, Emiliano, seemed unaffected by the tea. He had the look of a young man who was suspicious of everybody and everything. The other three were clearly in various states of euphoria. One appeared to be trigger-happy. His hand twitched on the trigger in time to a nervous tick in his left eye. Another smiled and moved in a sort of glide, gentle, calm. But there was no doubt from the look in his eyes that he'd enjoy a good killing. Far from rendering them harmless, the mercenaries looked even more villainous as a result of Madame Daeng's tea. Perhaps the head of the Federal Bureau of Narcotics had been right after all. Marijuana could very well be the most violence-causing drug in the history of mankind.

"Did you see me mowed down in a hail of bullets?" Siri asked Bpoo in a whisper.

"Stop it."

"Or that you'd be going with me?"

"I don't want to discuss it. All right?"

"What? You're the one who predicted all this. It's brilliant."

"Let's focus all our attention on getting out of it, shall we?"

"You may have noticed the odds have swung against us. I think you and I might have overpowered Miss Chin—just—and her short-fingered boss. But now I'm tempted to say they have the upper hand. And, no offence intended here, but if I'm about to be massacred, I'd rather like to be with my wife."

Siri stood and four gun muzzles swung in his direction. All the guards yelled.

"Siri, sit down," said Bpoo.

"Sorry."

Siri raised his hands as one does in such circumstances. The guards were now yelling in a frenzied version of their own languages. He ignored them and picked his way through the seated and sleeping bodies to where Madame Daeng resided. He smiled at her and, even though no Lao in any conditions under any circumstances would think of doing such a thing, he kissed her on the cheek as he sat. The hostages who noticed clapped and cheered. All the guards had assumed firing positions. They obviously wanted to kill someone. But, just as obviously, they were under orders to desist. Judge Haeng, who sat shuddering in front of Siri, was apparently unaware of this directive. There was a puddle beneath him which presumably did not originate from a burst water pipe under the flooring. Dr. Yamaguchi yelled something which caused the Americans to laugh, but Peach was deep in thought and didn't translate it. The guards were clearly out of their depth in such company. The fact that none of the hostages seemed to appreciate the awesome power they wielded made them look a lot like little boys playing soldier. There was no fear to feed off.

Civilai, who probably didn't need two and a half cups of marijuana tea to be cantankerous, called to the Thai- and Lao-speaking guards.

"Brothers," he said, "doesn't it concern you that you're behaving like trained monkeys, dancing to the tune of the American dollar? We're all of the same blood, you and us, yet you point your guns at your relatives. Would you do this to your own mother? Your—"

The shot exploded through the happy crowd like a split in the atmosphere. Civilai reached for his left ear just as the blood started to spurt. It was only a nick but there was no denying the fact that his brain was only a few centimeters from his earlobe.

"Ooh!" said someone in the audience. One of the sleepers awoke and asked what was happening. Emiliano, the Filipino, had fired his pistol left-handed from his hip. Whether he was related to Annie Oakley or merely couldn't care less whether he hit the old man in the forehead, nobody would ever know. But it was an impressive shot. The young man, still holding his AK47 in his right hand, leaned back against the wooden beams and rolled his cigarette with his tongue. He had almost everybody's attention which pleased him. Mr. Geung, holding his stomach, got to his feet and ran to the door. It appeared he was about to throw up. The smiling guard decided to let him go and laughed as he ran past. He was just another harmless moron.

"Now perhaps you'll all shut up," said Emiliano.

"Typical," said Siri, glaring directly at the marksman but talking to Civilai. "I lose an earlobe so what do you do? Rush out to get your own earlobe shot off. When is this jealousy going to end?"

Civilai was apparently feeling no pain.

"Did it come out the other side?" he asked Cousin Vinai.

Emiliano had raised his pistol again, this time taking aim.

"Did somebody ask a question?" Civilai shouted. "You'll have to speak up. This isn't my good side any more." He too smiled at the gunman.

It was just a question of discipline. Was the Filipino angry enough to override orders? Was he a soldier or a psychopath? Cool, cold—unable to take a joke. The pistol moved through the air from Civilai, to Siri, to Civilai.

"Please. After him." Siri gestured to Civilai.

"No, I insist. After him," Civilai replied.

Siri felt Daeng squeeze his hand just as Senator Vogal walked into the room. His hair was wet. He'd taken a shower, perhaps a few belts of coffee, and some downers or uppers or whatever it is that negates cannabis because he seemed more in control of himself than he had been.

"What's going on?" he shouted.

"Just playing with the locals," Emiliano smiled.

"Plenty of time for that," said Vogal. He had hold of Ethel Chin's wrist. He was squeezing and it was hurting. "Miss Chin here has decided to join the party." He dragged her across the room and threw her to the ground.

"What? You can't do this to me," she screamed. "After all I've done for you. After all you said. Our plans."

"Oh, do stop it," said Vogal. "You never could hold your drugs. Did you honestly think this was all going to have a happy ending?"

"You bastard."

"See? No control over your mouth. Never could keep it shut. Once a noisy chink, always a noisy chink."

"I didn't. I didn't tell them anything."

Vogal nodded to Emiliano.

"If anything else comes out of this mouth," he said. "Shoot it off."

"My pleasure," said the marksman.

The Lao had no idea what the couple was talking about but it seemed quite obvious they weren't getting along that well. Nobody bothered to translate and nobody really cared. But then it was Siri's turn.

"You!" said the senator.

"Moi?" said Siri.

Vogal called for one of the Thais to translate.

"You tell him he's the one," he said. "You tell him what's about to happen in this room is all down to him. It should have all been really simple. We find the pilot's body, make sure everything in the chopper was destroyed, the MIA story's a hoax, Potter kills himself but nobody's game to report it. We all go home. Everybody's alive at the end of it apart from some annoying drunk. You weren't supposed to spoil all that, old man. You know why we insisted on having you on the team? I'll tell you. Because you're a flake. Yeah, really. Ghosts and ghouls and travels through hell and back. Yeah, we get to hear about all that. We aren't completely without intel. You were supposed to be the coroner who knows nothing. You and the team of misfits your minister recommended were supposed to party your way through the week and not have a clue what it was all about. But you get your own team together, don't you? And you get nosy and you screw it all up. You're a serious disappointment. I don't usually like to get blood on my own hands but I'm really pissed at you. None of you other folks need to worry. I don't want anyone to panic. I'll just shoot the doctor here to make myself feel better then you can all go home."

No room was less likely to break out in a panic than the restaurant of the Friendship Hotel. Those who had a clue what was going on were watching it like a movie. They weren't in it. But Vogal was right about Ethel Chin. She really didn't know when to keep her mouth shut.

"Yeah? How stupid do you think they are?" she yelled. "They're all dead. Tell them wh—"

Like its predecessor, the bullet that silenced Ethel Chin sliced through the room and confused everyone. Toua and his wife had been sitting behind her and they were splattered with blood. They knew. But everyone else seemed mystified. Chin dropped onto her side, dead, and Emiliano put down his pistol, resisting the temptation to blow smoke out of the barrel. He looked proud, fulfilled.

"Ah! Peace," said Vogal. "You know? Murder is such a wonderful tool for discipline. I'm surprised high schools haven't cottoned on to the concept. Shoot the smart ass in the back row and you're guaranteed cooperation for the rest of the semester. It's on my next budget recommendation to the senate."

With Vogal's oratory and the henchman's struggled translation in the background, Madame Daeng turned to her husband and smiled.

"It's that scene, isn't it?" she said. "The one in your movies where all is lost, the assassins are about to massacre the innocent hostages— then, from nowhere, the hero swings in on a rope and rescues us."

"I think you were right up to the 'all is lost' part," Siri laughed. "I knew I shouldn't have fed Ugly this morning. If he was hungry there's a possibility he'd fight to the death to save me. Failing that. . . ."

"I was thinking more of Captain Boyd making an unlikely return from the dead."

"If we had a wish for every noodle we've ever eaten, it still wouldn't be enough to make that happen."

"He's dead, isn't he?"

"I'm afraid so."

"Us too."

"It's starting to look that way. If we made a rush for them they might do us the favor of laughing themselves to death."

Daeng looked around and chuckled.

"We are a ragged lot," she said. "Most of us wouldn't make it to our feet before the first bullets hit."

"When did we get too old for this, Daeng? What happened to those days when we were somersaulting through the air with a cutlass in each hand taking out the enemy twenty at a time?"

"I don't think that was us, love. That was Bruce Lee."

"You know, I think you're right. I often confuse myself with him."

"I'd sooner have you."

"And I'd want nobody else but you."

Their grips tightened.

"It's been an exceptional eight months together," she said.

"I'd rather been hoping for several more."

"Me too."

Something had happened. The guards were all moving to the same side of the dining room. Siri knew it was the precursor to a firing squad. He wondered what options there were. Rushing the guards was better than sitting back and waiting, but he wondered how many of the stoned hostages were in any fit state to attack. The senator was pointing at him. A guard came wading through the bodies.

"I get to do a solo," Siri said and gave his wife's hand a last squeeze before getting uncomfortably to his feet.

"Give them the recitation," Daeng said. "The really long one you bored everyone to death with at Dtui's wedding."

"Madam, that was my own Lao translation of a Marot sonnet."

"Try that one. It might work again. Siri. . . ."

He stopped and looked back.

"Yes?"

"Did you put clean underwear on this morning?"

"Yes."

"Well, then, that's something, I suppose."

He gave her a warm smile and followed the guard who hurried him along with the butt of his gun. From a far room came the sound of the generator starting up. The clattering of the loose washers and nuts was worse than ever. Auntie Bpoo sat erect and strained her ears. At the front of the room, Vogal, with a pistol in his hand, was attempting to force Siri to get to his knees. The doctor refused to do so. The sound of the rattling pipes grew louder.

Bpoo had it.

"Siri," she called, "put your fingers in your ears."

She saw Siri smile at the joke.

"Siri, I'm serious," she called again. "It's mid-afternoon. There *is* no generator. Do it."

Siri immediately understood and, to Vogal's surprise, pushed his fingers into his ears and began to sing.

"I rather doubt that will help him very much," said the senator, laughing.

"Daeng, you too," called Bpoo. "Civilai, if you're at all conscious. Now. Put your fingers in your ears and hum."

The last sound Bpoo heard before blocking her own ears and humming something from Perry Como, was a rhythmic metal clatter getting ever closer.

Vogal's pistol was at Siri's head. He'd given up on his attempt to make the old fool kneel. He had a few biting words to say before pulling the trigger but his tongue suddenly felt larger than his mouth. To his left, the Thai guards were nodding in time to some distant rhythm. Even Emiliano to his right was rocking from side to side and, apparently, dribbling. Vogal put it down to the lasting effects of the old woman's tea. He attempted to ask the Filipino what the hell he thought he was doing but the words that left his mouth were alien—not even his own voice. He looked at the hostages freaking out like hippies at a folk concert, waving their fingers, lost behind closed eyes. He looked up to see the Down's Syndrome guy enter the dining room, banging on a beaten-up tambourine with a stick. He had wads of toilet paper stuffed in his ears and the most infuriating smile on his face. Vogal attempted to level his gun in the retard's direction but it just swung back and forth in front of him like a conductor's baton. Then his mind left him completely.

Siri let out a nervous laugh and shook his head. Geung really had packed everything but the morgue sink. He'd brought along the shamanic tambourine. Those who could hear it had fallen into a ritual trance just like the children at Thong Pong middle school. No doubt the tea had weakened everyone's self-control and made them susceptible to its haunting beat. Nobody knew where they were. Not Vogal, not the guards, and certainly not the guests who rocked and drooled and spoke in strange tongues. Those who had blocked out the sound would have a few seconds to act when the drumming stopped. Siri nodded at Geung who ceased his banging. As quickly as he was able, the doctor relieved Vogal and Emiliano of their weapons. Auntie Bpoo and Daeng took the guns from the other guards. There was no resistance. Civilai had been unable to put his finger in both ears as one was missing so he had succumbed to the sound.

When Vogal and the guards came round they were staring down the barrels of their own guns. The Thais thought it was all quite comical; two old relics and a drag queen having the drop on them. But Emiliano was a professional. He knew your average citizen would never be able to fire at a living being in cold blood. He started to walk toward the kindly looking old lady.

"One more step and I shoot," said Daeng, realizing too late that he couldn't understand her.

He took one more step.

She shot.

The bullet made a mess of the fingers of his left hand but he was determined to call her bluff. He took another step. The second bullet went into his shin and he dropped to the other knee. He looked up into the woman's eyes and she smiled. And he knew this was no ordinary old lady. He and the other bodyguards could tell the next bullet would be aimed at his heart and there'd be no hesitation in pulling the trigger.

"And you think you can shoot me, too?" said Vogal with far less confidence than the words warranted. "I'm a United States senator. If I don't return in one piece it'll be enough to start another war."

Bpoo translated.

"Tell him he thinks far too much of himself," said Siri. He walked up close to the sweating senator and pushed the pistol into his belly. "The way I heard it, any old criminal can buy themselves a senate seat. Your country will be glad to see the back of you. You're a murderer. And there are twenty witnesses here who heard you threaten me and confess to Potter's killing."

Bpoo passed on the message.

"They don't know what they heard," Vogal tried again. "Look at them. They're all stoned."

"Then they'll just have to believe what we tell them, won't they. And there's a bullet in that poor Chinese girl over there which certainly matches your gun. Either way, you're in very deep manure, Senator Vogal."

"It won't work, little doctor. You have no idea about the process of international diplomacy. A deal will be made. They'll exchange me for some political prisoner and I'll be released with a clean record."

Both Siri and Bpoo laughed.

"Senator, where do you think you are? This is Laos. Diplomacy is a long way off for us. We can barely scrape together enough literate men to act as foreign ambassadors. We don't have any political prisoners. The only benefit our Politburo could possibly get from this situation is the enjoyment of watching you humiliated and your government squirm. We'll follow your case as it passes through the courts and have a little party when they lock you away. No, wait. I do believe you have electric chairs. That would be one to watch."

"You. . . ."

At last, the senator was lost for words.

23

GUERRILLAS IN THE MIST

The truck with Lit driving like a madman skidded along the gravel in front of the Friendship and bumped so hard into the front steps that three of them were destroyed. Both he and Phosy were out of the cab and into the Friendship before the engine had died. Dtui and John Johnson were close behind. They headed first for the dining room which was empty. Likewise the kitchen. It was Dtui who first noticed the stain on their way out.

"It's blood," she said. "A lot of it."

The search became more frenzied as they went from room to room along first the east wing then the west. None of them was locked and all were empty. All that remained were the cabins at the rear and the old opium warehouse. And it was in the open-sided godown that they found everybody. Civilai looked up to see them arrive. His head was wrapped in a white bandage. He looked like a Sikh.

"We need to touch on the subject of punctuality," he called to them. He was one of seven—the others being Daeng, Dr. Yamaguchi, Secretary Gordon, General Suvan and the two old musketeers—who sat on the edge of the raised concrete floor with their weapons trained toward the fence. And there, tied to the wooden posts, were Senator Vogal and the four guards. They were dressed in only their underpants. Whether they were shivering from the cold or from fear seemed hardly relevant. Rhyme was at the fence using the last of his film to snap Vogal in his teddy bear undies. Like the others, the journalist had remained stoned throughout the whole hostage drama. He'd learned what had actually happened from Siri and Auntie Bpoo. He fully intended to write it all up as a "live at the scene" piece which would include every one of Bpoo's exaggerations. The transvestite had been good to her word by drinking the cold tea in Potter's room and was now every bit as wasted as the others had been.

"My idea," she boasted. "Taking off their clothes. My idea." And roared with laughter.

Dtui, relieved that none of her fears had been realized, ran to grab her friends' hands and rub their backs—her own Lao hug. Those not assigned to sentry duty were seated around the large table with glasses in front of them. They all seemed to be squinting from the effects of the tea.

"What happened to your face?" Siri asked Phosy.

"Walked into a mountain," said the inspector.

"But it was a mountain full of gold," Lit added.

"There's gold in Laos?" Siri raised his bushy eyebrows.

"Absolutely not," Civilai called across to him. "Don't you think the Politburo would have announced it if there was? No, sir, they'd give everybody a chance to help themselves before the government could lay its hands on the stuff. It's all a rumor."

"Well, a little lump of that rumor accidently fell into my pack when I was treating my husband," said Dtui, pulling out a small nugget which appeared to be pure gold. She passed it around the table while Commander Lit explained the theory of what had happened toward the end of the war. Siri shared his own findings from Potter's documents and between them the neat logic of the operation became apparent.

"This was all about gold?" said Daeng.

"Enough to make some people very rich," said Lit.

"And a lot of others very dead," Phosy added. "They obliterated two villages in order to ship out their war booty."

"There's still plenty left," said Lit. "I don't know whether the local battalion are guarding it to share out amongst themselves or whether they have orders from above. But somebody has a whole mountain full of gold down there. I'll be making a full report about it."

"Well, I'm not having it," said Judge Haeng, now in a dry change of clothes. He'd been hiding at the far side of the table, invisible and silent since the fracas. "I'm setting up a national enquiry as soon as we get back. A good socialist. . . ."

Siri wrote something on a slip of paper and folded it in quarters before passing it on to the judge. Haeng read it and blanched. Whatever was written there terminated the latest motto and would keep his honor shut up for the rest of the day. Siri would tell no one what it said.

The newcomers sat at the table and sipped at the fine Scotch whiskey.

"Did the papers tell you anything else about Potter's involvement in all this?" Phosy asked Siri.

"I think he had suspicions about the illegal exploitation of air strikes, perhaps even the use of napalm. I found a copy of a letter addressed to Mr. Rhyme over there, asking him to take as many aerial photos as he could, focusing on cleared land and bomb sites. We know that the major suspected something was up in Ho

Chi Minh. He had access to the same paperwork as Vogal. He knew there were discrepancies in the work placement orders. He was sending memos to the embassy in Bangkok until Vogal got wind of it. Vogal went over the ambassador's head and had Potter removed. But the embassy was still on the major's side. Looks like Potter and the ambassador put this little excursion together. Isn't that right, Gordon?" he asked in Thai.

The second secretary looked up and listened as Peach did a more formal translation of Siri's findings.

"I . . . er. . . ." Gordon began.

"I have a letter here from the ambassador," said Siri. "It was in with Potter's papers."

"Well then, I guess he did," Gordon conceded.

"I don't think you really need to guess," said Siri. "Seeing as your name's right here in the letter. It says how the embassy would support Potter's nomination as team leader and the ambassador hoped that certain outstanding issues might be cleared up as a result. His trusted aid, Mr. Mack Gordon, would be included on the team to offer any support the major might need." Siri looked up at the American.

"You and Potter were working on this together. You've known all about this right from the beginning," said Siri.

Gordon put down his weapon and came over to the table. He looked around at the expectant faces.

"Not really," he said. "I had access to some of the things Potter knew but he didn't share everything with me. We had no idea what it was Vogal and Bowry had been doing here, only that it was illegal and it made them rich. There was other stuff I couldn't tell you all. I'm sorry."

He pulled out a chair and sat.

"The photographs sent to the embassy came with a note," he

said. "It was one of those blackmail letters you see in the movies, with the words cut out and pasted. It said something like, 'Hi, Dad, congratulations on the promotion. As you can see, I'm alive and well. Thanks for asking. The guy you got to sabotage my chopper wasn't the brightest. When you decide to kill your only son you really better do it right or he'll come back from the grave at the most inconvenient time.'"

The guards were distracted by Peach's translation. None of them noticed the senator slowly rocking back and forth. The fence post he was tied to was loose. By leaning against it and pulling upwards, he was slowly dislodging it from the ground. Emiliano on the next post looked across and he too started to edge his post out of the dirt.

"'I escaped to Thailand,'" Gordon continued to recall the note. "'I met a local girl and found work. It's a comfortable life. I almost forgot all about you and your disloyalty, et cetera. But I see from the newspaper that you're a bigwig now and you've got your finger in a money pie. So I've decided to claim my inheritance. I could use half a million dollars as soon as possible. Not a bad price when you consider everything I know. Everything I could tell them at your appropriations committee meetings.' And then there were suggestions on how to get the money over here. That was the gist of it."

"So that's why Senator Bowry was so confident that it was his son in the photos," Phosy said.

"Actually, no," Gordon said. "He didn't ever see the note."

"You held it back?"

"For two reasons. One, it would have diverted the senator's attention away from this MIA mission. We wouldn't have had any control at all if he went off in search of his son in Thailand. And secondly, we knew it wasn't Captain Bowry who sent the note."

"What?" said Daeng. "Then who was it?"

"Leon. The head mechanic at Long Cheng. We knew about him from Potter's files and embassy reports. We have quite a database of American expatriates living in Thailand, especially ex-servicemen. A lot of them find themselves a bar to run and don't move very far from it. The note gave a PO box in Pattaya as a return address. It was registered in the name of a guy who has shares in the same bar as Leon. Seems the older he got, the stupider he got."

"I know how that feels," said Civilai.

"It didn't take us long to get the connection to Leon. We went to see him, me and Major Potter. He was surprised we'd found him. It took us a while to convince him we were only interested in getting something on Vogal but if he didn't cooperate we had enough evidence to put him away. We told him we'd try to keep the police out of it if he told us where we could find Boyd Bowry. He thought that was funny. Boyd was dead, he told us. Leon had set up the whole thing with the photographs. He'd met a guy in a bar who bore a passing resemblance to Captain Boyd and shot some pictures of him at the local ethnic culture park. He'd thrown in the briefcase for effect. We asked him how he could know Boyd didn't survive the crash. He told us how the chopper was fitted with a tracer. Leon had a radar tracker. He knew exactly where the craft went down. He was working out of the same office as the flight control team. He was on duty late on the night of the crash. He was in a position to give false locations to the search and rescue teams. He hadn't really heard the explosion. It was just another way to confuse the search."

"As soon as Air America had given up on Boyd, Leon flew in there to take a look round. It appears Boyd almost made it. He'd somehow avoided the explosion. I guess we know how he did that now. Lowered himself down on the cable. Incredible that he should even try. Leon found his body mangled up in the trees. He dragged him down and buried him. Leon didn't actually confess to being the one who sabotaged the chopper but I wouldn't have put it past him. He did have a look about him. He undertook a discreet reconnoitre of the village nearby and that's when he saw the tailplane. I guess the germ of an idea took root then but it wasn't until the announcement of the MIA mission and Bowry's newfound influence in DC that Leon sparked into action."

"There were Lao girls working in Leon's go-go bar. One of them had family in Xiang Khouang. A couple of brothers. She'd been in Thailand since the early sixties but, with the war over, she was keen on the idea of visiting her home village. It was just outside of old Xiang Khouang town, not that far from Ban Hoong. Not so hard to cross the border if you've got friends on the other side. Leon paid for her trip in exchange for a couple of small favors. A bonus if she came back with results."

"The photograph and the rocks," said Daeng.

"She was the dragon's daughter," Civilai laughed.

"So the rocks. . . ?" Yamaguchi asked.

"Just another clue in case we were so dumb we missed the point," said Gordon. "Backup in case the villagers died of a group heart attack carrying the tail up through the mountains. Leon needed Vogal and Bowry to believe Boyd had survived. Then they'd be more likely to hand over his half a million. Leon's attempt to blackmail Bowry fitted right into our plans. We were certain someone would make a mistake and we'd be here watching."

"You didn't ask Leon what Boyd and the two senators were involved in?" John Johnson asked.

"Oh, we asked. But we'd gotten everything out of him we were likely to. He had a condominium with 180-degree vista of the ocean and a jet spa. He wasn't living that kind of lifestyle on an air force pension. He'd made that money the same way the senators did. He wasn't about to endanger his investment."

"But it wasn't enough for him," Siri said.

"He saw the other guys were living at the top end and he wanted to be up there with them. He got greedy. Two weeks after we talked to him he was dead."

"Do you think they found out he was orchestrating the blackmail?" Phosy asked.

"No, if they did they wouldn't have gone through with the MIA mission. I think they were getting jumpy. It was time to clean up. They eliminated the last two mechanics who knew what had happened. That left Captain Boyd and Potter. Through the blackmail note, the young captain had taken on a life all his own. Leon had reanimated him and we at the embassy decided to ride his luck. The major wanted to catch Vogal in the act of sabotaging the mission. But we underestimated him. By coming up here and shutting down all communications, Vogal was able to see off the major and make an alibi for himself. If things didn't work out he could wipe out the lot of us and blame some renegade bandit gang. He had it all covered."

"Actually, it's brilliant," said Civilai. "Splendid efficiency without a hint of conscience. No wonder they're the leaders of the free world."

"Vogal," said Dr. Yamaguchi.

"That's right," said Gordon.

"No, I mean, Vogal's gone."

They looked to the fence to see that the evening mist had rolled in fast from the plane. The foggy figures of three of the guards sat featureless at the perimeter, but beside them two fence posts lay on the ground. Vogal and Emiliano were gone. The two musketeers started to give chase. One of them reached the fence line before Commander Lit called them back.

"Wait!" he shouted. "I think this recapture might take care of itself."

Everyone stood silent, waiting for the inevitable explosions. Field mice weighing less than a hiccup had been known to detonate the temperamental ordnance on the plain. Even without clothes weighing them down, the runners would have to call on some ill-deserved karma to make it across. Everyone waited. Listened. Expectant . . . Nothing.

"Do you think we should call out, 'Be careful,' or something?" Daeng asked.

"I think they knew the dangers when they took off," said Siri. "They think their chances out there are better than the alternative."

The silence continued. Siri wanted to capture the moment somehow. The tension. The expectation. It would have made a remarkable cinematic image. He wondered whether it might be seen as inappropriate to discuss his screenplay concept with Civilai at such an occasion. He could see Kurosawa milking this scene. Two desperate men in their underwear lost in the mist on a landscape sown with explosives. Black and white. The only way to go. He looked around. Men and women holding their smoky breaths. Doubts fluttering. What if the endless blitz stories were all a myth composed by the propagandists? What if there were no—

It was less a bang, more a . . . a thunk. Like a punch. Loud, it was, and final. But not the boom you'd expect. There was no scream because bombies were renowned for their suddenness. By the time the shock had washed over you, screaming was the last thing on your mind. If your mind was still attached to your skull. Everyone wondered which of the escapees had been taken, but the thought was fleeting, because the second thunk seemed to leave a whistle in the air like a high-pitched ricochet.

24

A FAMILIAR HAUNT

Everyone agreed that being black had not distracted John Johnson from being a very fine helicopter pilot. He'd ignored the ban on flying during heavy smoke cover, hotwired one of the helicopters in the yard, and had so far made two trips to Muang Kham beyond the smoke zone. Siri and Auntie Bpoo sat on the broken steps of the Friendship Hotel waiting for the third shuttle.

"So. Mission accomplished," Siri said.

"I'd been hoping for something more exciting," Bpoo confessed, rethreading a necklace that had been broken during the troubles. "Thought I might have to drag you from beneath the wheels of a rapid locomotive."

"In a country without a railway?"

"It was a fantasy, old man. In a fantasy you can construct whatever damned engineering infrastructure you please."

"Ear-fingering was no less dramatic. And for that I thank you."

"Yeah, right."

"Now, is there any way I can return the favor?"

"No."

"Not even if you told me what's wrong with your health?"

She glared at the doctor with eyes wide as melon slices.

"What makes you think there's something wrong with my health?"

"I can see the future."

"Don't make me laugh. You can barely see the present."

"Conceded. But I am rather good with the past, and I recall seeing you together with Dr. Yamaguchi at every opportunity."

"He's a passionate man drawn to glamor. What can I say?"

"He's also a very fine researcher."

"The helicopter's late."

"I've been through his CV. Oncology."

"I think I'll complain to the airline. Get my money back."

"You've been asking him how long you have left."

"Do you ever stop being annoying—and wrong?"

"So, tell me."

Auntie Bpoo searched the sky for the return of Sergeant Johnson.

"I'm a fortune-teller," she said. "I don't need to ask *when*. I can give you a date and an exact time. I could sell admission tickets."

"So?"

"So annoying."

"Bpoo?"

"So, I want to know—"

"If it's preventable."

"Stop it, will you? I detest it when people finish sentences for you. It's very—"

"Frustrating."

Siri was smiling. Bpoo had to laugh.

"If I thought there were any way it could be cured I'd talk to a surgeon," Bpoo said softly. "Not a coroner. Yamaguchi's a pathologist. A doctor of the dead bits. I wanted to understand what it looked like. I mean, after it kills you. After it's done its evil work. Does it gloat? Does it swell up and boast of its ominous power, 'Look what I've done'? Or is it exhausted, embarrassed, full of remorse?"

"I doubt Yamaguchi's ever had to face questions like that before."

"I don't have the technical vocabulary. I could only ask in emotional, human terms like that. You see? I can live these last few months better if I don't hate it. If I don't take it personally. I want to love my tumor. I want us to go together, each playing his or her part. Partners walking hand in hand over a steep cliff."

"Hm. What did he say?"

"He ignored the question and counseled."

"Good for him. Was coming up here to save my life part of all this?"

"In a way."

"Do you want to explain why?"

"You're the only person I know who sees the dead."

"And?"

"If you were dead too you'd be completely useless to me."

"If I . . . ? Oh, my word."

"See?"

"Please tell me you aren't planning to haunt me."

"Guide, Siri. Ghosts haunt. Spirits guide. I'll never be forgotten in your mind. We'll be together always."

She started to sing. It was the Thai version of "Auld Lang Syne." Siri put his fingers in his ears and hummed.

"That won't help you any more," she shouted.

Siri removed his fingers and took her hand. She let him.

"I could really use a poem right now," he told her.

"No. Not in the mood."

25

THE CIVILIAN MEDAL FOR AN OUTSTANDING CONTRIBU-
TION TO THE SECURITY AND DEVELOPMENT OF THE
PEOPLE'S DEMOCRATIC REPUBLIC OF LAOS: SECOND TIER

The ceremony was scheduled to commence at 2:00 P.M. It was three fifteen. According to the Americans present, the minister was late. According to the Lao, if he got the day right it was a good sign. Apart from Major Potter and Ethel Chin, back in the States now and probably in the ground, and Senator Vogal who was still a little scattered, all the guests from the Friendship Hotel were in attendance. Gordon had spent a week in Bangkok writing reports and explaining things to committees. But he had returned for this special day. He confirmed that Senator Bowry had been arrested and that the CIA had solemnly sworn to conduct a full inquiry into the manufacture and use of this mysterious super napalm and other illegal activities during the last few years of the war. Dr. Yamaguchi had delayed his return flight in order to have a holiday and to attend today's splendid affair. Rhyme had stayed on because he needed these photographs to complete his Pulitzer piece.

The award would be presented on the small stage in the corner of the canteen at the Ministry of Education. Under normal circumstances, the Civilian Medal for an Outstanding Contribution to the Security and Development of the People's Democratic Republic of Laos: Second Tier, would be handed over by a member of the Politburo in the public gallery at government house. But given the short notice and the "delicacy of the matter," none was available to preside. The ministers of Justice and Information and Culture had refused point-blank and only the Vice-Minister of Education had wisdom enough to see value in the exercise. But even though he'd agreed to present the medal he had insisted on no more than two photographs. Neither was to appear in a publication available inside Laos.

John Johnson and General Suvan were in full military dress uniform. Of the two, the American looked less like a postal worker. Siri and Daeng, Phosy and Dtui, Civilai and his wife Mrs. Noy were in a cluster. Each held but did not drink from non-matching glasses with tissue paper jackets. The vessels contained some unlikely glow-in-the-dark Agent Orange concoction. Auntie Bpoo, dressed like a respectable lady undertaker, joked with Dr. Yamaguchi. Also in uniform was Commander Lit who, Dtui pointed out to her husband, looked particularly dashing. He'd done something to his hair to make it slick back and he'd left his glasses in his top pocket, which might have explained why he was constantly bumping into everyone.

"He looks a lot like Payao Poontarat today," Dtui said.

"The bath water salesman?"

"Olympic boxer. Very elegant."

"You're right. He does have that beaten and bruised look about him."

"I don't see Peach around anywhere," said Dtui, scanning the room. Out of the corner of her eye she noticed Siri and Civilai exchange a glance. It was enough to make her aware that, not for the first time, she was trailing behind the herd.

"What? What happened to her?" Dtui asked.

"Ooh, nothing, I expect," said Siri.

"Probably sealing insurgency donation envelopes with Mummy and Daddy in Indiana," said Civilai.

"In Indiana? She's gone back?"

"Yes," Siri nodded.

Dtui was bemused. "But she hated America."

"Probably not quite as much as she had us believe," Siri said.

"All right." Dtui put up her hands. "Let's not do the subtle, Inspector Migraine explanation of events. Just tell me what I've missed."

"She was denied the continuation of her visa," said Siri. "And it's Maigret."

"Did they give her a reason?"

"They told her she needed a university degree to work in the education sector. But that was only to cover up the actual reason."

"Which was?"

"Spying."

Dtui coughed. "Spying? Who for?"

"The CIA."

Dtui laughed.

"The CIA's recruiting seventeen-year-old daughters of missionaries?"

"No."

"Peach is under eighteen."

"Peach is under eighteen," Siri agreed. "But the girl who came with us to Phonsavan was a completely different fruit."

"Banana?"

"Cherry."

"I don't get it."

"The fruit family in Luang Prabang had four children," Siri

explained. "Peach was the youngest. Cherry the oldest. Two boys in between. Cherry left Laos when she was fourteen to continue her education in the States. She went to university. Before she graduated, she was recruited by a CIA desperate for smart people with Asian languages. She also had the good fortune of looking younger than her age."

"Not unlike me," said Civilai.

"That would only be true if you were actually 130," said Siri, and continued. "When the fruit family was asked to leave, the consulate orchestrated an audacious switch. When they passed through Vientiane, unbeknownst to the family, the consular office issued a second passport to Cherry under the name and age of Peach. Thus, as nobody knew the girls in Vientiane, Cherry became her little sister. She claimed that she didn't want to go to America. Wanted to stay to help the new regime. She tore up her air ticket in a display of national loyalty and was allowed to teach small classes at the lycée. When the mission came around, the Americans requested this new Peach as their interpreter."

"Which explains why, despite all the available bilingual half-breeds with decades of experience under their belts, they opted for a slip of a girl," said Civilai. "The evil CIA very badly wanted one of their own on this mission and they assumed we'd be sure to approve an innocent teenager with anti-American leanings."

"Amazing," said Dtui.

"And it worked," said Daeng.

"It worked until the good doctor here asked for an investigation into the whereabouts of the older sister," said Civilai.

"How could you have known?" Dtui asked.

"Didn't know, exactly," said Siri. "More an instinct. Henry James said that in the case of a young American woman, poise comes from good breeding and a solid education. I didn't see Peach's abilities coming from home-schooling in a remote village in the north of Laos."

"Not even from missionary parents?"

"Especially not from missionary parents. She was too fluent in central Lao dialect. Too worldly. Too diplomatic. I felt certain she'd studied overseas."

"What a mind. When did you bust her?" Dtui asked.

"Shortly after they approved my team selection," Siri told her.

"But that was before we left."

"A week before."

"So why wasn't she kicked off the mission?"

"Aha, enter the intelligence division," said Civilai. "More commonly known as the limited intelligence division. After a lengthy meeting in a secret location, the LID decided it would be of huge national interest to allow her along and feed her with false information which she would pass on to her superiors. And who better to be entrusted with this duty than Comrade False Information himself, Judge Haeng? Assuming she was now completely full of both the judge and the information, they let her go. It's being hailed as a huge espionage coup at the LID. I went by there yesterday. They were having a party to celebrate."

"How did you know where to go?" Daeng asked.

"What?"

"If they meet at secret locations. . . ."

"There's a wooden sign in front."

"Not surprised."

And talking, as they were, of the devil, Siri noticed Judge Haeng at the table of inedible snacks. He excused himself from the group.

"Be kind," said Madame Daeng.

"Ah, Siri," said Haeng when the doctor arrived beside him. "I was about to come and talk to you. You'll be pleased to hear I've solved that little problem you told me about. I explained to the air force command that, given the circumstances of that last day in Phonsavan, it would be only fair to overlook your disregard for regulations by smuggling a live animal onto an official government flight. I suspect none of them could imagine that . . . dog being of domestic value. I've torn up the report the pilot wrote."

"Well, Judge, that's decent of you."

"Brothers, Siri. You and me. If there's anything. . . ."

"Actually there is one more small thing."

"Oh."

"Nothing a man of your stature couldn't deal with. My wife and I are being blackmailed."

"What? Blackmailed? That's terrible."

"A petty criminal came by the noodle shop a few days ago when I was out and threatened to tell the police that I have a library of foreign language books in my back bedroom."

"The police would never believe such a blatant lie."

Siri looked around for something recognizable to eat.

"It is a blatant lie, isn't it, Siri?"

"No."

"You have a library?"

"Back bedroom. Several hundred books. French."

Judge Haeng was a dark-skinned man so when he blanched he turned a shade of gray.

"I . . . well, I . . . I suppose as long as they aren't being distributed to the people they aren't doing any harm."

"That's the way I look at it. Madame Daeng gave the blackmailer your telephone number and told him to call you. Then she hit him over the head with a skillet. He might get in touch."

"I'll . . . I'll take care of it."

"You're so kind."

"You're welcome, Doctor."

They shook hands warmly. Siri stood and watched the little judge walk away. Anyone overhearing their conversation, anyone who knew of the stormy history between the two men, might assume Judge Haeng had sustained permanent nerve damage as a result of the marijuana. But those nosy parkers who shouldn't have been eavesdropping in the first place wouldn't have known about that last manila envelope in Siri's secret under-floorboard hiding place. And they wouldn't have any idea that inside that envelope was a letter applying for political defection to the United States written by one Judge Haeng. It had been handed to the head of the USMIA mission on the night of Potter's death. Unfortunate that it should go astray, considering what was written in it. The letter claimed that Judge Haeng was being persecuted by members of the supreme council as a result of his fearless diatribes against communism. As a result of threats, he now feared for his life. He claimed to have in his possession a number of top secret documents that the CIA would find particularly interesting. If the American consulate would consider smuggling him out of the country he could make those documents available as well as his personal experience as a ranking member of the Party. At the end of the letter was the flowery and pretentious signature which nobody would ever be able to fake. Like a good coward, by running away Haeng would have his revenge on all those who had bullied him.

Major Potter had obviously thought the offer interesting enough to secrete the envelope in his whiskey crate before drinking the coffee that would render him unconscious. People like Judge Haeng seemed to have an innate knack for bad timing. He probably confessed to Peach, not passing on any false information at all. Saw her as a potential ally in his escape to capitalism. As long as Siri had that document, he knew the judge would be a much more pleasant person and infinitely useful. Siri would enjoy this relationship for a while but deep down he knew he'd be returning the letter. How dull would retirement be without Judge Haeng snapping at his heels?

At exactly 3:25 the vice-minister hurried in the door with a secretary beside him, apparently briefing him on why he was there and what he had to do. He recognized and shook hands with General Suvan, Judge Haeng and Comrade Vinai. He recognized and ignored Siri and Civilai, whom he looked over his glasses at, causing him to trip over the step to the stage.

"Don't tell me you've offended that one too." Daeng shook her head.

"Have we offended that one?" Siri asked.

"Don't recall," said Civilai. "Wait. Isn't he the one whose limousine we filled up with ducks?"

"No. That was the Vice-Minister of Agriculture."

"Of course it was. So, no, madam. I can honestly say we haven't yet offended this man."

The vice-minister blew into the microphone and his breath bellowed from speakers at the four corners of the canteen. Siri noted that the microphone was no more necessary than the volume control permanently set on "uncomfortably loud."

"Is the man who's getting the medal in the room?" the minister asked.

"He's here," called Siri.

"Very well." The vice-minister squinted as he searched for the name hidden in the text. "I would like to invite Mr. Geung Watajak to come up to the stage." He was surprised to see everyone bow deeply like Japanese courtiers, but it was only in order to put their glasses on the floor and have both hands free for an ovation fit for a king. Mr. Geung was looking every bit the hero in his Mahosot Hospital blazer, white shirt and a black tie borrowed from Civilai. To his left, looking equally ravishing in her khaki hospital shirt and a navy blue *phasin* skirt, was Tukda. Whereas her smile flashed around the room collecting others, Geung held his jaw square and his lips compressed. He'd been to the Soviet parade earlier in the year and decided that the military slow march would be appropriate for such an important ceremony as this. His foot hovered in the air before each step.

"He should get to the stage by November," Civilai whispered.

"Can you walk a bit faster, son?" came the vice-minister's voice from four directions. But the morgue assistant would not be hurried.

Of course, Mr. Geung's heroic act at the Friendship Hotel could not be written up in the commendation exactly as it had happened. A man could hardly receive a medal for banging a middle-school-band tambourine. Not even if that tambourine was possessed by an evil spirit. But everyone apart from Siri and Bpoo had been in a shamanic trance at the time. So nobody actually knew the details of what really happened that afternoon. As Mr. Geung was a stickler for the truth, he'd refused to let the doctor tell anyone he'd charged at the dangerous thugs with a machete and hacked them to death. It had taken several rewrites of the statement before he was satisfied.

"Geung Watajak," read the vice-minister, who couldn't wait for Geung's arrival on stage, "in the face of overwhelming odds, you did fearlessly attack five armed men in the dining room of the Friendship Hotel in Phonsavan. This was made all the more remarkable by the fact that you were carrying only a stick." (He did have a stick to beat the tambourine, so, technically, not a lie.) "In the confusion resulting from your heroic charge, you and your colleagues were able to overwhelm the terrorists and disarm them, thus saving the lives of several high-ranking dignitaries and foreign experts. For your bravery I am pleased to award you our nation's top civilian honour, the Civilian Medal for an Outstanding Contribution to the Security and Development of the People's Democratic Republic of Laos: Second Tier."

Geung had just reached the top step when the ribbon was removed from its box. His hair was disturbed during its placement over his head and he became a little fixated with trying to get it back in order. But when he turned and looked out at the cheering audience, he was in control. His hair looked impeccable. He gave a general nod to everyone but one specific nod to Tukda. Yet, not once did he allow the smile, so desperate for freedom, to pass beyond his lips.